THE
TRANSFERENCE

KATHRYN RUFFELL

CRANTHORPE
MILLNER
PUBLISHERS

First published by Cranthorpe Millner Publishers (2025)

ISBN 978-1-80378-323-9 (Paperback)

www.cranthorpemillner.com

Cranthorpe Millner Publishers

For Dad
Xx

ACKNOWLEDGEMENTS

Thank you to Oliver, Heather, Jess, and Jay who had the perseverance to read my initial draft and provide motivation and feedback all in one kind parcel. Thank you to the rest of my wonderful family, Dad, James, Helen, and Alex for always supporting me. Thanks to Brian for the meticulous attention to detail and guidance through my manuscript development. Shout out to Dave and Ruth for your insightful input.

And thank you to my husband, Simon, for everything, always.

CHAPTER ONE

She came awake with a start, heart thundering as she struggled to make sense of her surroundings. Lying flat, her hands registered the feeling of linen sheets beneath her. Trying to take slow breaths, she willed herself to think, to understand where she might be.

Slowly, her heartbeat returned to normal, her mind registering details, eyes searching for objects she could recognise in the gloom. Raising herself up on her elbows, she groaned as she became aware of a dull ache spreading throughout her body. She could discern a small amount of light coming from the moon, shining through a long, thin window set in the stone wall. Instinctively she rejected the conclusion that her eyes were leading her to.

'It can't be,' she murmured.

Looking around the room, taking in a detailed tapestry hanging on the far wall, she realised she was in a four-poster bed in what must be one of the castle's bedrooms.

A girl from the town, Sionan had no business being in a room as luxurious as this. Confusion clamoured with rising alarm. The last thing she remembered was being invited by the duke's steward to work at the castle for a banquet being hosted in a month's time. The opportunity to earn some coin and the excitement of seeing the nobles gathered in their finery meant that she had been delighted to accept.

Sionan searched her memory, laboriously thinking, step by step, about what she could recall. She remembered agreeing to the generous payment offered by Onway, the steward, and sharing the news of her good fortune with her family and childhood friend Kayton. He had begged her not to take the work, believing wholeheartedly the rumours circulating in town of sinister events at the castle. Sionan, more pragmatic in nature, and with the offer of paid work available, had been dismissive of the stories, preferring to focus on the opportunity this work provided rather than ghostly tales.

She recalled packing a bag of clothes, and Onway had ushered her into a fine carriage. She had been alive with excitement, waving at folk she knew as the carriage wound along the road from town up to the castle.

Onway, taciturn by nature, had not spoken on the journey. The steward was in his later years, and Sionan recalled thinking how tired the grey-haired man appeared. He had politely assisted her from the carriage and through the main castle square, then left her to wait in a small, comfortable room for further instruction from the household staff. Refreshments had thoughtfully been left, and she remembered drinking a cup of water but could remember nothing after this.

Sionan shook her head, fighting to focus on the present and break through the fog of confusion muffling her senses. The heavy feeling of exhaustion in her limbs made it difficult to sit up. Hearing voices approach, she looked towards the large oak door set in the wall on the left of the room.

'How is our guest faring, Onway?' a warm melodic voice asked.

'She has not woken yet, my lord, but does not appear to have any wounds or broken bones'.

'Excellent, Onway, excellent. She was the perfect candidate, you see. Full of life and vitality. Look at how results have improved with our methods already. This is a fine art we practise, and we must celebrate our successes over these last weeks.'

'Yes, my lord,' the steward replied.

Sionan knew instinctively that they were speaking about her and pulled back the covers in alarm, but she wasn't in her clothes, only a full-length nightgown. Nothing was right about this situation. Frantically, she looked around the circular room but saw only the walls and a singular oak door. There would be no easy way to hide.

Pretend to be asleep, she thought, *there must be a way out.*

Trying to calm herself, Sionan laid back down, forced herself into stillness, and closed her eyes. A nagging doubt warned her that the strange happenings she had mockingly dismissed as superstition were now gut-wrenchingly real.

The door opened, shedding light into the room from the corridor.

'Ah, Onway, it appears our guest is still sleeping. Light a candle in case she wakes. We do not want her to become alarmed at these new surroundings.'

'At once, my lord,' Onway replied.

Sionan heard movement as the steward returned to the hall to light a taper. The soft glow of candlelight danced across her closed eyelids as a candle was lit on the bedstand. Her mind screamed at her to keep still, to breathe slowly, even as her jumbled thoughts tried to make sense of the strange discourse.

'I shall sit with our guest for a time, Onway. I would like to be here when she wakes.'

Sionan listened as the steward carried a chair from the side of the room to the bedside; she could hear him plumping cushions for the man's comfort.

'Thank you, Onway. Rest for the night, now, I shall not need your assistance again.'

'Thank you, my lord. Good night to you.'

'Good night.'

Footsteps receded and the door closed. Sionan heard the man take the seat beside her and rustle his clothing as he made himself comfortable.

She waited, keeping her breathing even for what felt like an eternity. There was no movement from the man beside her at all. He merely sat. Her feeling of panic changed to suspicion and the need to know why she was in this room. Opening her eyes in tiny slits, she observed the man. He appeared to be of average height, slim, with dark hair and was clean-shaven. His face was handsome, with light wrinkles around his blue eyes and forehead. Sionan immediately recognised the middle-aged, scholarly man as the duke. She desperately tried to think why he would be here. Sionan could feel no threat emanating from him, and with a sinking feeling, knew she would need to speak to find out what was happening.

The duke was clearly not intending to move, and looked relaxed in his soft woollen tunic, black hose of the finest quality, and polished, black, knee-length boots. The only adornment she had seen glinting in the candlelight was a gold chain with an amethyst amulet hung around his neck. Sionan, a tailor's daughter, had only ever seen Duke Gelanson from afar at parades, surrounded by his guard, and usually in a fine carriage. To be this close was not something someone of Sionan's station would ever expect to happen, nor was she sure how she should behave to extricate herself from this unnerving situation.

The duke leaned forward, smiling slightly, gently rounded shoulders from years of study reinforcing his lack of physicality. 'Ah, so you are awake!' he exclaimed with delight.

Pretending to be startled, Sionan opened her hazel eyes fully. 'Where am I?' she asked.

'Please allow me to introduce myself first, my dear.' The duke smiled warmly. 'I am the Duke of Clasterne, Duke Gelanson. Do you recognise me? You are in my home. You have, I understand from my steward, been in a terrible accident, falling down the kitchen stairs while preparing for the banquet.'

'I fell down the stairs?' Sionan echoed in alarm.

'Yes, but do not worry, my dear. I am happy to say you have been recovering well, but you must continue to rest for some time yet. Do not concern yourself with the banquet tomorrow.'

Sionan frowned in confusion. She could not remember anything about an accident. In fact, she could not remember anything at all after she entered the castle. When she had arrived, there was still a month of preparation to go before the celebration banquet.

Does this mean I've been in the castle for nearly four weeks?

As if sensing her anxiety, the duke leaned forward and patted her hand reassuringly. 'The servants informed me you gave your head quite a bang, my dear, so do not worry if you cannot recall anything for now. Relax and take your time to get well, you are perfectly safe here.'

Sionan wanted to feel gratitude for the duke's apparent kindness but her sense of disquiet grew.

Why would someone of the duke's importance be taking the time to speak to a lowly servant? she thought.

Perhaps she was being uncharitable by showing a lack of trust, but she felt increasingly embarrassed by the duke's attendance to her, and refused to ignore her own intuitive warnings.

'Thank you for your kindness, Duke Gelanson,' Sionan carefully replied. 'I feel well enough to return to my family now. I do not wish to cause you further trouble.'

'It really is a little soon for you to travel back to the town and your family.' The duke rose from the chair with a quiet sigh to pace slowly across the room. 'I am glad to hear you feel well but you really have taken quite a fall. Onway informed your family that you would not be back for another week due to the business of the castle and the banquet occurring soon, so do not fear, they will not be worrying about you. Oh,' Gelanson added with a kindly smile. 'And we have, of course, ensured they are recompensed for the time you are spending here.'

Sionan looked at the duke, hiding her unease. She knew her mother would have been breaking down the castle door to see her if she had been informed of the accident.

Surely the rumours can't be true? But then why insist I remain here to recuperate?

A memory of Kayton's face pleading with her not to accept the work flashed in the forefront of her mind. Sionan had always thought he was naive, willing to believe any farfetched, ale-soaked tales of travellers at the inn where he worked.

As they had grown from being children to working age, she had stopped believing folk stories, but Kayton never had. Over the last years she had noticed him taking a more romantic view of her and had thought his pleading was partly due to him not wanting her to be away from him. She thought of his face, flushed with anger and embarrassment, when she had laughed at his fears. She had so wanted to prove Kayton's childish beliefs wrong, but now, as she looked at the duke, she questioned herself.

Have I made a terrible mistake?

'Thank you again for your kindness, my lord. I greatly appreciate your care and attention to me, but I would feel much more comfortable in my family home at this time. If you would just return my clothes to me, I will be on my way.' Sionan sat up in the bed, ignoring her nagging tiredness. 'I really do feel well enough to reach home, my lord.'

She tried to rise but was stopped by Gelanson pressing her shoulders gently to encourage her to lie back down, a kind, fatherly expression on his face as he pulled the covers back over her.

'Now, I insist you rest, my dear,' the duke responded, smiling. 'Get some sleep and we will talk again in the morning.'

Sionan felt dread growing in the pit of her stomach. He was not going to let her leave, whatever she said. Allowing Gelanson to carefully pat the covers back in place on top of her, she knew she would need to get out of the castle alone. She refused to give in to panic.

"One stitch at a time," her father had always told her. Her mind raced as she tried to think of the best way to get out. No one was likely to stop a servant leaving for the town at such a busy time in the castle. There would be so many folk coming and going with the banquet preparations, she just needed to get lost in the crowd.

She settled back into the bed, appearing to capitulate to the duke's wishes. 'Actually, I do feel a little tired… and dizzy,' she said, relaxing her shoulders. 'If you don't mind, my lord, I will take some more rest now.'

'Of course, my dear, of course. Please relax whilst you are recuperating. I will leave you to your rest. Onway will return with your breakfast in the morning. Sleep well and we shall have the physician check on you again tomorrow.'

Sionan watched the duke exit the room and offer her a final, warm smile as he closed the door. She listened as his footsteps receded and waited a few more moments to ensure no one returned. Gingerly, she felt over her face and scalp, but there was no pain, no bruising, to support the duke's tale that she had banged her head. Despite Gelanson's kindly words and actions, she had seen an emptiness in his eyes, a lack of warmth sharply contradicting his smiling, benevolent actions.

Sionan clambered out of the bed.

A short woman, taking after her mother in stature as well as nature, she had been encouraged from an early age to be independent. Now, she believed in her own ability to escape from this predicament. What worried her more was how to escape without causing offence. Whilst she may not believe or trust Gelanson, he was still the duke of these lands and she could not risk raising his ire. If she did, the ramifications for her and her family were unthinkable.

She paused, mind racing.

Perhaps if she could quietly leave the castle during the night she could relay to any interested party that she had not wanted to cause the duke any further trouble with the banquet approaching. Satisfied that this approach was the safest, Sionan went to the window to find her bearings. She looked out of the thin aperture, trying to shake the heavy tiredness from her limbs and communicate the urgency of her situation to her exhausted body. She could see that the bedroom was inside the turret on the west side of the castle. The town sprawled out far below, to the south. Craning her neck to look down from the small opening, she realised that she was much higher up than she had hoped. Huge grey stone walls stretched away from each side the turret. Sionan swayed back from the view in shock. She had been deliberately placed in a room that was difficult to access or escape from.

She crossed back to the bed, shoulders bowed in disappointment, hugging her arms across her body. A sharp pain in both arms caused her to stop and look at the crooks in her elbows. On each there was a small, distinct, star-shaped bruise. In the wavering candlelight, Sionan peered more closely, having no knowledge of where this bruising had come from. She shivered, unable to shake the feeling that these bruises indicated something ominous.

Galvanised into action, she crossed to the oak door, gently lifted the latch, and peered out into the corridor beyond. There were no guards or servants moving around. In fact, for a castle that should be in the throes of organising a big event, this corridor was eerily silent. Sionan left the room cautiously, quietly latching the door behind her.

Creeping down the corridor, she descended the first set of winding stone stairs, the flagstones cold on her bare feet. The light from the torch back in the hall threw flickering shadows around her as she descended the stairwell. She knew she needed to find some clothes first and then try to blend in with the servants leaving the castle for their errands in the town.

Sionan crept down the steps until she reached another small landing. Following a short corridor, she saw another door, mirroring the one she had just left, to what she could only assume was another bedroom. The corridor remained silent, a single candle shedding only a small amount of light. Listening outside for a moment and hearing only silence, she gently opened the latch and inched into the room to try and find some clothes.

Silently standing, she waited, allowing her eyes to adjust in the darkness. The room smelt vaguely of decay, like rotten fruit left at the end of a market. Sionan's nose wrinkled at the unpleasant odour.

As her eyes became accustomed to the dim moonlight filtering in from the window, she saw a woman lying on the bed. The figure looked ancient, with thin, grey, wispy hair splayed out on the pillow. Skeletally thin arms lay on top of the bedsheet.

Knowing she should not wake the woman but feeling drawn to the bedside, Sionan leaned in to take a closer look, the unpleasant odour growing stronger. Then, reeling backwards, Sionan gasped in horror as she recognised the elderly woman's features. Had she not seen this *girl* each morning, carrying her tray of lovingly arranged loaves from the bakery to market? Could this decrepit form in front of her truly be Leetha, the young girl she knew?

Sionan looked in terror upon the decayed form, her eyes drawn to the bruising on Leetha's arms, a blue-black hue of marks spreading all the way from wrist to shoulder. Sionan took a sudden intake of breath. The shape of a star in the crooks of her elbows matched Sionan's own lighter marks, but Leetha's marks were dark, gaping star-shaped sores, with yellow pus dribbling onto the bed cover.

Sionan recoiled from the bed, startled as she suddenly noticed the girl's eyes were open and watching her. Before Sionan could react, Leetha spoke in the faintest whisper, uttering only one word:

'Run.'

CHAPTER TWO

The young man entered the inn, eyes searching the gloom for the renowned fighter he had heard spoken about with awe over many a year. The heroic tales had kept Kayton dreaming about becoming a captain in the Overlord's army, fighting for royalty, gaining justice for the people, and righting the wrongs of the world. He was barely able to hide his excitement that, if luck was on his side, he would soon be meeting the legend himself.

Making his way to the bar he raised a hand for the barkeep's attention. 'Can you direct me to Captain Chancer Landry, sir? I've been informed he is currently in this town.'

The barkeep grunted in response, gesturing to a man slumped forwards on a table in the corner of the bar. 'His tankard is as dry and empty as his money pouch,' the barkeep replied. 'He's not managed to pick up any guard work for some weeks and he's taking up good table space. Unless you're here to settle his debt, I'd suggest you steer clear of where he's heading. He's outstayed his welcome in this town.'

Kayton tried to hide his surprise and dismay. Walking over to the table, he saw the drunken man did not even notice the increasing noise of revellers entering the bar as folk finished their work for the day. Kayton squeezed onto the bench opposite, taking care not to knock his bruised torso; the reminder from his final altercation with the duke's guards reassuring him again that seeking help was his only course of action.

As he sat gingerly on the seat the man did not stir. Kayton was unimpressed with what he saw. He observed the man's greasy brown hair, beard streaked with grey, and clothes that had seen better days. The stench of stale ale rising from the slumped form was nearly enough to send Kayton away again… *nearly*. But he had come a long way for help and had to believe there was some truth in all the stories he had heard, and he knew, down to his core, that there were no other choices left open to him. He searched out the server and gestured for assistance, swiftly ordering food and ale for himself and the captain.

The server returned, placing dishes and tankards on the table and giving a none-too-friendly shove to the inebriated form. Bleary eyes opened to focus on the bowl. Without questioning where the meal had miraculously appeared from, the captain tucked into the stew. Kayton appraised him with a hopeful gaze as the bowl of food was demolished.

'Good afternoon, Captain Landry,' Kayton stated formally, wishing to impress despite all he had observed so far.

The man winced in response. 'Captain is not a form of address I go by. It's just Chancer now. And you are?'

'I'm Kayton Stratton, I've travelled from the Manor of Clasterne to find you, Capt— Chancer. I have come seeking your help to rescue our townsfolk who are being held against their will by the duke.' Internally Kayton winced, his words sounded pompous and ridiculous.

'Clasterne is a long way to travel to from here,' Chancer replied irritably. 'Why don't your own people help you? Don't you have local heroes for that type of work?'

Kayton took a moment to gather his thoughts before replying, wondering how he could better present the danger people were in. He recalled all the heroic stories he had heard of Captain Landry and began trying to match them with the man who sat across from him, supping ale.

The captain had been given the nickname of Chancer by his men for his daredevil antics. Celebrated for his bravery, he was renowned for risking all on one chance of success. Luck had smiled on the warrior during the years of war, strategies had paid off and he became one of the most famed soldiers of the Overlord. However, the stories Kayton had heard did not speak of the time that had passed since the campaign, and clearly the warrior had fallen a long way since serving the crown.

A jumbled mix of inebriated arguments, lively discussions, and shouts for more beer intruded on Kayton's thoughts as he watched Chancer empty his tankard. The man grunted with disapproval when the drink ran out and he gestured meaningfully to Kayton that the empty vessel should be refilled.

'I understand you do not know me, but please hear me out,' Kayton said, ignoring Chancer's unspoken request for more ale. He had resolved not to let down, Sionan, and he leant forward with determination.

'The duke of our Manor is a man of dark ambitions,' Kayton said solemnly. 'People are disappearing from the town, and everyone is too terrified to stand against him. Those who disappear, we never see again, or they return as empty shells with no life in them. They just exist.'

'And the ones that return? What do these people say?' Chancer asked, clearly hoping that by continuing the conversation, more ale would be forthcoming.

'They say that the duke has treated them kindly, and they return with gifts of money and food. They say they have a *wasting disease* that the duke has tried to save them from, to no avail.' Kayton's voice rose with indignation 'It is all lies! Something dreadful is happening to them, and fear for their families prevents them from speaking the truth.'

'So, let me make sure I understand you,' Chancer interrupted, losing patience as his tankard remained stubbornly empty. 'You can't petition the Overlord because people make no complaint against your duke, their families make no complaint against the duke, and the only person who is convinced that this disease is a falsehood and that people are disappearing is you?'

Kayton watched, frustration mounting, as Chancer called for the server directly, gesturing with the tankard.

'I know how this must sound,' Kayton replied. 'Other people believe it is happening too. I've discussed it with folk in the Three Crowns.'

'Ah,' said Chancer. 'People in your local tavern also accept it to be true. Would these people be drunks nursing grievances against the duke?' Chancer's eyebrows rose with the question, irritation flickering across his features.

Kayton felt his face flush at Chancer's disbelieving tone.

'You have to believe me,' Kayton urged with mounting tension. 'People live in fear for their lives. Those who have spoken out have simply disappeared, or worse. Their families also disappear, so that no one will dare to protest now for fear of their loved ones never returning. Please, we need someone to help us. I had thought that with your reputation, you would be able to provide us with the aid we need.'

Chancer laughed, the sound devoid of humour. 'You thought one man could achieve all the things that a whole town could not? Frankly, young man, your story sounds far-fetched. Let me guess: your beloved has been stolen away?'

Kayton's face flushed crimson, deepening to an uncomfortable puce as he pushed away the embarrassing memory of Sionan turning away from him, of her humour –which quickly gave way to annoyance – at his pleas that she decline the offer to work for the duke.

'Ah, so you *wish* the girl was your intended?' Chancer continued. The server placed two more tankards on the table, and Chancer, swigging ale again, spoke more gently to the crestfallen lad. 'I am sorry for the troubles that have taken someone you love from you, but I am not a physician to cure a disease, and I am certainly not going to stand against a duke.'

'I can pay you,' Kayton interjected quickly. 'I can pay one bronze per day for your time.'

Chancer leaned back on the bench, bloodshot eyes appearing to appraise if Kayton was serious. A bronze a day was not to be dismissed lightly.

'Please, Captain,' Kayton continued. 'Please just come and see for yourself what is happening. You will know we need your help when you see it with your own eyes.'

'Maybe the time has come for me to move on, if you're serious, and can pay,' Chancer replied, stretching his back out, stiff from another day of sitting on the bench. 'I've not travelled to Clasterne before, and clearly my current reputation has not preceded me if you're here for my help, so maybe a change of town would be beneficial to us both.' Chancer attempted to stand, swaying slightly before righting himself and holding the table for support. 'We'll leave tomorrow,' he announced decisively.

Kayton's jaw dropped in astonishment. 'You'll do it? You'll come to Clasterne?'

'Yes. How could I refuse to help a town in need of a hero,' Chancer responded with a touch of sarcasm. 'One bronze per day is the deal.' Sticking out his hand, he grabbed Kayton's arm in the warrior's grasp.

Kayton returned the grip with enthusiasm. 'We'll leave at first light?' he said eagerly.

'No,' Chancer replied. 'Why do you youngsters always think journeys need to start when the cockerel rises? We'll leave late morning, after we've had a chance to break our fast and gather supplies. I take it you have money for those items too?'

'Yes,' replied Kayton.

'And you'll need to settle my account here,' Chancer added in a loud voice.

As Kayton turned to leave, he found the barkeep blocking his path with a smile and a hand held out. 'That will be four bronzes, sir.'

Kayton paid with a sigh, quietly hoping he had enough funds to see them back to Clasterne. He saw Chancer hold out his hand and smile as the barkeep reached below the bar and returned a sword in a beautiful scabbard and a baldric containing what appeared to be an impressive array of throwing knives. Chancer buckled the sword scabbard onto his belt and tightened the baldric of short knives across his chest to sit diagonally from left shoulder to his hip.

Kayton's face lit up with delight at the imposing picture Chancer now presented. Fully armed, the baldric of knives increased the breadth of the warrior's shoulders, and the quality of the sword would be worn only by someone who knew well how to use the weapon. This was the lion-hearted warrior Kayton had searched for. His confidence in their mission soared, only slightly dented as Chancer bumped between the tables and tripped as he exited the bar.

Kayton followed Chancer outside and noted how large the man appeared now he was standing. Despite the drunken stupor he had been in when Kayton arrived, Chancer was clearly still someone to be reckoned with.

As the evening sun shone down on the inn, Kayton's heart was lighter than he had felt for days. He knew he may sound naïve, but he had convinced the captain to help him, albeit with the assistance of the offer of coin. For the first time, Kayton felt there was a chance of success.

'Off on our bold quest,' Chancer joked, slapping Kayton on the shoulder, only just staying on his feet while Kayton assisted him along the road. 'It'll take us a week or so to get to Clasterne,' Chancer continued, looping his arm around the boy's shoulder. 'I'm feeling generous, so I'll teach you how to fight along the way. How's that for a fair deal? Two fighters to save a whole town.'

Kayton nodded eagerly in response, his mind filling with images of a daring, courageous rescue. 'I'm staying in a guesthouse around the corner, we can organise our supplies and lodge there overnight, if you wish?'

'*You* can start organising supplies,' Chancer replied grumpily, his generous mood quickly evaporating. 'I'm going to sleep off this headache.'

Chancer followed Kayton to the guesthouse, the large man banging his head on the door frame as they entered the small, pristine hallway. Kayton quickly ushered him to his room before the landlady spotted them and could refuse entry, quietly shutting the door as the noise of Chancer's sword and baldric of knives clattered to the floor.

Chancer sat heavily on the bed, barely managing to kick the boots free from his feet before falling backwards, comatose. Kayton eyed the snoring form, quickly deciding it was probably best to leave the captain to rest.

Leaving the guesthouse, he headed into town to gather food and supplies for their journey.

I'm heading home, he thought, whistling with the happiness of hope returning.

As the dawn sunlight filtered through the shutters on the guesthouse window, Kayton rose from the floor where he had spent an uncomfortable night.

His mind flickered back to his parting from Sionan two weeks ago. He had been frantic with worry, almost shouting as he willed her to understand the danger she would be in. Unfortunately, the more Kayton spoke out against the duke, the less willing Sionan, and others, had been to listen to his warnings. The increasing frequency of his angry confrontations with some of Gelanson's guards had caused a rift between him and his oldest friend, and he knew people thought he was a fool.

On the third day of Sionan's departure, Kayton had taken it upon himself to visit her at the castle. He was gruffly turned away by the castle guards, and when he had persisted, they had given him a sound beating. A fortnight on and the bruising on his ribs had faded to a mottled brown but the soreness was still there every time he picked up his travelling bag, reminding him of their violence.

Desperate for help, he had set out to find Chancer the day after the beating, the guards' stern threat not to return to the castle or he'd be thrown in the cells ringing in his ears. In Kayton's eyes, the beating, that was so clearly meant to silence him, was firm evidence that the whispered rumours were true. What Kayton had needed was a warrior of action, someone who would know how to stand up to the duke and wouldn't be afraid to show the people of Clasterne the hidden rot in the centre of their own town. Kayton had set out to find a hero: the famed Captain Chancer Landry.

Now, with new determination, he repacked the travel bags again, checking how much money he had after purchasing supplies. Kayton had sold everything he possessed and taken his meagre savings to fund this rescue attempt, and he knew the bronzes would quickly run out.

Making as much noise as possible, with an aim to waking Chancer, Kayton clattered around the room, washing his face with the jug of water and bowl provided on the nightstand. Looking in the small mirror, he decided to leave the light growth of sandy beard that was starting to show.

Perhaps Chancer, and Sionan, will take me more seriously if I appear older than my sixteen summers, he mused.

Groaning, Chancer sat up and rubbed his temples, clearly trying to ease the throbbing pressure of a headache. 'Crow's bones, boy, do you need to make so much noise?' he growled. 'Clearly there is no more sleep to be had here.'

The captain swung his legs out of the bed and pulled on his boots, muttering under his breath. Kayton hid a smile as he watched the hungover man leave for the outhouse.

A fearsome-looking elderly lady stood barring the guesthouse doorway when Chancer tried to return. Kayton watched as the woman took the captain to task.

'You'll not sit in my house until you've washed,' she commanded. 'I run a clean establishment here and I won't have the likes of *you* bringing it to disrepute. The water butt is to the side of the house, there's a jug and soap by the side.'

'Of course, good lady,' Chancer replied with a mocking bow, winking at Kayton. Returning outside to the water butt, he removed his shirt and doused his hair and upper body. He scrubbed the grime from his skin with the hard soap.

Kayton stood at the door, staring at Chancer in awe. The captain's torso and arms were criss-crossed with the scars of a man who had fought many battles. Without looking at Kayton, Chancer put his shirt back on and re-entered the guesthouse.

'Any chance of an ale with breakfast in this fine establishment?' Chancer asked, eyes taking stock that this was indeed a much better hostelry than the usual barns and taverns frequented for overnight stays; clean rugs, pastel-coloured curtains, and no straw on the floor. The elderly lady frowned at Chancer's question, not deigning to reply and gesturing them to the table in the dining room.

Both men sat on the bench as she placed bread, apple, mutton, and a hot drink in front of them. Kayton watched with amusement as Chancer tasted the drink and grimaced at the flavour of nettle tea sweetened with honey. There was definitely no alcohol in it. Kayton thoroughly enjoyed the beverage, thanking the lady profusely for her kindness in serving the impromptu guest he had bought with him.

As the mollified landlady left the dining room, Chancer spoke. 'Right then, lad, let's get our bags. How long did it take you to journey from Clasterne and find me?'

'Around two weeks. I had to travel through towns searching for information about you. We need to get back as quickly as possible. Sionan will be in desperate need of our help. Who knows what will have occurred by now.'

'Ah, Sionan, is it?' Chancer said. 'So, the beloved intended has a name. This is the girl who has got you on this foolhardy quest?'

Kayton's eyes dropped to the food on his plate, trying to suppress the embarrassment welling up again. 'Sionan is dear to me,' Kayton said carefully. 'She's not my intended, though. We've been friends since we were children. She's wonderful, we've been through so much together over the years, we even have the same day of birth, which we celebrate together every year. She's amazing, so strong and smart and always there to help anyone in need.' Kayton petered out, realising he was gushing like a schoolboy.

'Hmph, it's like that, then,' Chancer replied

sympathetically. It was clear for anyone to see that Kayton was yearning for more with this young woman. 'Well, let's see what a daring rescue mission will do to change things.' Chancer gave a short laugh. 'And don't worry about how long it will take us to return. Now that you've found me, we can take a much faster route through the forest. I know someone who can guide us.'

Returning to their room, Chancer hefted one of the packs Kayton had prepared on to his back, put on his weapons, and strode towards the door.

'Come on then, lad, let's get moving,' he called over his shoulder.

Kayton scrambled to place his pack on his back and buckle his short sword, a poor cousin indeed to Chancer's fine weapon. He paid the landlady, whose eyes raked over Chancer's departing form with obvious distaste.

'Be careful of the company you keep, young man,' she said. 'That one will only lead you into trouble.'

'That is exactly what I'm hoping for,' Kayton replied with a broad smile as he left the guesthouse with a spring in his step and followed Chancer down the road.

CHAPTER THREE

Chancer led them into the forest towards the border between Ascalion and Katlesa. The pair made good time on foot, quickly leaving the town in the distance. The air felt milder in the woods, without the crisp bite of frost early in the morning.

As darkness fell on the second day, Chancer bade the lad to stop and make camp whilst they awaited another traveller. Kayton sat staring into their campfire, waiting as instructed.

'I wonder how Sionan and her family are faring,' he pondered, looking at Chancer. 'They are tailors by trade. These clothes were a gift from Sionan's parents on my birthday. They are the best clothes I have ever owned.'

Chancer could see the joy the simple gift had brought shining from the lad's face. 'You're close with the parents too then?' Chancer asked.

'Oh, yes,' Kayton replied, 'They always watched over me, ever since my parents died.' Kayton's speech tailed off and silence fell.

'It's warmer this evening, the change in season is coming.' Chancer interjected, clumsily trying to distract Kayton from what must have been sad memories. 'Winter will be chased away by this early spring sun. All the better for travelling.'

'Yes,' Kayton agreed. 'And the faster we are back in

Clasterne the better. How long are we waiting for this friend?'
he asked.

'As long as it takes,' Chancer replied. 'Two warriors and a
young lad from the town storming a castle to rescue a maiden
have much better chances of success than just one warrior.'

Kayton looked at Chancer sharply. 'Don't you believe we
can save her?'

Desperation was shining in Kayton's eyes, and Chancer
could see that now was not a good time to continue his
attempt at a joke. The captain had been increasingly sharp
and sarcastic with the lad over the recent days, while his body
screamed for ale, wine or spirits. Even leftover dregs from the
bottom of the barrel would do, but he knew he should not be
taking it out on the boy.

'I believe we will do our best to try and save her, Kayton, *if*
she wants or needs our help. But if everything you say is true,
you need to prepare yourself for how hard this will be. You
are talking about standing against a duke. I am not a miracle
worker. I am only a man who will do the best I can for you…
for one bronze a day.' Chancer smiled, taking the sting out
of the words. He saw Kayton's shoulders relax in acceptance.

Chancer ran a hand through his greying hair and
wondered if he had ever been so idealistic. He still marvelled
at how Kayton had managed to find him at all. In the two
days it had taken them to journey to this point, he had seen
very little travelling knowledge exhibited by the lad. He had
met youngsters like him before in the army, where their lack
of awareness of danger seemed to somehow keep them safe
as they breezed, unaware, past mortal threats. Chancer knew
that when this naïve bubble burst the result would be painful

for the lad, just hopefully not deadly.

Perhaps once, at the beginning of his time serving the Overlord, Chancer had been like the boy, truly believing he was battling for what was right and just, fighting to bring peace to the lands. When the heralds had moved through his town, calling people to arms, they had spun a tale of dark dangers of Ascalion rebel forces, and Chancer had joined up without a second thought. As time passed and he saw the rebels first-hand, his sense of justice eroded as he realised these were only people like himself, fighting for their view of freedom. He had learnt, with some bitterness, that there were no righteous good and sinister evil forces at work, only people battling for what they believed was right. Coupled with this, he had witnessed, and been subject to, the fickle whims of nobles. He had quickly come to understand that justice was always in the eye of the winner, not the righteous. From that point on, Chancer had made it a rule to remain emotionally detached from any work he undertook, joining mercenary bands or guard details for short periods of time, and leaving as soon as he had enough coin to winter over in a town.

Despite his own rule, he now found himself warming to this young man who had sought his help. Feeling old and jaded, with heavy memories, Chancer thought it was about time he was involved in a story with a good ending for folk. *Maybe I can live up to the heroic reputation… if I can just manage to stay away from the drink.*

His smiled wryly to himself and set to work building up the fire with dry wood, and then finally added some green boughs, creating smoke in the breeze. He walked wordlessly to the stream nearby, dampened a small square of blanket, and placed it over the fire to prevent too much smoke rising from the flames. Then he quickly pulled the blanket off the fire and watched a single puff of white cloud from the flames.

'Why do you do that each evening?' Kayton asked, intrigue evident on his features.

'Wait and see,' Chancer replied, glad something was distracting the lad from his worry.

Chancer completed this action four times and then loaded more green branches and left the fire to smoke for a time before repeating again. Once completed, he banked the sides of the fire, leaving it to die down to soft embers as the night drew in.

Both men got into their bedrolls whilst darkness fell. Chancer watched over his young travelling companion. Smiling to himself again, he was relieved to see that, despite Kayton's worry for Sionan, the lad quickly dropped into a deep sleep.

Chancer woke suddenly in the dead of the night. He lay still, listening, unable to discern any sound or interruption to the normal rhythm of nocturnal creatures that may have woken him. He knew he was no longer alone.

As he stretched his senses out into the dark to find what had awoken him, he suddenly felt something press against his face. A cold wet nose prodded him none too gently.

'You took your time getting here,' he said, looking at the large brindle-brown dog towering over him.

The dog responded with a lick to Chancer's face, then sat

back on its haunches and allowed Chancer to ruffle it behind the ears.

'Are you speaking to Scase or me?' a female voice asked with amusement.

'The dog, obviously,' Chancer replied. The massive hound looked like a cross between a duke's war dog and one of the wolves that were abundant in the forest.

Climbing out of his bedroll, Chancer stirred the embers of the fire to life. Across from him stood a woodsperson dressed in brown wool tunic, doeskin trousers, and moccasin boots. She was tall and athletic with short, tightly curled black hair and arresting sea-green eyes. Her mouth turned up in a smile, clearly delighted she had caught Chancer unaware. Her skills as a forester evident in her posture, completely relaxed in the darkness of the trees. A quiver of arrows and unstrung bow was held across her back, along with a journey pack for travelling and a wickedly long hunting knife buckled on the left-hand side of her belt.

'How are you keeping, Hirae?' Chancer asked. 'Life appears to be treating you well.'

'Can't complain, Chancer. Winter has been kind and here we are, a beautiful spring knocking on the door already. You should try it some time, living out here away from all the distractions of town life.' She paused, an eyebrow raised, looking at Chancer's dishevelled state. 'It seems life has not been treating you so well?'

Chancer grunted in response, knowing that his body was still coming to terms with his new life on the road and lack of ale. His muscles were slowly returning to strength after hours of walking and sword practice each day with Kayton, but he was still a shadow of his former self, and most definitely not in his prime.

'Ah, but Hirae, who would keep the innkeepers in business if I moved out to the forest?' he retorted.

Scase padded over to the fire and laid himself down close to the remaining warmth radiating from the embers. No longer interested in the exchanges between his mistress and Chancer, and sensing no food was available, the animal promptly went to sleep.

'Clearly Scase is also keeping well,' Chancer continued. 'Some breakfast?'

'Sure,' Hirae replied. 'But not any of your travel rations. You can keep those.'

She reached inside the hunting bag attached to the right side of her belt to produce two dead rabbits. Chancer knew this would be a welcome meal for both Kayton and himself. Whilst he may have been untouchable with a sword, he was not a good huntsman, and with Kayton's limited experience they had been feasting on hard bread and dried meat since leaving the town.

Hirae set to work preparing the rabbits for the cooking pot. 'Does the young one ever wake?' she said with a nod at Kayton, who remained asleep in his bedding roll.

'Not unless he can help it,' Chancer replied, grinning.

'So, what's the story?' she queried. 'I saw your signals, and now here I am.'

Chancer paused before speaking as he thought about how unbelievable their story was going to sound. Quietly, he outlined how Kayton had travelled to find him, hired him to help rescue a girl from the Duke of Clasterne, even though there was little evidence that she had actually been abducted against her will in the first place.

Hirae listened in silence as he finished his tale, and watched the young man still sleeping. 'That's a tall story, Chancer, and no mistake. Why have you got yourself involved in this? Surely there is some better way to earn money.'

'He believes it, Hirae, with every fibre of his being. If I don't try and help, he'll do something foolhardy.'

Speaking the words made Chancer realise how true they were. After only a few days of Kayton's company, Chancer was already starting to feel responsible for the young man. His mind veered away from the knowledge that his life had become so empty that a stranger with a tall story was enough to give his life a purpose.

'You're not his captain,' Hirae replied softly. 'It is not your duty to keep him safe.'

The pair fell silent as they looked at Kayton's sleeping form and settled to wait for the young man to wake and share his tale.

As morning approached, the light from the fire flickered and dwindled, Hirae looked at Chancer with sadness. During the night, she had reflected on the foolhardiness of their scheme but knew that nothing she said would dissuade him from this venture now that he had set his feet on the road.

Crouching down, she poked the fire back to life viciously with a stick. This had always been Chancer's problem: he became too personally involved and ended up more damaged with each disappointment from life.

Hirae had learnt fast as a young woman that people had to help themselves. Her mother had fled to the forests with her after the then Duke of Ascalion had killed Hirae's father. The noble had cut down a loving father in a fit of pique when her mother had rejected his unwanted advances. During their first winter in the forest, they had nearly died as her mother battled to learn how to survive in the wilds. Hirae's burning hatred for the nobility was born during that cold winter, and when the Duke of Ascalion caused more anguish and terror than the people could take, Hirae had been first in line to lead the rebellion. She had grown to adulthood relying on nature to provide, and her skills in the forest had been invaluable to the growing band of rebels.

Hirae had found a strange kind of peace in the uprising. At least when she was battling soldiers, she felt she was taking a stand for her father and all the other people who had suffered, simply because a vicious, egotistical man had been born into a place of power.

The idea of unseating the Ascalion duke had taken hold fiercely, and the rebellion had spread like wildfire. Then the Throne became involved. The rebellion was crushed as quickly as it had started when the yellow-liveried Overlord soldiers arrived in their thousands. The bitterness of defeat had driven Hirae back into the forest, and only a few people from those years remained close to her. One of them was sitting in front of her now. Although the irony that one of her most valued friends had been one of the crown's most venerated soldiers was not lost on her.

'What has the fire ever done to you?' Chancer asked with

amusement, breaking into Hirae's reverie as she continued to jab the stick into it. 'The lad is paying one bronze a day,' he continued. 'And one bronze is better than none. Who knows, there might be more work available in Clasterne when we get there.'

'And remind me, why do you need me?' Hirae left the question hanging. She did not like towns. The forest was her home.

'I signalled for you because, if the girl needs rescuing, I think we'll need your superior skills to get in and out of Clasterne and through the forest silently.'

Hirae snorted in response to the blatant flattery. 'And why would I leave my comfortable cabin to get involved in this foolhardy scheme? It doesn't appear to me that this lad can afford two bronzes a day.'

'I'll split my bronze with you: five coppers each a day. It will be an adventure. Come on,' Chancer cajoled. 'We'll be there and back in a few weeks and you'll have coins to stock up on salt for next winter. Besides, when's the last time we had an adventure together? Scase will love it.'

Hearing his name, the dog opened one eye and observed Chancer with interest.

Hirae sighed and paced the small clearing. She stopped and leaned against a tree, breathing in the crisp air and watching the waning moonlight reflecting silver on the trees. She needed salt, that was true, but more than that, she could see in Chancer's eyes that he was set on helping this lad. She knew what was driving him on: the desire to save this young man and assuage the irrational guilt he carried for every soldier under his command he had failed to save. In war, folk died, you couldn't save everyone, but Chancer didn't see it that way.

Shaking her head, knowing this was not a good idea, but also knowing she would not leave Chancer to take the risk alone, she found herself conceding.

'I'll talk to the lad when he finally wakes up. See what he has to say for himself. Then I'll decide.'

Chancer's responding grin was brighter than the sunlight breaking through the trees as the new day dawned.

Kayton awoke to the smell of rabbits cooking on the fire. He yelped as he saw a massive hound standing over him. Hirae laughed at the alarm on the young man's face, clicking her fingers for the dog to return to her.

'Don't worry, he won't hurt you.'

'Who are you?' Kayton asked, clearly embarrassed that a large dog and a stranger had arrived in the camp and he had not woken.

'I'm Hirae, and this is Scase.'

'You're the friend Chancer has been signalling?'

She nodded in response. Removing the rabbits from their spits over the fire, she divided the meat up between three platters made from tree bark. Kayton watched as a large portion of the meat was also thrown to the giant dog who fell upon the food with gusto.

'Tell me your story, Kayton. Why is Chancer here helping you?'

Hirae listened, eating the rabbit and watching Kayton intently as he recounted the events in his town, the beating he received when he tried to see Sionan, and the fear everyone laboured under.

'…And that's why I need the help of Chancer. Every town has heard the stories of his bravery during the campaign. He's our best chance of success.'

'What happens after you have Sionan back and this duke takes someone else?'

Kayton stammered to a halt and hung his head. Clearly, he had not thought that far ahead. Hirae sighed inwardly, wondering how addled Chancer's mind must have been from years of alcohol misuse to agree to this escapade. She observed her dog, who, having finished his breakfast, padded across to sit by the lad.

Kayton fidgeted uncomfortably under Hirae's piercing gaze. After a long pause, she continued in a lighter tone. 'Well, Scase clearly likes you, and that's good enough for me. We'll help you,' she said, turning to Chancer. 'Five coppers a day, half a bronze.'

Kayton whooped with delight.

'Now don't you go thinking I'm a hero like the captain here,' Hirae replied, smiling at the young man's infectious response.

'I set off to find one fighter and now we are a warrior band of three, four including your huge dog!' Kayton replied with enthusiasm.

Scase tilted his head, as though in agreement, powerful jaws opening appearing to mimic a smile. Kayton rubbed the dog on the head, before looked to the east.

'We're coming, Sionan!'

CHAPTER FOUR

'*Run!*' the emaciated girl repeated.

The dawn light coming through the window accentuated the thinness of her face and desperation in her eyes. Her silver hair gave her a ghostlike appearance as her haunted eyes darted around the room in fear and pleaded with Sionan to escape whilst she could.

'I can't leave you here like this,' Sionan whispered urgently. 'I have to get you out of here!'

'It's too late,' Leetha replied, her voice weaker. 'Don't trust them. Whatever they say, don't trust them.'

Feeling helpless, Sionan held the girl's hand. She could see that Leetha was struggling to draw breath to say something more.

'What have they done to you?' Sionan asked with trepidation.

She leaned in, desperate to hear any words the girl may speak and to understand what had befallen her. Leetha's eyes drifted to a close. In panic and desperation, Sionan grasped the girl's shoulders, gently shaking her frail body to stir her back to wakefulness. The girl's sunken eyes did not open. Her laboured breathing rasping in and out was the only sound in the room.

'Please, please, speak to me!' Sionan urged desperately, swamped with choking fear that she would be left alone with no answers to her many questions.

Leetha slowly opened her eyes, the monumental effort draining the last of her energy. Sionan grasped her hand, and just when she hoped that Leetha would speak again, the last breath exhaled from the girl's desiccated body.

Sionan looked at the girl in disbelief, unable to accept that someone she had once seen each day was now this aged, lifeless husk.

She clutched Leetha's wrinkled hand, hoping for any sign of life, but knowing deep down there was none left. Fighting back grief and fear, Sionan was unable to reconcile her mundane act of accepting a few weeks of work in the castle with the horror she had just witnessed. She stood and backed away from the bed, choking back a sob of terror whilst she looked at the shrivelled body.

Sionan had to escape, she had to get to freedom. Leetha's family needed to know what had happened here. No, not just the family: the whole town should know. The insidious evil of the duke must be stopped. She might not know exactly what had occurred, but she knew the girl in front of her had died because of the duke.

Sionan froze as she realised she was massaging the bruising on her arms again. The purple star-shaped marks had a more sinister meaning now. A wasting disease was the rumour in town, which was frightening enough, but Sionan had never heard of a disease that caused such bruising, or the festering star-shaped sores on Leetha's arms. She had heard Gelanson speak of "practising a fine art", and she would wager that his words were linked to what had been done to them. This was no natural illness that had robbed Leetha of her youth and life.

Sionan looked round the room for anything that could help her. In the corner by the window was a small trunk. Opening it, she found some clothes that must have been Leetha's. The tunic was a little long in the arm and the trousers long in the leg, but they were still a vast improvement on the nightdress she had been wearing. She grabbed a hat from the base of the trunk and tucked her hair up inside. Searching the room for anything else of use, she found a pair of soft leather shoes under the bed. Hands shaking, she fumbled as she put them on. She hid her nightdress in the trunk and closed the lid quietly.

Taking stock of herself, she knew what she wore wasn't much of a disguise, but at least she could try to blend in with the people coming and going. Sionan could see through the window that the sky already had a lighter quality, the morning sun giving ever more urgency to her actions. She had to move quickly if she was going to make it out of the castle before anyone returned to her room as the new day dawned.

She left quietly, closing the door behind her, and listened for any sounds of movement. All she could hear was the thundering of her own heart as her fear heightened.

If I am caught, will they do to me what they did to poor Leetha? she thought.

Creeping along the corridor, hugging the shadows as best as she could, Sionan slowly made her way down the turret stairs. Her descent was agonisingly slow, as she stopped every few steps to listen for movement. She believed she was about halfway down the stairwell when she heard footsteps approaching from below. Quickly, Sionan darted into a side corridor and her eyes frantically sought a room to hide in. She spotted a door and lifted the latch, hid behind the door and left it slightly ajar. Peering carefully through the small gap, she recognised the steward, Onway, taking a tray of food up the stairs. Whether it was for her or Leetha, she did not know, but either way she had only a short period of time before her disappearance would be discovered.

Waiting a few more heartbeats for Onway's footsteps to fade away up the stairs, Sionan's feet flew down the remaining steps, sacrificing caution for speed. She felt at any moment she would hear Onway's deep tones shout out for the guards.

As she reached the bottom of the turret, she slowed in her headlong flight upon spotting the backs of two guards blocking the entrance. She clenched her hands in frustration, realising there was no way past them without being seen. The guards in their purple livery were standing, pikestaffs crossed, barring the way of anyone who wished to enter or exit the turret. Clearly only Duke Gelanson and Onway frequented this area of the castle.

Sionan tucked herself behind a pillar, her forehead creased in worry, trying desperately to think of some way past. This was her best chance of escape. She would be hard-pressed to explain why she was in the baker's daughter's clothes, and Duke Gelanson would know she had seen Leetha. She questioned herself as she struggled to make sense of everything.

What's happening here? What caused the strange, star-shaped bruising on my skin? Is that what killed poor Leetha?

Sionan was rubbing the crooks of her arms again. She felt

alert, though it was probably only the fear pumping through her veins that was keeping her upright. She had to think quickly and get past these guards. If she could just get home, her parents would know what to do.

A distraction was needed. She looked for something suitable to throw; perhaps the guards would move off long enough to investigate the noise. Her eyes searched frantically for any object.

Onway's shout suddenly cut through the still of the dawn air. 'Guards! Guards!'

Sionan shrank down behind the pillar as the two guards raced into the tower and up the stairs. Reacting rather than thinking, Sionan took this golden opportunity and shot through the entrance onto the walkway which ran across the main castle square. She raced along the corridor, and when she reached the corner, she stopped and looked through the decorative stone arches to gain her bearings. She could see the main castle gate not far to the south. There were only a few short yards to make it outside the castle.

Catching her breath, Sionan watched the sun peek over the horizon, and within moments the castle square started to fill with servants about their dawn chores. Four guards stood at the main gate, talking to the milkmaids delivering the day's dairy to the castle kitchens.

Taking a moment to steady her breathing, with her heart thumping, she walked with feigned confidence towards the gate. Expecting a hand to grab her shoulder at any moment, she tried to walk slowly across the courtyard. As Sionan reached the gate, she heard the chatter of the milkmaids returning from the kitchens with their empty pails. Spotting an opportunity, she walked over to the women.

'Can I give you a hand with those?' she asked, smiling and gesturing to the pails. 'I'm on my way back to town and we may as well share a load. I know how busy it gets when the duke has one of his big events coming up.'

'Thank you,' one of the girls replied in surprise.

Sionan lifted a pail, amazed that her voice was not shaking with terror. The girls launched into a sunny conversation as they walked, discussing the amount of milk that had been requested by the cook for the forthcoming banquet, and regaled Sionan with rhetorical questions about the duke and nobles who would be visiting. Sionan forced herself to laugh light-heartedly at their comments and focus on the conversation while they neared the gate and walked through unimpeded. Pails clanging, they passed from the castle onto the road to town. The shadow of the castle loomed behind them as they strode down in the morning sun, the milkmaids oblivious to Sionan's discomfort.

Sionan's heart squeezed in terror as she heard shouting and commotion from the castle.

'What's all the noise back there then?' one of the girls asked.

'Who knows?' another replied. 'But we've got three more trips to make this morning, so we can find out on the way back. C'mon, the herd master will have our hides if we don't get a move on.'

Sionan realised she was holding her breath as the girls continued down the road with her in tow. In mere moments, the traffic on the road increased, enveloping them in noise and bustle as more and more townsfolk travelled to start their daily work. Sionan forced herself not to look behind her as they approached the town. Seeing the side road to the milksheds, she returned the empty pail to the girls.

'You're welcome to help us carry the next load up if you want,' one of the girls laughingly said.

Smiling in response, Sionan politely declined and bade them to enjoy their day. Watching the girls with envy as they walked away carefree and chattering, Sionan mingled with the folk flowing into town. As her heartbeat slowly settled into a normal pace, she allowed herself a look over her shoulder. With relief she noted there were no guards coming from the castle towards town yet.

As joy at the escape and exhaustion warred within her, Sionan moved off towards her home, her mind racing as she tried to plan her next steps. All she really knew was that the duke would be coming for her, and she had to reach her family before the guards. Hurrying forwards, she allowed herself to be swallowed by the crowds gathering for the market.

She may not yet know how, but she would find a way to keep herself and family safe from Gelanson.

CHAPTER FIVE

'This will not do, Onway.' Duke Gelanson shook his head, disappointment etched on his features. 'It is a deep regret of mine that these townsfolk cannot understand the importance of the work they are contributing to.'

He paced the room, holding his hands behind his back. The beat of his steps on the floor marked the tempo of his irritation that the girl had escaped.

'There is nothing else for it, Onway. I have tried kindness, and have allowed them freedoms, but they just do not have the intelligence to understand. We shall have to place a locked door on the tower so there can be no further disappearances. We can allow no freedoms to those privileged few selected for our study.'

'Yes, my lord,' Onway replied, head and shoulders bowed.

'And see to it that everyone is informed that the door is being placed there to contain people who are sick from the wasting disease.'

'Yes, my lord,' Onway repeated, keeping his eyes fixed on the floor.

When Duke Gelanson was unhappy, someone would suffer, and not from anything as obvious as five lashes or time in the stocks.

Gelanson paced the well-appointed study. Beautiful pottery from Sahjashorn and luxurious rugs from Ascalion were lit by the afternoon sun beaming through the leaded glass windows. Delicate statues of all types of creatures and animals adorned carefully crafted display cases. Rooks with emerald eyes and stags with bejewelled antlers stared watchfully from their shelves. The large fireplace remained empty in this room because the duke could not abide too much heat. Gelanson often remarked he could never understand how people could feel so cold in a climate as mild as Clasterne's, but then privately thought that maybe it was their aging blood that caused the chill in their bones.

The walls of the study were lined with precious volumes from throughout the lands of the Overlord and further afield. Gelanson had acquired a wealth of intelligence from the four Manors. Knowledge was priceless to the duke; with it he had ensured Clasterne was becoming one of the most wealthy and powerful Manors in all of the Overlord's lands.

Today, his concerns lay far closer to home, with the missing girl. The duke paced back and forth in his stately, full-length robe of white with the amethyst medallion of office ever present on his chest. He paused to sip from a goblet of watered wine that was on a silver tray on his grand mahogany desk.

'The girl must be found, Onway. We cannot have her telling tales. Put the word among the townsfolk that we have discovered the disease is infectious. That will stop anyone offering to help her.'

The stress of the situation was now causing a headache to burgeon behind his right eye, and Gelanson could not abide pain. He had been a sickly child of an uninterested mother and a father who was a powerful fighting man. Growing up, Gelanson's solace and only joy had come from books. In his mind, the one thing his father had got right was to hire the Principality's best tutor, reputed to have come from far across the Western Seas. Certainly the mystic discoveries taught to the young noble were not based on any of the Principality's lore.

As Gelanson's interest grew, his tutor had encouraged his fascination, always reiterating to the boy that there was no danger in knowledge. One had a duty to science, to understand the mysteries of the world. The impressionable youth had absorbed these lessons and began his own experiments at the tender age of twelve. If anyone thought it odd that animals his parents gifted him kept dying or disappearing, no one dared to comment.

It was at the age of fourteen that Gelanson had killed his mother.

He had not intended to cause any distress, he was merely interested to see what would happen when he applied one of the higher-level incantations from an ancient scroll on a human being. His mother had died in excruciating pain as blood poured from her eyes and nose while she choked on the fluid filling her lungs. Gelanson had been horrified, not at his mother's suffering, but at the distasteful mess and noise of the event.

At that moment, the young boy knew his purpose; he would devote his life's work to recovering the ancient skills of the dark arts and bring them into the light of modern-day science. Gelanson had felt alight with optimism and the glory of direction for his lonely existence. He was committed to a path of discovery.

In his eighteenth year, Gelanson had the epiphany that he would be better than his father at governing the Manor. Not only would the people benefit from Gelanson's superior intellect, it would also allow him greater access to wealth for the pursuit of his ambitions. By this time, he had refined his art to remove the physicality of drowning in blood that his mother had suffered. In fact, the manifestation of the blood pouring from his mother's eyes and nose during her death throes was an unnecessary and clumsy part of the incantation, as far as Gelanson was concerned.

After a successful hunt, his father had been eating at the top table of the hall, talking in his overly loud, brash voice. In the middle of another boastful tale about his hunting prowess, the large man had simply dropped dead. The banquet hall had exploded into uproar and horror that their beloved duke had died. No one had noticed the quiet, studious son sat at the end of the table. No one had heard his whispered chanting amidst the noise of the musicians, jesters, and raucous laughter at the duke's tales.

After the necessary mourning period, Gelanson had stepped in to take control of the Manor. During the Ceremony of Recognition, where the Overlord formally recognised Gelanson as Duke of Clasterne, people commented on how well the young man was coping with his grief. If they noticed how much taller he appeared to stand, it was only to remark on how well he was meeting the expectations of his people as the new duke.

Gelanson stirred from his thoughts, opening a small black

box on his desk. He lifted a green star-shaped stone from the box, his headache from the stress of the escaped girl needed to be resolved so that he could focus. He walked to his faithful steward, lifting the man's hand and placing the small stone in his palm. Gelanson did not notice Onway flinch at the cold touch of the stone.

Gelanson's melodic voice filled the room as he spoke an incantation, and the stone embedded in his Chain of Office glowed, changing from amethyst to vibrant green. The duke breathed deeply with pleasure as the twin green stones pulsed silently with a cold light. His headache faded, and tensions left his body.

After only a few short moments, Gelanson felt fresh and rejuvenated, he removed the star-stone from Onway's hand, barely noticing the deeper wrinkles around the steward's eyes or white hairs that had appeared in the servant's beard.

Placing the star-stone back in the box, Gelanson closed the lid as the stone on his chain changed back to amethyst. 'Find the girl, Onway, and we can return some life to you,' he said in a reasonable tone.

'Yes, my lord,' Onway replied, rubbing at a star-shaped bruise now present in the palm of his hand. The Steward bowed and left the room, stumbling in a body that had aged five years in just a few moments.

Gelanson turned his back on the steward, the unfortunate man already dismissed from his mind.

CHAPTER SIX

Daylight pierced the canopy of trees, dancing across the rabbit trail Scase was snuffling along. Hirae's knowledge of the Ascalion forests allowed a swifter route towards Clasterne than Kayton had travelled, and they were nearing the Gashon crossing, which would take them to only a day away from the castle.

Kayton could feel time marching up his spine but comforted himself with the knowledge that they would still be at the castle before the duke's banquet. Surely Sionan would be safe before the big event. Kayton hoped that with so many nobles and dukes from neighbouring Manors visiting Clasterne, even Duke Gelanson wouldn't wish to jeopardise such an important affair with any intrigue.

The group made steady progress on foot from sunrise to sunset and fell quickly into a comfortable routine. Each day Hirae and Scase would hunt together for rabbits, pigeons, or even small deer, and gather berries, tubers, and greens for the evening meal. Kayton spent his time learning how to track animals and gather food. He was pleased to find a natural affinity for the woodlore Hirae shared with him.

Whilst the meat was roasting over a small fire each evening, Chancer would invest time teaching the boy sword techniques, which Kayton was not such a natural with. However, Chancer commented that, with time, the lad would improve.

'It's all in the feet,' Chancer relayed to Kayton one evening as they settled down by the fire. 'You need to rest on the balls of your feet. Here, try and pivot on your heels, see what happens.'

Kayton rocked back onto his heels, tried to turn quickly and stumbled.

'Try it again on the balls of your feet,' Chancer instructed.

'I feel like a dancer prancing about, not a fighter,' Kayton grumbled.

Chancer's deep belly laugh rolled out in the clearing. 'Lad, some of the best swordsmen I know are trained in dancing. How do you think they move so quickly? Practise your balance and stance every day. That is what will save you in a sword fight, not waving the sword around in front of your nose. Come on, try the basics again.'

Kayton gave a long sigh, sounding more like a petulant teenager than the young adult he was. However, he dutifully pivoted on the balls of his feet, with a little more success moving to the resting stance he had been taught. Standing, left leg in front of him, foot pointing forwards and his right leg behind, and both legs slightly bent for stability. Kayton did not question the stance anymore, not after one lesson where he had decided it would be better to stand with both feet together rather than this long shoulder width stance. Chancer had delighted in sending him sprawling with the first block Kayton had tried to make during that lesson. He did not make the same mistake again. At the end of each day of practising the pattern of moves prepared by Chancer, the sound of Hirae removing the meat from the fire brought relief, becoming Kayton's cue to stop for the evening.

Kayton watched, fascinated, as Hirae broke open the clay she had dug out from a stream bed earlier that day and baked in the fire to form a solid outer skin. Inside the pot, the smell of succulent, roasted pigeon filled the clearing with a mouth-watering aroma. Scase sat, patiently waiting, with large strings of drool hanging from his jowls. Hirae repeated the action with three more pots that had baked in the fire, stripped meat from the carcasses, and shared it amongst all four of them. Scase happily wolfed down his portion before gazing soulfully at Kayton, who had never seen a dog eat so much – but then he had never seen a dog so large before. The hound had quickly picked him out as the softest touch for food, and Kayton, as he did every day, gave Scase some of his dinner, unable to resist the soft brown eyes of the dog.

Whilst Kayton had enjoyed the first week of travel, feeling more comradery and belonging than he had experienced as an orphan in the town of Clasterne, Chancer's experience was not so pleasurable. Over the week, Chancer had felt the vicelike grip of the need for ale begin to loosen its hold on his body. However, he still found himself reaching for a tankard that wasn't there, particularly at night when waking from nightmares. Often he would awake in a cold sweat to Hirae's steady gaze, knowing that she was aware of his inner turmoil. On those nights Scase would come and lay his solid, warm body against Chancer's bedroll, and the comfort he drew from the dog's steady companionship lulled him back to sleep.

Despite Chancer's inner torments, the young lad's enthusiasm for the rescue was beginning to rub off on the jaded captain, although Chancer knew the thin veneer of security, comfort, and naïve optimism would crack as soon as they left the forest. For now, Chancer enjoyed the days of peace before the danger that would surely come, if the boy's tale held truth. For the first time in many years the captain did not anticipate the start of each new day with a dull feeling of emptiness.

'We'll need to make our way to the Gashon crossing,' Chancer broached as they finished eating.

'Why not take the main crossing?' Kayton asked.

'I do not believe you travelled quietly to find me, Kayton, and if you've already taken one beating from the duke's guards, I don't think you will be greeted any more warmly when you return with an armed swordsman in tow. Let's err on the side of caution and approach a little more quietly on the way back. Hirae will scout ahead and see if the way is clear. No one knows you are travelling with us.'

Hirae nodded to Kayton and moved ahead, quickly leaving the men behind as she faded from sight into the forest.

'I know you find these delays hard, lad, but we need to approach carefully. The duke is powerful, and that makes him dangerous to people like us.'

The duo settled down to wait and, as usual, the first sign of Hirae's return was her dog's wet snout pushing on Kayton's hand.

'It's not good news,' Hirae announced. 'It may be nothing, but there are six armed soldiers at the ferry crossing.'

The Gashon crossing was a small ferry with room only

for a handful of passengers and one horse and cart at a time. To have this many armed men at a small border crossing was certainly unusual.

'Kayton, this is perilous,' said Chancer. 'If those guards are there for you, we may not make it to Clasterne at all. We should take another route.'

Kayton leapt to his feet, frustration exploding. 'The banquet is only a day away. I've been too long already. We have to get to Sionan!'

'Hirae, thoughts?' asked Chancer.

'I don't like it, but if Kayton's right and we delay too long there may be no one to save. Anyway, when have you ever taken the safer route, *Chancer*?' she asked with a smile.

'Okay, we'll try for the ferry,' responded Chancer. 'But Kayton, if anyone asks you, we are travelling to Clasterne in the hope of work. I am looking to work for the duke as a guard, and you are looking for an apprentice role in a trade.' He raised an eyebrow at Hirae. 'And you, in your woods gear?'

'Obviously I am looking for work in the stables and kennels as a hunt master,' she replied with a straight face. Chancer nodded in agreement, smiling. There really was nothing else Hirae could be with the distinctive hound walking beside her.

The trio and dog left the cover of the trees and walked purposefully down the dusty track to the ferry. As they approached, Chancer assessed the six soldiers. Three men and one woman were a similar age to himself, and looked like seasoned fighters. They leaned on the wall of the ferry tollhouse, taking their rest where they could. The two younger men were clearly new to the role and strutted around with the impatience of youth. All wore the purple livery of soldiers from Clasterne.

'Morning to you all,' Chancer called. 'How long is the wait for the ferry?'

'Depends who's asking,' one of the young men replied brashly.

The woman, taller than the men, glanced with annoyance at the rude young soldier. Her arms were corded with muscle, tempered from daily sword practice and work. The golden eagle on her leather breastplate covering the cloth denoted her as captain of the squad.

'Excuse the young man,' she said to the newcomers, whilst eyeing the young soldier pointedly. 'Dellen, go and check the horses.' Turning her back on the soldier, she thrust out her hand to give Chancer a brief but firm shake. 'Captain Stegen.'

Chancer noted the callouses on her hand, like his own, reflecting the many hours she must have held a sword. Chancer introduced Hirae and Kayton, neglecting to provide their real names, and enquired again about the ferry.

'The ferry should be back before the sun is fully risen,' Stegen responded. 'The crossing only takes an hour at this point of the river. Where are you folk travelling to?'

'Trying the town and castle in Clasterne for some work,' Chancer responded. 'Do you know of anyone hiring guards?'

'Ah, one of the Overlord's old soldiers, are you?' Captain Stegen remarked with a knowing nod. 'I was one of the luckier ones. My brother and I got taken on by Duke Gelanson when the campaign ended. I don't think there's any guards needed, but it's always worth trying. There may be some work available in town for your wife and son. Join us for a bit of breakfast and tell us your news. We haven't travelled much out of Clasterne for a while now.'

'That's kind of you,' said Chancer, knowing he could not refuse without arousing suspicion. He did not disabuse the captain of her conclusion they were a family unit and deliberately ignored Hirae's unamused stare.

They sat on the ground whilst one of the guards provided some biscuit, dried fruit, and meat. After the freshness of the food from foraging in the forest each day, the soldier's rations were not the most appetising, but Chancer was grateful that there appeared to be no danger.

Captain Stegen eyed the dog. 'Is it friendly?'

'Generally, yes,' Hirae replied. 'Especially if you are feeding him.'

Stegen threw a couple of strips of meat to Scase, laughing as the dog caught each one in mid-air. Scase sat on his haunches, steadily watching, waiting patiently in case any further food came his way.

'So, what news is there from over the border?' Stegen enquired, looking directly at Kayton.

'Ah, well… that is to say—' Kayton stammered.

'You know the young ones,' Chancer interrupted. 'They don't notice anything further than their own nose. We've been travelling from Sendar, in Ascalion. Do you know it?' Chancer ploughed on without waiting for a response. 'There are still the same rumours. The Overlord expanding east across the mountains or west across the sea, depending on which tavern you're in. Taxes are too high, wages are too low, the usual complaints. We're just trying to keep food in our bellies and look for somewhere to settle. We've heard that Duke Gelanson is a fair ruler. Hopefully Clasterne will be the place we can find work and put down some roots.'

'Ah, so you haven't heard our rumours from Clasterne?' Stegen asked with a satirical smile.

'No,' said Hirae. 'What rumours?'

'The duke's none too happy, I can tell you. There's been a rumour started by some townsfolk that he's not treating his people well. Far-fetched but, like you say, it's the usual story created by folk unhappy with paying their taxes, you know how it is. You can't let these things get out of hand, though. First there's rumours, then there's unrest, and then the next thing you know, you have a rebellion like Ascalion all over again. That's why the duke is taking it so seriously. No one wants to go back to the way things were before the peace.'

They all nodded their heads in agreement.

'So, here we are,' continued Stegen. 'Just keeping an eye on those coming in and out of the Manor. We're on the lookout for a young lad. Apparently he's trying to get people to join him in a rebellion. Although, truth be known, the townsfolk seem to think he's more upset about a young lady rejecting his advances and accepting work at the castle.'

Chancer felt Kayton tense next to him and prayed the boy would not be foolish enough to respond.

'I don't get involved in the gossip,' Stegen continued. 'I just follow my orders to apprehend any armed groups led by a young man.' Stegen eyed the trio carefully.

'Thank you for the heads-up,' Chancer replied. 'I hope you locate the culprit. The last thing we need is unrest.'

'He'll give himself away in time,' Stegen said with confidence. 'Then justice will be served. You'll enjoy Clasterne, they're honest people, and the duke is a good man, holds Justice Day every week without fail. Everyone has their opportunity to air grievances in front of Duke Gelanson, even if the grievance is about the duke himself. Just recently, a father accused him of making his daughter sick with a disease, caused a right ruckus; protesting in town and trying to stir up trouble. Sad, really. His grief about his daughter's health had obviously driven him mad.'

'What happened to the man?' Hirae asked.

'Only thirty days in the cells with labour to complete. Our duke is a generous man, that's for sure.'

'A lenient sentence indeed,' Chancer responded before Hirae could comment.

The group finished their food as the ferry appeared in the distance, negating the need for any further conversation. They watched as the pulley operator winched the ferry to shore.

The distraction of the ferry was a welcome relief, Chancer could see that Kayton was struggling with the knowledge that his friendship with Sionan was a source of gossip and amusement.

'Well,' Chancer said. 'I'm glad we're travelling to a place where the duke is so intent on justice and order. It's good to know we will be in safe lands.' He shook Stegen's hand and thanked her for sharing the food and information.

As the trio walked down to board the ferry, Captain Stegen called out to them. 'Keep your eyes open as you travel. The boy we're looking for is headed for a long drop on a short rope. Don't get caught up with him. Guilty by association, and all that.'

Hirae responded with a wave as the ferry bumped against the shore. The operator deftly jumped onto the pier and tied the ferry to the sturdy posts jutting from the bank. When he had made the small vessel safe, he beckoned the trio and dog on board. Scase looked at the river with interest, wagging his tail at the sunlight glistening and sparkling on the water.

The ferry was basic but sturdy in its construction: felled tree trunks lashed together and wooden panels nailed to create a flat floor. On a sunny, calm day like today, crossing the river would be a gentle float as the winch pulled them back.

Once onboard, the operator released the ropes from the mooring with a practised flick of the wrists. Jumping back aboard, he used a long wooden pole to push the ferry from the bank. As the vessel caught in the river flow, it groaned against the winch rope, and then the pulleys took up the slack as the raft was winched safely across. The ferry moved steadily away from the shore, and Chancer and Hirae waved to the soldiers again.

Kayton could barely contain himself. 'I am *not* trying to start a rebellion and Sionan has *not* rejected me. We just had a difference of opinion about her taking work at the castle. I *know* she is in danger. Leetha, the baker's daughter, went there for work and hadn't been seen for weeks when I left. Her father was treated shockingly.'

'It's okay Kayton, relax, we trust you. You're going to hear all sorts of rumours now. The duke can't exactly admit the truth,' Chancer said.

'It's interesting, though', Hirae remarked. 'It seems a lot of effort and expense, sending armed soldiers and stirring up stories about rebellion, all just to silence a few townsfolk who are unhappy.'

Chancer mumbled his agreement.

The ferry operator approached for payment. 'One copper a person and a half for the beast.'

Chancer paid the ferryman and, turning to Kayton, spoke quietly whilst the ferry operator went about his work.

'Clearly there is something to your story. No matter what Captain Stegen said, a duke does not fund armed guards at small way stations, looking for a young man spreading rumours. There must be more to it. Duke Gelanson is clearly hunting you, Kayton. We're going to have to be a lot more careful now in our approach. We were lucky back there, I'm not sure we will be that lucky again.'

Kayton nodded, worried.

'For everyone we meet now, we are a family travelling to try and settle in Clasterne,' Chancer continued. 'And Hirae, try and look a bit less, you know, wild.'

Hirae raised her eyebrows in disgust. Scase, after the initial excitement of watching the flowing water, was less excited now that the ferry had set off, gently bobbing along through the current. He sat down beside Hirae, eyes watching the approaching shore.

Eventually, the ferry bumped gently against the opposite bank. The operator deftly leapt on to the jetty and repeated the action of tying the ferry up on the mooring. Scase leapt with one huge bound up the bank and ran around like a puppy, chasing imaginary rabbits, clearly enjoying the feeling of being back on land. Hirae also seemed to be thankful, her features relaxed from the tense scowl she had been holding on the journey.

They headed up the track towards the trading road that would take them to Clasterne town. As they walked over the rise of the bank, Kayton tensed, his gaze frozen on a group of soldiers standing at the top of the bank. Chancer looked from the four guards in their purple livery to Kayton's face. He could see fear written plainly across the lad's features.

It would appear that their luck had just run out.

CHAPTER SEVEN

'I know him,' Kayton hissed urgently. 'He's one of the castle guards. What is he doing here? I've served him at the Three Crowns. What if he recognises me?' The words tumbled over themselves, fear evident in the boy's voice.

'There's nothing we can do now,' Hirae replied calmly. 'We can't go around them, they've already seen us. We'll have to go through them.'

Hirae and Chancer eyed the four armed men. One had a wicked scar down the right side of his face, and he spoke first as they walked up the rise from the riverbank.

'Morning, all. How was your trip across the river?'

'Good, thanks,' Chancer replied, standing in front of Kayton, trying to unobtrusively block the soldiers view of him. 'We're a little delayed,' he added. 'We were hoping to get to town tonight, but I suspect it won't be until tomorrow now.'

'You're right there,' the soldier replied. 'On foot you've got another day or so's travel, but there's a good wayside inn that you'll reach before nightfall. You can rest up there.'

Hirae smiled in response as she and Kayton headed down the road. Kayton stayed on her right, head down, as far from the soldiers as he could be without drawing unwanted attention.

'Thanks,' replied Chancer as he hefted his pack, appearing to make it more comfortable on his back but Hirae knew he was carefully freeing his range of movement in case he needed to access his knives or sword.

The trio strode away from the soldiers purposefully. Hirae could feel her back itching ominously – exposed. Her stomach sank as he heard a shout.

'Stop!' a younger soldier with a fresh face called. 'Sir, that's the boy from the town that the duke wants arrested! He's the one!'

The rasp of steel filled the air as the four guards drew their swords.

'Drop your weapons and stand fast!' shouted a soldier.

'Run!' bellowed Chancer, breaking for freedom with Hirae and Scase. Kayton stood transfixed as the armed guards ran to try and surround them.

'We can't let them escape!' screamed the young soldier, sword raised, leaping forward at Kayton.

Hirae, sprinting away from the guards, looked over her shoulder to see Kayton still rooted to the spot with fear, the young soldier's sword slicing through the air to strike. Her hunting knife flashed into her hand and without pausing, she spun towards their attackers, drew back, and threw the knife with power. The blade glittered in the sun as it arced smoothly across the gap to land solidly in the chest of the young soldier. Kayton watched aghast as the soldier looked down with confusion at the large knife handle protruding from his chest, blood rising to bubble from his mouth as his legs crumpled and he fell to the ground.

Two further guards also dropped, with Chancer's

throwing knives embedded in their throats. Strange gurgling noises echoed on the riverbank as their lifeblood poured out, trickling down to join the river.

In mere moments, only the man with the scar on his face remained standing, and he backed away towards the ferry, knowing he could not win this fight. Scase followed the soldier, growling threateningly, hackles up, looking even larger with his brindle hair standing in a crest along shoulders and back.

The seasoned soldier eyed the dog fearfully. His look said that he had no desire to throw his life away now he has outnumbered. The ferry owner huddled behind the winch in terror at the sudden violence as the scar-faced soldier backed onto the ferry.

'Cast off!' the soldier instructed the frightened man, eyeing the trio on the bank and their vicious dog.

Hirae and Chancer exchanged a quick look. They could cut the rope the winch ran on and leave the ferry and its occupants to drift to their fate, or they could run the risk of Captain Stegen and her armed unit coming back after them.

'Cut it!' Hirae urged. 'They'll ground further downstream, it will buy us more time.'

'Leave it,' Chancer replied, looking at the colourfully painted ferry winch. 'I do not have the stomach to destroy an honest man's livelihood just to save our own skins. We can make good time now,' he said, gesturing at the soldiers' horses that were picketed this side of the bank.

'Still soft,' Hirae said, shaking her head at him in mock disappointment as they strode towards the dead men's horses.

Kayton still stood frozen, staring at the three corpses. He

had barely breathed since the terrifying violence erupted.

'You killed them…' he croaked. 'You killed them!' Horror and dismay created sharp, accusing edges to his words.

'What did you think was going to happen on this journey?' Hirae asked as she and Chancer retrieved their weapons and cleaned them on the clothes of the dead.

Sliding his throwing knives back into their sheaths, Chancer paused and looked at Kayton's grief-stricken face, the lad's barely grown sandy beard making him look even younger than his years.

'Kayton, you need to decide if you want to go through with this before more lives are lost,' Chancer said. 'Now is the time to walk away if you want to. No one will fault you, but if you want to go ahead with this, people are likely to die. Hirae will not allow herself to be taken by the guards and nor will I. Think on it, and think carefully, but for now we have to move.'

Scase leant his massive body against Kayton's legs, appearing to offer comfort. Leaving them, Chancer and Hirae moved off to the horses, removed the purple tailcoats of Gelanson's livery, and adjusted the stirrups and reins.

'In for a penny,' Hirae murmured as she searched through the soldiers' packs. As she rummaged for useful supplies, a handful of papers fell out of the pack belonging to the young soldier whose actions had triggered the cycle of violence. Hirae's eyes flicked over the name recorded on a wage note – *Jabad Stegen.*

She passed the paper to Chancer. 'What do you think?' she said. 'Younger brother to the captain across the river?'

'Either way, he's dead now,' Chancer replied. 'And it means

nothing good to us if he is a relative, that one has the look of eagles about her.'

'You're right there,' replied Hirae, gazing at the ever-dwindling ferry on the river, returning to Captain Stegen and her men. Sighing, Hirae returned to the packs and took out all useful supplies, including a money pouch, and transferred them to their belongings before leaving behind the saddlebags, which had the troop's eagle emblem stamped into the leather. Seeing Kayton still not moving, Hirae returned and gave him a rough shove.

'Move. You can grieve for them later.' Kayton was clearly in shock, but she had neither the time nor inclination to nurse him through what, to her, was an obvious outcome of the journey. She bent down with her hands cupped as a step up for the lad. 'Get on the horse, Kayton. We have to go.'

The urgency in Hirae's voice seemed to reach through to the lad, and he climbed into the saddle with her help. Hirae tied a lead rein on to the horse's bridle to control his horse and held on to it as the group set off with Scase loping along beside them.

'Hold on to the pommel,' Chancer shouted to Kayton as he kicked his horse into a canter. The sudden lurching movement snapped Kayton into holding on with all his strength. The horses leapt forward, smoothly building to a gallop down the road.

Hirae knew they had only a couple of hours' head start before the chase was on. The thudding of the hooves as the horses galloped down the hard-packed earth road was like a clock pounding down on time. Aware that their lead was slowly ticking away, she spurred the horses on.

After a hard ride that must have felt like a bone-jarring eternity to Kayton, Chancer held up his arm to signal the group should slow to a walk. Hirae remained in control of Kayton's mount and gently encouraged the lathered horses to slow.

Scase had dropped back as the horses had cantered for five leagues. The hound would continue to lope along at a wolf's run, chewing up the distance slowly league by league. Hirae was unconcerned as they slowed the horses, knowing the dog would reappear in his own time, quite probably after hunting some dinner along the route.

'We need to lay some false trails, or they'll be on us in no time.' Hirae viewed the surrounding land critically. 'We're only a few hours' travel from Clasterne, but we cannot risk staying out in the open any longer. The woods will provide us cover,' she continued, signalling to move to the left of the road where a woodland stretched as far as the eye could see. 'We keep the sun on our right, that way we'll still be heading in the correct direction. I can keep us safe in the woods.'

They guided the horses off the road and into the trees, following her instructions, Hirae still leading Kayton's mount by the rein. It was clear the young man was no rider; his knuckles were white from grasping the saddle pommel and his face was set in a grimace of pain.

They followed a deer trail deep into the woods as dusk fell and Hirae finally announced it was safe to stop. Kayton groaned as he tried to get off the horse, but his feet were trapped in the stirrups. Hirae chuckled at the lad's distress. Taking pity, she released the boy's feet, and pushed his leg up and over the saddle as Chancer helped him down the other side. Kayton fell to the floor with a muffled shout.

'I can't believe people ride for pleasure,' the lad grumbled through clenched teeth.

'You'll find you enjoy it more when you know how to do it,' Chancer replied.

'It helps if you don't sit like a sack of potatoes,' Hirae quipped.

Chancer frowned at Hirae. She was a tough woman who had seen much in her life, which made her short of patience with people, especially when it related to them not knowing how to look after themselves. She quirked an eyebrow at Chancer but held her tongue from further criticism.

Kayton stood slowly, bent over like an old man. He tried to collect firewood whilst Hirae removed the saddles and packs from the horses.

'No fire tonight,' Chancer said. 'It would be too easily traced'.

Kayton sank to the floor and lay there unmoving, looking at the sky through the canopy of the trees. The peacefulness in the wood made the violence of only a few hours ago feel like a lifetime ago, but Kayton knew it was real, and there was no going back now. Whilst he may be young and naïve compared to Chancer with his fighting skills and Hirae with her cold competence, he was not stupid. He understood clearly now the ramifications of what he had set out to do, but he still held the unwavering conviction that they were doing the right thing. Something bad was happening in Clasterne, and he had to try and stop it.

He levered himself up on his elbows to speak. 'I'm sorry I didn't draw my sword, and I'm sorry for the way I reacted to what you had to do.'

Hirae paused from unsaddling the horses. 'It's no bad thing to stop and question whether violence is necessary, Kayton, but you need to understand that if Chancer and I deem any of our lives are in danger, we will act. Always.'

Kayton looked up with fresh eyes at the tall woodswoman who was returning his gaze earnestly. He realised how efficiently she would kill if she believed it necessary. He saw an inner strength, and knew innately that she would never back away from a fight. There was an unshakeable loyalty between Hirae and Chancer that would always drive them on. Kayton understood now he had been a fool to think no one would get hurt. His resolve strengthened.

'So, Kayton, now you know how it will be. People will die, and we might die. You must be unshakeable in your faith that we are doing the right thing. We are here because of you. If you are doubting your cause, now is the time to speak up,' Chancer spoke firmly.

'And with the money pouch from the soldiers' saddlebags we'll have enough salt for winter, we can disappear from Clasterne.' Hirae added, looking at Kayton.

Kayton paused, weighing his words carefully. 'I've never seen people killed before, and in all honesty, I hope not to see it again, but I am still certain someone must make a stand against the duke. I will be ready next time if we must protect ourselves.' He made to stand and draw his sword to mark his words, but the pain of cramp from horse riding reduced his intended dramatic flourish to a feeble hobble. The tension lifted from the group as laughter peeled out.

'Relax, Kayton. We know you are brave. When the

time comes, you will be ready to fight. Trust me,' Chancer reassured the young man. 'Hirae, what about you? Do you wish to continue?'

'I say we carry on,' she responded without pause. 'Something does not feel right here, and you know my feelings about the nobility. There were too many guards stationed for something as inconsequential as a disgruntled youth spreading rumours. Besides, when have I ever walked away from a fight?'

Chancer smiled in agreement. 'The die is cast now. Kayton, be assured we will fight only when there is no other option. You must never attack because of damaged pride. Only draw your weapon to prevent capture or loss of your life. When you do fight, you must be completely committed. Give everything you have.' Kayton listened intently as Chancer continued. 'When swords meet, there is no room for second-guessing. You must fight until your opponent yields, cannot continue, or lies dead at your feet. Do you understand?'

Kayton considered these words carefully and nodded in solemn response, hardening his heart to always follow Chancer's rules of engagement.

'Hirae,' Chancer continued. 'You have the best skill in the woods. We'll wait for a few hours, and you lead the horses to the south-east, so they think we're still heading directly to the town.'

'I'll take them a couple of leagues and then Scase will drive them on for a while. Don't worry, they won't find our trails back.'

Hearing his name, Scase emerged from the woodlands like a ghost. His brindle marking allowed him to blend into the background, almost invisible. Tail wagging, he trotted over to Hirae, who crouched to scratch the dogs' ears.

'What's your plan?' she asked Chancer.

'We'll circle Clasterne, staying in the woods, and then approach the town from the south side. If we keep moving at forced march, we'll make good speed. Kayton, rest now. You're going to need your strength.'

Kayton took the opportunity to stretch out on the ground, which was covered with a soft bed of moss perfect for his aching muscles. He watched Hirae head off back down the trail, leading the horses with Scase.

'Will she be okay?' Kayton asked.

Chancer laughed as he spread out his bedroll and laid down. 'I haven't met anyone or anything who can best Hirae in the woods yet. She's safer than we are.'

Without further ado, Chancer rolled onto one side, cushioned his head on his arm, and closed his eyes. Kayton lay, feeling the aches and pains in his body. A heavy melancholy gripped his spirit as he remembered the men who had died today because of his decision to seek help for Sionan. His mind drifted while he thought about the journey, wondering, as he had many times, why Hirae and Chancer were so close. Their relationship was an enigma to him.

'Are you and Hirae... together?' he ventured to ask Chancer.

Chancer opened his eyes and raised his head to look at the young man. 'Together?'

'Well, yes, you know, close,' Kayton replied, feeling himself blushing and wishing he had never started the conversation.

'I would trust her with my life,' Chancer replied, laying

his head back down and closing his eyes again.

Kayton knew he was not going to get any further information and sighing, turned over onto his side to try and sleep, and seek some solace after the long eventful day.

The moon was high in the night sky when Kayton awoke, a dog's face looming to his left. He was becoming used to Scase's wet snout waking him. Gently pushing the dog's head away from his face, he scratched Scase behind his left ear, on the beast's favourite spot. The dog grumbled in contentment.

Chancer was already up and Hirae was sitting on one of the packs, eating what looked like berries and tuber roots. Kayton saw a small pile set aside on a dish for him and smiled his thanks as he made short work of the food.

'The horses will be leading the soldiers on a merry dance now,' Hirae said as she rose and grabbed her pack. 'I took them two leagues onto another trail. Scase drove them on down, didn't you, boy?'

The dog leant on her, as she rubbed him on the back.

'They won't find our trail back here,' she said confidently. 'Now we just have to ensure this town lad doesn't leave a trail as wide as the road when we move on,' she added, her eyes wrinkling with the trace of a smile to take the sting from the words. 'Follow me closely, Kayton, and we'll be just fine.'

They moved off slowly in the opposite direction from where Hirae had taken the horses. Their progress was slow as she checked and re-checked that her companions were leaving no sign of their passage.

When they reached a stream, Hirae instructed them to remove their shoes and roll up their trousers. Kayton did not fully understand why, but complied. All became clear when he saw Hirae enter the stream and wade against the flow upstream for an hour.

'That'll fox any scent-hounds they have,' Hirae remarked to him as she moved off into the woods.

Night passed into day as they edged their way closer to Clasterne from a circuitous, southerly route. Kayton curbed his impatience as Hirae led them through the woods without incident for the remainder of the day before they were finally in sight of buildings and ready to make a foray into the town.

'Tonight, we camp here, and we will move into the town at daybreak. We need to gather information. Where do you suggest we start, Kayton?'

'Sionan's home,' Kayton instantly replied. 'Sionan will have definitely tried to contact her mother.'

'Very well, get some rest, we will move at first light,' replied Chancer.

It had been nearly four weeks, all told, since Kayton had left the town. He ached with anxiety to know what was happening to Sionan, but knew he had to trust Hirae and Chancer's expertise. If they said to wait one more night and move at sunrise, then he would respect their wishes.

As they all settled in their bedrolls, with Scase curled up by his mistress, Kayton couldn't help but envisage the look of wonder and gratitude that he would see on Sionan's face when they rescued her. He fell asleep with youthful dreams of basking in her adoring glory, blissfully unaware of the events that would unfold with the coming dawn.

CHAPTER EIGHT

Sionan soon became lost in the ebb and flow of people surrounding the opening market stalls. She felt the relief at the success of her escape wash over her, but she knew she needed to plan her next steps carefully. Thoughts tumbled through her tired mind.

How can I make people believe what I saw? How can I stop the duke without jeopardising my family? Who can help me?

She halted, looked at her surroundings, and realised she was making her way home out of habit, but that was surely the first place the castle guards would search for her. Remembering Leetha dying in front of her eyes, she knew that she had to go to the bakery first and tell the girl's parents all she had seen.

Feeling braver now she had a set plan, Sionan headed into the market, turning away from the street that led to the tailor's shop and her family home. Being sure to keep to areas where the crowds were busiest, she headed towards the bakery. The familiar shouts of the market sellers and smells of baked pies lulled her into a sense of security and wrapped her in comfort.

Although the sun had not yet reached its zenith, the morning was quickly slipping away. Rounding a jewellery stall with brightly coloured necklaces and trinkets sparkling in the morning sun, Sionan saw the vendor eyeing her with mistrust. She must look like a vagabond in these ill-fitting clothes, which may well be serving as a better disguise for a tailor's daughter than she could have hoped.

She hovered in the shadow of a spice stall to observe the bakery opposite. Keeping her head down, she looked back furtively and could see no guards in the market crowds. The smell of the saffron spice and warm, fresh loaves drifted on the gentle spring breeze, and Sionan felt her stomach rumble despite the danger she knew she was still in. Watching for a moment more she decided to enter, taking one last look around, she darted across the road and entered the open door of the bakery.

At the counter a large woman welcomed her with a warm smile but sad eyes. Sionan felt her heart wrench at the news she would have to give her.

'Sorry, dearie, I've nothing for you yet, but come back at closing time and you can have anything that is left. Better it goes to use than ruin.'

It took a moment for Sionan to realise the baker must have thought she was a beggar trying her luck for some food. Tendrils of the woman's grey hair escaped from the sides of her cap, similar to the one on Sionan's own head. The baker's frame was powerful from years of kneading dough, and softened by the curves from the good pastries she clearly enjoyed each day. The sunny voice did not match the sadness in her eyes.

Sionan had heard about the incident where her husband had accused Duke Gelanson of making his daughter ill to the point of death. At the time Sionan had agreed with other townsfolk that it was the poor man's grief at his daughter's dwindling health driving him to irrational talk. She knew better now.

'I've come from the castle, I saw your daughter.' The words burst out, and Sionan saw a light of hope enter the mother's eyes.

'You saw Leetha?' the large woman asked quickly. 'How is she? Is she any better? They won't let me see her!' The baker wrung her hands together, worry for her daughter etched in her face.

Sionan looked into the woman's eyes and tried to find the right words. She felt a tear roll down her cheek unbidden as she struggled, Leetha's husk of a body haunting her mind. Sionan laboured to describe what had happened.

Fearful understanding dawned on the baker's face. '*No,*' the woman whispered as she grasped at the shop counter to steady herself.

'I'm sorry, I saw her with my own eyes,' Sionan choked out.

'You were with her when it happened?'

'Yes,' Sionan replied, her head dropping with the pain of the memories.

Carefully, she told the baker all that had happened, from her waking in the tower to the final words she had heard Leetha say.

'I'm so sorry, your husband was right, I don't know what is happening, but it is something terrible.'

The baker's body shook as she cried with grief and the defeating knowledge that they had not been able to save their daughter. 'What can be done, what can be done? Where do we get justice for my daughter? They punished my husband and killed my child, and no one will listen!'

Sionan felt helpless in the face of the woman's impassioned plea. 'Truth will out, you'll see, ma'am.' Sionan tried to sound convincing, but did not truly believe the words herself. People had steady work and regular food now, and the taxes were moderate. Everyone spoke with excitement about the festival days Gelanson held to celebrate the changing of the seasons, and if there were any disputes they were always aired on Justice Day. In this comfortable setting, folk did not want to hear dark tales of strange happenings.

'There must be justice for my Leetha!' The baker's voice hardened with rage. 'Duke Gelanson may be the law in this Manor, but even he has to answer to the Overlord!'

Sionan nodded, dumbfounded at the baker's words. To petition the Overlord was unheard of. Perhaps it was the grief taking its toll.

If our own townspeople won't believe what is happening, Sionan thought, *why on earth would the Overlord turn on a tax-paying duke?*

The baker, shoulders shaking with grief, stumbled from the counter towards the back of the shop. 'My poor child, my darling Leetha, how could they? How *could* they?'

Sionan tried to think of some comfort she could offer, but just as she was about to speak again, she heard the terrifying sound of marching feet on the street outside. She knew with sickening certainty it was the guards searching for her.

'I must run, they're coming for me,' she said, her voice shaking with fear as she realised that she had stayed too long.

Hearing the desperation in Sionan's voice, the baker

quickly hustled her through to the back of the shop, pushing a small loaf of bread into her hand as she went.

'Thank you for bringing me the truth, child,' she said, briefly clasping Sionan's hands. 'Go!' she urged as she ushered her out of the back door. 'Flee, child!' she pleaded, closing the back door firmly behind her.

Sionan ran for the woods, knowing her life depended on it. Her mind raced, fear making it difficult to think. Everything was happening so fast, and her pursuers could be only moments behind her. The woods surrounding the town felt further and further away as her breathing laboured. Her heart thumping in her chest was louder than her footfalls as she made it into the trees. She ran on, stumbling over tree roots, her frightened mind imagining the heavy thud of soldiers' feet behind her.

When her lungs screamed at her for air, Sionan collapsed behind a large oak tree, gasping for breath, her legs on fire. Scouring the woodland around her, she could not see any tell-tale flashes of purple from the duke's guards. She panted for breath, held onto the sturdy tree, and looked at the bread still clutched in her hand. Her stomach rumbled noisily in its insistence for food. Sionan slowly clambered to her feet again and ate her crushed loaf as she travelled.

When she recognised the small stream ahead of her, she knew that she had instinctively run towards her home. Stooping to drink some water in her cupped hands, her heart ached to see her parents, only a short distance away from the edge of the woods. She crouched on the tree line, watching the small house where she lived with her father, mother, and two younger siblings. The town of Clasterne was growing fast as the fertile lands and rich woodland surrounding the area supported more and more people to settle here.

Sionan's parents had worked hard at their trade over the years to buy their little house set back from the main street. Sionan had taken the work at the castle because she felt strongly that she was of an age to share the responsibility of providing for the family. She ground her teeth in frustration at the thought of the harm she had brought upon them instead. She had to tell them what had happened.

Sionan cautiously made her way into the back of the house. She crept gingerly up the stairs to her room and used some precious time to dress in her own clothes and sturdy boots for travel, although she had no clear idea where to travel to. The only thing she knew for certain was that if she stayed in Clasterne she would be taken back to the castle, and she was certain there would be no opportunity to escape from there again. Sionan looked in the mirror and tried to see the same self-assured young woman who had left for the castle weeks ago. However, only a frightened face stared back at her.

She descended the stairs and took her hat, cloak, and a bag off the hook. With no clear idea of what to do, she decided to wait for her parents to take their lunch, not wanting to risk entering the shop for fear of being seen. Perhaps she could then travel to the next town for work until any interest in her whereabouts had died down.

Suddenly, the hallway door leading from the shop opened and her mother walked through. They were the image of each other in looks separated only by time. As her mother's eyes rose in surprise and pleasure at seeing her daughter, Sionan ran to the safety of her arms. Before she could stop herself, the terror of escaping the castle came flooding back and she found herself sobbing in her mother's warm embrace.

Hearing the commotion, her father poked his head around the door and, seeing his eldest daughter's distress, he called to the two youngest children, Sasa and Venni, to mind the shop. He ushered his wife and Sionan into their small parlour.

'Now then, child, what is all this upset?' her father asked in his usual steady tones.

'We thought you were at the castle for another week,' her mother added. 'The steward was here only three days gone, and he told us how excellently you were fulfilling your duties and that you had been asked to stay longer. What's happened? Has someone treated you cruelly?'

Her father's strong arms led Sionan to sit in one of the comfortable chairs. In faltering words she told her parents all that had happened and everything she had seen.

'I don't remember having any accident at all. Leetha thought something awful had happened to her, and look –' She lifted her sleeves to show them the star-shaped bruise on each arm. 'These match the weeping sores she had. The rumours are true, something awful is happening in that castle. We're all in danger.'

'Sionan,' her father said gently. 'I'm sure it was deeply distressing seeing poor Leetha pass, but I heard from the miller on the town square that she had contracted this terrible wasting disease everyone is talking about and was taken to the castle for care. It really doesn't mean something awful has happened. Perhaps in her delirium from the illness, she was unaware they were trying to cure her and make her better.' He paused. 'If you have the same bruises, we need to get you to a physician, and quickly, we can't risk you developing this awful illness.'

'Yes,' her mother added. 'Let's see if we can get the doctor to attend now, Stanton. Go and fetch them. Sionan, let's get you into bed to rest and get some hot food for you, you're home now, and we'll make sure you get well, don't worry, child.'

Sionan was stunned. Her gaze flickered from her mother to her father, and she realised that they had utter confidence in their misplaced belief.

'Although I do find it a little odd,' her mother continued. 'That the steward was here recently and did not mention you may have been exposed to this awful disease. That troubles me greatly.'

Her father looked worried. He was a good, solid, caring man who could not recognise any sort of wrongdoing or abuse of power in a person such as Duke Gelanson. He shared the same belief as many of the townsfolk that the nobility fulfilled a duty of care to the people they ruled, and Sionan should be as safe in the castle under the care of the nobility as in their family home.

Hopelessness welled up inside Sionan. If her own parents were unwilling to accept her word, then how could she convince anyone else? On her last meeting with Kayton, she had been so confident, mocking his childish belief in the stories. Her face burned at that memory, and now no one believed *her*.

'I know what I saw, and I know I am in danger, this is not a natural disease,' she asserted, trying to sound strong, but the words came out as though she were a spoiled child.

'You are perfectly safe here with us,' her father interrupted. 'Come and take that coat off and rest. We can send a message to the castle to let them know you will be recuperating at home, we need to get you some help for those bruises.'

'Please, Sionan, stay and rest, you have nothing to fear in your own home: we will keep you safe.' Her mother reached out to pull her back on the chair to rest.

Sionan looked at her mother's honest face and castigated herself for her selfishness in coming home at all. She could not jeopardise her family by being here any longer. Her instincts screamed at her to run. Spending more time trying to convince her parents would be a futile waste.

'I must go. I know you feel you can keep me safe, but I don't believe *anyone* is safe,' she said with conviction. 'If the steward returns, promise me you will not tell him you have seen me. If they know I have been here, you will be in trouble. I am sure of it. I must go.' She walked from the parlour, her parents shocked gaze following her.

'Go where, Sionan? This is your home,' her mother insisted.

'To the Overlord,' she replied, trying to sound assured, wondering where the words had sprung from. Hadn't she thought a short time ago that the baker was mad with grief to think of begging clemency from the Overlord?

The astonishment on her parents' faces matched her own doubt whether this was the right path, but not knowing where else to turn, perhaps any action was better than none.

Taking the opportunity presented from their stunned silence, Sionan made for the back door. Flinging it open, she stepped determinedly through, her conviction that she must run carrying her forwards.

She was stopped abruptly by a purple-liveried chest blocking the doorway, and looked up to find herself face to face with a guard from the castle.

CHAPTER NINE

Sionan frantically stepped back from the guard, trying to close the door, but the guard, seeing her intent, blocked it with his boot. Through the doorway five more guards obstructed her escape from the house.

'Now then, miss, there's no need for panic. The duke just wants you to return to the castle so he can ensure you are fully recovered. We can't have you running about town if you have this nasty illness that's going around,' the captain of the guards said reassuringly, employing his most charming smile.

All colour drained from Sionan's face. She turned to run through the house, thinking perhaps she could escape out the front. Seeing her objective, the captain reached into the hallway and grabbed her roughly by the arms.

'No, you don't! We have orders to take you to the castle and that's where you're going. Out you come.' He pulled her from the house and pushed her towards a wiry old guard who grabbed her arms to restrain her.

Sionan heard her mother shriek at seeing her daughter manhandled. Her father came piling out of the house.

'Stop that!' her father shouted. 'Don't you start roughhousing my daughter. That's completely unnecessary!' he stated firmly, moving to his daughter's aid. 'I will bring her to the castle myself to see the physician, you can take your hands off her right now.'

Roaring panic filled Sionan's ears, merged with her father's voice shouting at the guards to let go of her. Dread for her family rocketed through her body. She pulled and wrestled, breaking the hold of the guard. As she turned to run, a pain exploded across her face, driving her to the ground. Her father, seeing his daughter struck down, swung a punch at the guard.

Time slowed as Sionan looked up from the ground to see the guard step back and draw his sword at the same moment as her father, who was not a fighting man by nature, overbalanced when his punch missed and went sailing harmlessly past. Stanton spun full circle, following the swing of his arm and stumbled backwards.

Sionan heard screaming from a distance, vaguely recognising it as the sound of her own voice, as she saw the guard's sword enter her father when his momentum carried him backwards onto the weapon. His own face mirrored the shock on the guard's face as the armed man stepped back, pulling the sword out, leaving her father to collapse to the ground.

'Stanton!' her mother cried with anguish as she ran to him. She fell to her knees, trying frantically to stop the blood pouring from his chest. The choking noise that came from Sionan's father was deafeningly loud in the silence that had befallen the group. Her mother held her husband's face and shouted his name in desperation. Then, there was utter silence as his last breath exited his body.

The captain of the guards looked on the scene, distaste

plainly written across his features. A simple arrest had now become a full incident, and there would have to be an inquiry on Justice Day. If there was one thing Duke Gelanson did not like, it was an inquiry involving his guards.

'It was an accident!' the guard shouted, looking in horror at his bloodied sword.

The captain shook his head at the man. 'That'll be for the duke to decide on Justice Day. Right, come along, let's not have any further difficulty today. Take the girl!' he instructed the guards, and turned to Sionan's mother, who was kneeling on the ground sobbing. 'We're sorry for the incident, madam,' he said, looking dispassionately to the dead man on the floor. 'Rest assured Duke Gelanson will look into this fully.'

Sionan's mother looked at the captain like he was a madman. In the space of a few moments, their world had been destroyed, and now it was being dismissed as an *incident*.

'The undertaker will be sent to you shortly,' the captain added before turning away.

Two guards grabbed Sionan and began to drag her from the house to a waiting black carriage. There were no windows and only one door at the back with a small grill. As they pulled her away, Sionan's rage at the injustice of her father's death exploded, galvanising her into action. She bit, twisted, kicked, and scratched with the whole strength of her being, not caring if she was injured in the process. She fought with undiluted hatred for these soldiers who had destroyed her peaceful home. There would be no more quiet evenings by the fire, sewing and listening to their father's comical tales. Nothing. Their life together as a family was gone. They had murdered her father and she knew there would be no justice.

Sionan felt the grip of the two soldiers on her arm loosen as her frenzied resistance took them by surprise. She wrenched herself free and ran to her father's body. The guards eyed her with more caution now. One of the men wiped blood from his nose where the back of Sionan's head had connected solidly during the struggle.

Sionan swung to face the guards with animosity as they approached her again. She became aware of someone else running towards her and turned, ready for a new attack. She stopped in astonishment as Kayton, brandishing a sword, came running from the woods.

'You'll not touch her again!' he shouted.

Sionan struggled to comprehend what she was seeing. Gentle dreamer Kayton was standing with a sword in front of her father's body, and he looked deadly serious about using it. His open, kind face was set with determination. A tall woman with a wicked hunting knife approached to stand on Kayton's left, and a well-muscled, heavily armed bearded man approached his right side with a sword.

The guards froze as a deep, rumbling sound echoed through the air. The dog's growl was like the warning of thunder before the destruction of a lightning strike. The hound bared his teeth, his whole body poised ready to attack.

The guards looked to their captain for instruction. What should have been a simple arrest had resulted in a man dead, and now they faced armed enemies and a vicious looking hound.

'I am placing you all under arrest for dissent and aggression to the duke's own guard,' the captain announced. 'Take the girl!' he commanded the guards and ran at the bearded warrior.

Sionan watched the tall woman spring into action, ducking a sword swipe from the nearest guard, the woman flowed under the swing, and stabbed the guard in the side with her hunting knife before pivoting away out of his reach. The dog erupted, snarling white teeth flashing as he leapt at the guard who had attacked. With a savage growl the dog bit into the guard's sword arm and bore him to the ground. The crunching sound of bones under the power of the dog's jaws was echoed by the guard's shrill scream.

Sionan watched in shock, but the tall woman was already moving towards the next opponent, calmly throwing the hunting knife in one fluid movement. The unfortunate guard dropped to the floor without a sound, the knife jutting from his chest.

Kayton ran screaming with anger at the wiry guard who had killed Sionan's father.

The guard easily blocked Kayton's wild strike and stepped forward to deliver a direct thrust, but the training had sunk in and Kayton furiously parried with speed born of fear, then stepped back and gave ground. As the guard moved to strike again, Kayton turned the blade with his own sword before lunging forward to stab the man in the chest, the sound of the sword cutting through the guard's flesh reverberating through the air as the man fell to the ground.

Meanwhile, the bearded warrior fought with the economy of an experienced swordsman, whirling between the swords of the captain and one of the guards. Everywhere they tried to strike they found air or were blocked by the warrior's sword. As the captain lunged to deliver a killing blow, the warrior sidestepped before delivering a deadly riposte, stabbing the man through the heart. The warrior then deftly spun away from an overhead strike from the remaining guard and savagely slashed the man's wrist, severing the sword hand. The guard fell to the ground, screaming in agony, and was quickly dispatched with a clean thrust through his chest.

The trio of fighters turned to face the last guard, but the fight was already over. The guard had dropped her sword and backed away from the group. Turning, she ran for the tree line and had almost made it when a throwing knife lodged in her back. The guard fell face forward on to the earth and lay there unmoving.

Sionan stood in horror, staring wide-eyed at the blood soaking into the ground. Her mother was covering her father's body with her own as if, by protecting him from the fight, she could bring him back to life.

Sionan could not process the violence she had observed, and could not believe how quickly everything had spiralled out of control. All she had wanted to do was escape from the castle, and now her father was dead and her terrified mother and sisters were in mortal danger. She felt someone gently take her arm and looked up into Kayton's concerned gaze.

'Sionan, are you hurt? I'm sorry we weren't here in time to save your father.'

Sionan looked at Kayton blankly. Shock had set in and she could find no words to respond.

'Chancer and Hirae travelled with me to save you,' Kayton continued. 'We need to get you somewhere safe.'

Sionan turned away from him and went to kneel by her mother, wrapping her arms around her sisters who ran to her, as they wept inconsolably. She ignored the approach of Kayton and his comrades.

'Please, Sionan!' Kayton pleaded. 'If you stay here the guards will come for you. We are here to rescue you.' Kayton's words faltered, the empty and naïve words dropping into the silence.

'Rescue?' Sionan choked out. 'No, this is no rescue, if I run with you, my mother and sisters will be in danger. I should have just stayed at the castle, then Father would still be alive.'

She hung her head, the weight of the words almost too heavy to bear. Sionan's voice was so quiet the group barely heard her continue, 'I have to return. It's the only way my family can be safe. I was foolish to leave the castle in the first place. It has only bought sorrow. Duke Gelanson will never allow me to be free. If I return now, my mother and sisters may be spared.'

'Please, Sionan. Your mother and sisters can come too,' Kayton urged. 'We must get away. If you go back, you'll die!'

'You want me to doom my family to a life of hardship, running from the duke, always running? No, Kayton. I will go back.' She looked up at him, his blue eyes were shining with sincerity, but she barely recognised the young man in front of her now. 'You must stay away from my family. There is no help to be had here, nothing to protect folk like us.'

Chancer clasped Kayton on the shoulder.

'She's right, lad,' he said. 'Her family will be safer if she returns to the castle.'

'Then what was the point of it all?' Kayton shouted in frustration. 'Why did we kill the guards if we're just going to let her go back? What if Gelanson decides to kill them all anyway? There must be something we can do!'

'There is,' Hirae interjected, her voice a pool of calm. 'At the moment we don't know what is happening in the castle or what is being covered up. If you truly want to stop Gelanson from doing this to others, Kayton, we need more information. If Sionan goes back, she can try to find out. We don't know what we're up against, so we don't know how to stop it.'

'So, you are suggesting that we *rescue* Sionan again?' Kayton asked incredulously. 'Don't you think that's going to be a little difficult, given all that has happened?'

Sionan laughed mirthlessly. 'You didn't rescue me the first time, Kayton, I rescued myself. All you've done is make things worse by killing the guards.'

'Kayton,' Chancer interjected before the lad could respond to Sionan's stinging response. 'The guards were dead the moment you ran from the trees. Hirae's plan is audacious and has risk, my favourite type of strategy.' A ghost of a smile spread across Chancer's face. 'And it buys time for the family to escape.'

Sionan's face lit up with hope at the confident warrior's words. Any possibility of keeping her mother and sisters safe was a plan worth following.

'If they all try to run now, they will be captured within days.' Chancer continued, 'Look at her sisters, Kayton. They are too young to travel fast. If Sionan is returned to the castle, focusing the duke's attention on her, that allows her mother and sisters an opportunity to get away. That could work.' Chancer walked to Sionan and knelt down beside her, looking into her sorrowful brown eyes. 'Sionan, I am Chancer Landry. You don't know Hirae and me, but I give you my word, two nights from now we will come for you in the castle. Learn everything you can and be ready for us. It will give your mother and sisters time to prepare for travel.'

'Travel where?' Sionan asked. 'Nowhere is safe in the whole Manor.'

Chancer turned to address her mother. 'Go south towards Sahjashorn, travel with any merchant you can find as they leave the market. You must leave before the second night. They will come for you when we free Sionan. Do you understand?'

The woman nodded dully at Chancer's words, her eyes never leaving her dead husband.

'I have a friend in Hamden,' Chancer continued. 'Go to the Barge Inn on the river and tell the owner you are friends of Captain Chancer. Tell him I am calling in the favour owed. He will keep you safe until I can come for you.'

Chancer repeated the information to the grieving woman. The trauma of her husband's death appeared to be preventing Sionan's mother from absorbing the instructions fully. 'Two days is only a short time to prepare to travel and complete your farewells,' Chancer said, looking towards Stanton's body. 'But as a tailor, you have skills to offer along the journey which will keep you all safe and fed with merchant wagons.'

As Chancer and Hirae moved away, Kayton halted them with his words.

'I'm staying with Sionan. Two people in the castle will be better than one. Besides, if we tell them I have killed the guards then they won't be searching for you.'

'Without wishing to upset you, Kayton, do you really think Gelanson will believe a boy from town managed to kill six guards? I think it's unlikely,' Chancer responded.

'His thinking is sound, Chancer. Even if they don't fully believe his story, it will create some breathing space whilst they figure out what has happened and two pairs of eyes will be better than one in there,' Hirae added. 'Although, I don't like it. What if Duke Gelanson decides to execute you on the spot, Kayton?'

'He won't,' Kayton said with confidence. 'He will need to make an example of me at the next Justice Day. The townsfolk will want to know why one of their own has been killed, and that gives Gelanson the perfect opportunity to lay the blame at my door.'

Hirae and Chancer looked at each other, weighing the lad's words.

'There is merit to the plan,' Hirae said to Chancer. 'If we remain invisible, it will greatly increase our chances of success, and if we strip the guards' bodies of money maybe the duke will believe it was a robbery gone wrong.' She whistled Scase to her, who was still worrying at the arm of the guard who had bled out on the ground.

'How long until the next Justice Day?' she asked.

'Three nights from now,' Sionan responded.

'That's the decision made then, we'll come for both of you in two nights,' Chancer repeated emphatically. 'Sionan, tell us everything you know about the castle's layout and what happened last time you were there.'

Sionan told them in a shaking voice about Leetha and where they had been held. Chancer questioned the girl carefully, but the grief was taking its toll and she stammered to a halt, eyes resting on the still form of her father.

Hirae handed Chancer his throwing knife and retrieved

her hunting knife. Sionan watched them clean their weapons on the tunics of the dead guards and move to leave.

Hirae looked towards the woods. 'We can stay no longer. Be safe, Kayton,' she said, taking his arm in the warrior's grip. 'Stay strong, we will come for you.'

'Wait!' Kayton suddenly said. 'I haven't paid either of you. In case I don't come back…'

'We never really did this for the money,' Hirae said with a flashing smile, her green eyes dancing. With a wave, she turned and walked towards the tree line, Scase close at her heels.

'Two nights from now,' Chancer repeated, squeezing Kayton's shoulder. Nodding at Sionan, he turned to follow Hirae.

Within moments they had disappeared into the woods, and all that was left was the quiet weeping of a family over the body of a beloved father.

CHAPTER TEN

Hirae sat with her back against a tree, focused on trying to enjoy the warmth of the afternoon sun and the comfort of Scase lying parallel to her, resting his huge head on her lap. The air smelled of pollen from trees coming into flower, and the sound of birds singing was joyous after the death and violence of the day before. Life had become dangerously complicated since agreeing to help Chancer, and despite her outwardly cold demeanour, killing always disturbed Hirae.

Chancer and Hirae had camped deep in the woods overnight, trying to come up with viable options for their rescue attempt. Hirae knew that a heavy melancholy had risen in Chancer to replace the thrill of the fight. The knowledge that the dead guards, may have had loved ones and people who depended on them sitting uneasily on both of their minds. Chancer had scouted dangerously close to the edge of the woodland to view the castle through his farsight lens. They had taken watches throughout the night, observing through the magnifying scope, learning everything they could about the building's layout and the guards' movements.

During the rebellion, the Overlord had invested in providing a farsight lens for all her captains. Something so simple had given the crown an advantage over the less well equipped Ascalion rebels. The Overlord's troops watched the rebels' movements from afar and gained intelligence on their numbers and equipment, which had allowed her army to stay one step ahead and ultimately win a decisive victory.

Hirae wondered how Kayton would react if he learnt she was actually an Ascalion rebel fighter and had fought against Chancer rather than with him, as the young lad had assumed. When you lived in a town like Clasterne, you relied on news from afar announced by the town crier. She was pretty sure this news would not have favoured the Ascalions.

Chancer's squad had attacked Hirae's band when they had retreated to the very north of Ascalion in the Kaweot Pass. After a bitter winter, the mountains were treacherous, and the clashing of swords and shouts of battle had caused a deadly avalanche. She and Chancer had been battling under an overhang, and they had turned in disbelief as the roar of sliding snow deafened the sounds around them. In a split second, all fighting paused as the men and women stopped, horror on their faces, to see the cascade of snow and ice rushing towards them like a waterfall. With no time to reach safety, the troops were swept away. Hirae had only moments to grab Chancer and push them both as far under the overhang as they could squeeze. They gripped the rock face in sheer terror for what felt like a lifetime as snow thundered past them. She would never know why in that moment she had chosen to save her enemy, other than that it had felt like the right decision to save any human life in the face of nature's anger.

In the weeks that followed they battled, not with each other, but together, to stay alive, escape the pass, and reach civilisation. The hardships they faced finding food, shelter, and warmth as they painstakingly picked their way out of the mountains built a lasting respect and loyalty between them. They had never spoken about the Overlord or the rebels – they left that war in the past as they focused on survival – but Hirae knew that Chancer held himself responsible for the loss of his troop, having confided in her that he was the one who had chosen the spot for the ambush.

When they finally made it out of the pass, the friendship they had was forged strong as steel. Hirae had disappeared into the forests of Ascalion to regroup with the rebels, but shortly after returning, news of the daredevil Captain Chancer winning a decisive victory for the Overlord echoed through the towns and villages. The rebellion was over.

Hirae had watched with sadness as Chancer had descended into drink during the years after the campaign ended. He was a "ghost captain", as they called it in Ascalion. A man who carried the deaths of all his soldiers with him and could not let them be free. Helping Kayton and the girl seemed to have given Chancer a purpose again, and that was reason enough for Hirae to stand with him, although she had to wonder how the two of them were going to succeed. There was unlikely to be a happy ending to this. Ruefully, she wondered if Chancer had just found a different way to self-destruct.

'So, are you going to come up with one of your crazy, famed, Captain Chancer strategies?' she asked, trying to lift her mood.

'Well, I was thinking of silently scaling the hundred-foot turret wall during the change of guards in the dead of night, skilfully negotiating my way past the guards inside the castle, and spiriting Sionan and Kayton away.'

Hirae laughed. 'I see your sense of humour is still terrible.'

Chancer smiled, sitting next to her in the sun. He paused, the weight of the task they had undertaken appearing to press down on him. 'It won't be possible to get into the castle unnoticed,' he said. 'The guards are well disciplined. I haven't seen any idle sitting around, no sentry falling asleep on watch. I think our best approach is through the front door.'

'Hide in plain sight?' Hirae asked.

'Yes, how do you fancy becoming baroness of some far-flung place?'

'With my knowledge of the nobility?' she quipped, raising her eyebrows in disbelief. 'I don't even know which knife to use at dinner. How about you be a baron and I'll be your personal bodyguard? That may be vaguely believed for half a day. Although, we can't exactly turn up as we are.'

'Agreed. I've been watching nobles arriving for the banquet Sionan spoke of. That's our best way in. Let's look for a nice nobleman who wants to help us out,' Chancer replied, a wicked gleam in his eye.

'I think I prefer the scaling-the-tower-at-night idea,' Hirae mumbled under her breath as they moved down towards the road. After some time scouting the area, they found the ideal spot for their trap– a bend of road which was out of sight of the castle. The pair took it in turns to watch the road through the farsight from the safety of the trees. Scase, becoming bored with waiting around, wandered off in search of something more interesting. Hirae watched the dog with envy, wishing her life was still that simple.

The sun had started to dip behind the horizon when they saw the perfect opportunity: a small carriage with only one driver and one liveried guard on the stand plate. With no additional entourage, this was likely some minor noble who would not be immediately missed. Clearly, they were running late, as the horses were lathered but now walking with heavy legs, their heads hanging low from exhaustion.

Hirae shook her head in disgust. The horses' fatigue would make it easier to stop the carriage, but neither she nor Chancer had any respect for people who did not care for their animals. On the road, your horse was your life, and if you cared for them, they rewarded you with loyalty and would carry you away from danger.

Hirae whistled for Scase, and he soon reappeared from the undergrowth. Swiftly, they moved down to intercept the carriage as it reached the apex of the bend.

'Hold!' Hirae called, pointing to the front of the horses. Scase ran to cut the horses off, and they whinnied in fear at the sight of the large hound in front of them. With nowhere to run, the horses backed up, stamping their hooves as the driver brought them under control. Simultaneously, Chancer appeared by the carriage and grabbed the guard's legs, pulling him off the stand plate and efficiently clubbing him on the back of the head.

Hirae turned to the driver, who was watching the events with resignation.

'I'm just trying to earn an honest living here,' the driver explained. 'All I want is to get home to my family in one piece.'

'Down you get, then,' Hirae replied in a jovial voice. 'We'll have to knock you out, though, or your lord will have your hide.'

The driver nodded in surrender and climbed down. He turned to face the horses, and Chancer clubbed him with the hilt of his sword, then caught the weight of the man and carefully laid him on the ground.

'Why have we stopped? What is this disruption?' a plummy voice shouted in anger from the carriage.

The door was thrown open and Hirae moved to welcome the occupant with her knife.

Seeing the steel in front of him, and his guard and driver sprawled on the ground, the noble's eyes widened in horror. 'You will release my carriage at once! I am Sir Dennier, and Duke Gelanson is expecting me for the banquet this evening. You will stand aside or suffer the consequences, you ill-bred oafs!'

'Well, you have to admire his pluck,' Hirae remarked with amusement to Chancer. 'Come on, out of that carriage, your lordship. These ill-bred oafs have a different evening planned for you.'

She reached forward to grab the lord and pulled him roughly from the carriage. Off-balance, he fell out and landed face-first on the ground. Hirae placed her foot on his back to prevent him getting up and held her knife to his neck.

'Kill or quiet?' she asked Chancer.

Chancer looked at the state of the poor horses, as if to consider the option of killing their owner who had so mistreated them. 'Quiet,' he responded.

Hirae calmly reversed her knife and used the handle as a club to knock the noble out. 'That was easy,' she said, checking the men were still breathing. 'Let's hope our luck holds.'

The pair dragged the three men into undergrowth of the woods, stripped the guard and noble, changed into their clothes swiftly, and pocketed the noble's money pouch. Sir Dennier appeared to be a man unused to physical exercise, as the silk shirt stretched to breaking point across Chancer's biceps and chest. Chancer put on his own sword belt – not willing to enter the castle unarmed, and deeming his sword fine enough to be worn by a minor noble – and handed Hirae his belt of throwing knives.

Hirae's guard uniform seemed a better fit, although she ditched the cloak with the noble's house emblem of a stag sewn in garishly large silver thread on the back. She tightened the baldric of throwing knives across her body, and with her hunting knife ever present, she looked menacing enough to pass as a personal guard for a noble.

Using strips of leather from the carriage harnesses, they tied the men up at their hands and feet and bound them to a tree. Knowing how verbose the lord had been, they gagged them as well.

'Guard!' Hirae instructed Scase, who moved over to sit and watch the men.

Returning to the road, they saw the tired horses had not moved, content to crop grass growing along the verge and rest.

'My lord,' Hirae said to Chancer as she opened the door with a flourish. 'Your carriage awaits.'

Chancer climbed in and Hirae settled herself into the driver's seat. She flicked the reins to start the tired horses, who began walking at a sedate pace to the castle.

Pink hues streaked the horizon as evening approached.

Hirae could only hope Kayton and Sionan were surviving as they approached their second night in the castle.

CHAPTER ELEVEN

Sionan dried her eyes on the back of her hands, her mind returning again and again to the day her father died. How could something so terrible have happened? Her grief was all-consuming. Her mind taunted her: if she hadn't been so hell-bent on proving Kayton wrong about the duke, would she have accepted the work at the castle in the first place?

Her last moments with her family had been brief and full of pain. Knowing she would soon be taken away, Sionan had given her mother and sisters fierce hugs, admonishing them repeatedly to follow Chancer's instructions no matter what. It had seemed only moments before more guards arrived. Two had moved to restrain Kayton, who placed his sword on the floor, offering no resistance. They were both quickly loaded into the windowless carriage, the darkness within a balm to Sionan's wounded soul. There was no sunshine to make mockery of her grief. In the dark, her heart could break without her family seeing her debilitating guilt for having brought them to this ruin.

The guards had spoken to her mother, but Sionan could not make out the words. She heard no response from her family, but her last view through a crack in the door was of them weeping over her father's still form.

Creaking wheels, jingling of harness and traces, and horses' hooves striking the compact earth along the road back to the castle – all prevented the quiet that Sionan knew Kayton would have filled with words. For now, Sionan herself had nothing to say, how could she? Silent tears tracked down her face and dripped to the floor in time with the carriage bumping along the uphill road.

Now Sionan sat in a small, dank cell wondering how much time had ticked by. She had been brought water but no food. When she had first been placed in the cell, the rank stench of previous occupants' unwashed bodies and urine stung her eyes. Perversely, she found at first that she preferred to be in the cell rather than the luxurious bedroom she had awoken in before. At least her current surroundings honestly reflected her situation. There was no pretence that she was anything other than a prisoner of Gelanson.

She had heard the guards talking as they walked away from her cell that first night.

'Horrific! A girl caught up with that lad from town. Murdering her own father, all for money,' they had remarked to each other with morbid fascination. 'How terrible to be killed by that boy with your own daughter cheering him on.'

One guard had remarked that he had it on good faith from a friend of a friend that they had been stealing from the tailor's shop to run away together when the father had tried to stop them.

At first, Sionan had been too stunned to protest.

How can people believe such a ridiculous tale? she thought. *But then, people do love a murder story to get their teeth into. I'm just a tailor's daughter. Why would they believe me over their duke?* Sionan held on to the priceless knowledge that the guards were talking of her mother and sisters with pity. *Surely,* she thought, *that means they are safe, and people will show them kindness rather than persecution.*

At first, her grief and anger at the duke kept her fear at bay. However, as time crept on, she felt that the walls were closing in on her. The coldness of the stone was sucking the warmth from her body, and with it the heat of her anger gave way to dread.

A rat scurrying across the floor sounded like a monstrous, taloned creature coming to attack her. Sionan's fear rose like a ravenous beast to engulf her. The rat ran over her foot, and she jumped up from the straw-covered pallet to stamp her feet, hoping the noise would drive the vermin away.

I shall not succumb to fear, she told herself firmly. *I shall not allow Gelanson that victory.* Although she had only met Hirae and Chancer briefly, she believed with certainty that they would come for her, and that she would have to be ready when the time came for her and Kayton's rescue.

Sitting in this tiny cell was not affording her any more knowledge than she had before they arrested her, how could they stop the duke if they didn't know what was happening, and where was Kayton? Why wasn't he in the cells with her?

Sionan realised she was subconsciously rubbing the star-shaped bruises on her arms again. Although she couldn't see them in the gloom of the cell, she could still feel the tenderness of her skin. This strange marking was the key. If they could find out what had caused it and expose Gelanson, then surely there would be some hope that the townsfolk would believe her.

She knew that all people from the Manors were allowed to petition the Overlord if they felt their grievance had not been fairly resolved at Justice Day. It was this very system, put in place after the Ascalion rebellion, that had ultimately maintained the peace between the Manors, but Sionan had heavy doubts about whether someone such as she could gain an audience, let alone be believed by the Overlord.

Sionan sighed, self-doubt and fear creeping through her bones as the minutes ticked by in the small, windowless cell. The sounds of the busy castle above were muted through the layers of stone and with no window or torches burning outside her cell, it was impossible to tell the passage of time. She knew she was hungry, and had been brought water twice now. On the second occasion, the door at the end of the corridor had opened to reveal torchlight in the room beyond.

Needing to do something, anything, she started shouting for the guards. Maybe if it was night-time and she made enough of a nuisance of herself, she could at least learn how long she had been in the cell. She shouted until her voice grew hoarse, calling for the guards, Kayton, and even the duke himself. She demanded food and a clean bucket to toilet in. She demanded everything she could think of. As her voice echoed around the empty cells and corridors, hopelessness dragged at her.

She still didn't know where Kayton was.

When they had reached the castle, the prison carriage had drawn straight to the west wall of the castle, where the cells were below ground. Sionan was unloaded and taken straight to this cell, where she remained. She had not seen or heard anything of Kayton since they arrived, and now concern fogged her mind.

She continued to shout and beat her hands on the door, and just when she thought she would lose her voice, she heard the grating of the heavy bar on the door at the end of the corridor. She pulled herself onto her tiptoes and peered through a small grill to see who was coming. Her stomach sank with dread as she saw Kayton's limp form being dragged between two guards. They opened the door of a cell opposite to hers and threw his unconscious body in there.

'What have you done to him?' Sionan screamed at them. 'Kayton, are you okay? Kayton!'

The guard came to the door and sneered through the bars at her. 'Calm down, you little bitch! Your lover boy is still alive, he's just been helping us with some questions.' He barked a cruel laugh.

'Everyone has a right to stand at Justice Day!' Sionan yelled. 'You can't do this to him!'

'Believe me, he'll be on the stand for Justice Day. You think the duke's going to let him get away with murdering good honest men like your poor father and our people? You're lucky I don't come in and save the duke some time by killing you myself, you murderous vermin. Execution's too good for you.'

Sionan took a step back, stunned by this man's hatred pouring down on her. The guard hawked and spat through the bars as she backed into the corner of her cell. She listened with relief as his heavy boots stomped back down the corridor, where the heavy door clanged shut.

Doubt flared as she wondered how they would ever escape, until she realised that the glimpse she had seen of the room at the end of the corridor was no longer lit by dancing torch flames. One night had passed, then. Sionan's resolution firmed as she remembered that Chancer and Hirae could already be on their way to rescue them. She must get out of the cell and find some answers.

'Kayton, can you hear me?' she called softly. 'Kayton, please answer me! Are you okay?' Sionan strained her ears, listening for any sound of movement. All she could hear was rats scuttling along the corridor and the drip of condensation from the stone roof of the cell. 'Kayton, I'm here with you, we'll be okay, just hang on.'

Sionan could hear nothing from Kayton's cell. With no response from him, all Sionan could do was wait. She sat leaning on the cell door, drawing her knees up to her chest and wrapping her arms around them for warmth. If she was to be stuck here, she would conserve her energy for any opportunity that presented itself. In the meantime, she carried on speaking to Kayton in the hope that her voice would rouse him. Sionan shared tales of her family, but mostly she spoke about her father, and in sharing her memories, she allowed her grief to pour out. After a time, her voice fell silent, and still she could not hear any movement or response from Kayton. Sadness overwhelming her, she leaned her head forward on her hands until exhaustion overtook her tired mind, and she drifted into an uneasy sleep.

Kayton aroused to consciousness from a pain-ridden dream of someone calling to him. The despair of all that had happened hit him like a hammer blow. There had been no dazzling rescue, no grateful Sionan falling into his arms with love shining on her face. There was only soul-wrenching grief and the promise of living day to day trying to escape Duke Gelanson's wrath. Groaning with pain, he sat up. He heard a voice through the dark.

'Kayton, are you okay?'

Relief blossomed through him as he realised it was Sionan. 'I'm here, Sionan.' he croaked in response.

'What have they done to you?' she asked.

Kayton leant on the door to try and stand. What *had* they done to him? He was in agony. He didn't think any of his bones were broken, but he wasn't sure. The first blow from the guard to his stomach had made him crumple, gasping for breath. The boot that had followed it caused a cacophony of agony, shooting through his abdomen to encompass his whole body. The next kick had landed in the small of his back. He had lost track of the number of blows that were landed upon him until he recognised the voice of Onway from the doorway, instructing the guards to place him in a cell.

'We understand your vehemence, Sergeant. We know you have had comrades killed by this criminal, but as you know, the duke is committed to justice. The boy will remain in his cell until Justice Day. There will be no further incidents such as this.'

The guard grunted in response, ordering his men to stop. Kayton watched Onway turn and walk away. The guards must have been unimpressed with having their version of justice curtailed. However, everyone in the castle knew Onway's word was final, and they would not risk crossing the duke's favourite servant.

As Kayton was lifted by the arms between two of the guards, the pain across his back and ribs drowned him. It was more than he could cope with; his vision faded to a small pinprick of light as blackness descended. He didn't fight the blessed release and passed out.

Kayton had come to in the cell and lain for a time listening to the dripping walls and feeling sharp pain with every breath. At first, he did not understand why they had struck only his body, but with Onway entering the room to stop the beating, he realised that Gelanson would not want a prisoner to appear as though he had been mistreated in any way. That would not aid his reputation as a fair provider of justice to the people. Bruising on a defendant's body could be hidden. Bruising on his face could not.

When he heard Sionan's voice, Kayton took his time trying to stand. His legs and arms felt fine, but the excruciating, stabbing spasm in his chest and belly tormented him. He took tiny gasps for breath.

Then his eyes met Sionan's through the bars.

'This rescue isn't going quite the way I had planned it,' he said with a small smile.

Sionan laughed shakily in response. 'I never said thank you, Kayton, for coming for me. I'm sorry I ever agreed to the work at the castle. You were right about Gelanson. I wish I had never doubted you. You are the truest of friends, Kayton.'

She looked as though she were about to say more, but two guards approached along the corridor.

'You leave him alone!' she shouted through the bars. 'Haven't you done enough? Everyone will hear about this brutality on Justice Day!'

One of the guards turned and laughed at her. 'Don't worry, it's *you* we're coming for.' The malice in his eyes bore into Sionan. He unlocked the door and made to grab her. Sionan pushed him away, but the second guard grabbed her arm. She twisted and screamed, but the guards' hold was like a vice on her arms, imprinting bruises as they pulled her from the cell.

'Leave her alone!' Kayton tried to shout, but the words came out with a wheeze of pain from his chest. He pulled at the bars of the door, but it was locked steadfastly, and what little strength he had left after the beating was fast running out. Kayton watched helplessly as Sionan was hauled past his cell. The solid *thunk* as the bolt bar was slid back in place in the door at the end of the corridor cut off Sionan's shrieking anger.

Kayton sank to the floor of the cell. Every idea he had come up with to try and help had ended in failure. He could not believe how naïve he had been in thinking that he could stop someone as powerful as the duke. All he had done was make the situation worse, the killing of the guards would surely sign the death warrants of his companions and himself.

As the darkness of the cell clamoured in on him, the cold brought a new dimension of torture to his already aching body. He struggled to keep his faith that they would win. His shoulders drooped in dejection. The pain of his body was nothing in comparison to the agony of not being able to protect Sionan. Kayton knew with certainty that the happy ending he had painted in his imagination would never happen and hung on desperately to the hope that Chancer and Hirae were coming for them.

CHAPTER TWELVE

Sionan's eyes adjusted to the light in the guard room. Blush-pink rays of evening sun shone through the ground floor window. The second night was falling, and she was losing time to gain information. Realising that fighting the guards may result in her being put back in her cell, or worse, she stood firmly with her chin raised and stopped struggling against their hold.

The guards watched her suspiciously as the captain addressed her.

'Now, young miss. The duke himself will speak with you this evening. He's a very busy man with the banquet tonight, but he has some questions that you will need to answer. Don't you go messing him about, and you mind your manners.' The captain towered over her as he leaned in menacingly to add weight to his words. 'And mark me well, if you try any funny business, I will be right there to beat it out of you!'

Sionan could not conceal the fear from her eyes as she looked into his.

The captain stared at her a moment longer, seemingly weighing up whether she would cause any further trouble, but appearing satisfied that her fear was real, he instructed the guards to release her arms. They pushed her out of the guardroom and along the covered walkway towards the northern corner of the castle. The captain set a brisk pace at the front, with the two guards flanking Sionan.

As they walked the perimeter of the castle square, Sionan noted the frenzied activity of servants preparing for the banquet tonight. She could hear carriages arriving from the main entrance to the south. There were people coming and going, and in this hurried activity, the idea that this would be the best time to escape goaded her.

But what of Kayton, Hirae, and Chancer? No, she must stay strong and await their escape together.

Grand carriages trundled through the south gateway, depositing nobility in the castle square, where they began walking along the impressive stone cloister to the Great Hall. As the carriages emptied of their occupants, the drivers and guards moved to the eastern wall and exited to the stables and carriage outbuildings. Branches of cherry blossom festooned the hall's impressive doorway, and ornate displays of spring posies stood in stone urns. Sionan could just hear the nobles' well-spoken voices remarking on the grandeur of the event.

In the entrance of the Great Hall, she could make out Onway standing in a rich emerald tunic with Gelanson's emblem of an eagle stitched in fine gold thread on the chest. Sionan felt her hackles rise as she saw the man that had lied and duped her into coming to the castle.

Onway was bowing, formally welcoming nobles to the banquet before ushering them into the hall. Gelanson was sparing no expense at impressing the nobility of Clasterne and surrounding Manors.

Sionan thought about screaming for help, but realised it

would not help. Why would a visiting noble intervene? The idea was ridiculous, and in all the hubbub they may not even notice. Her steps faltered slightly. She knew they were heading back to the castle tower where she had previously been held, and the dread that she may not escape from there a second time sank into her.

A small carriage entered the square. There was only one driver, and by the looks of the knife at her hip and baldric of throwing knives across her torso, she was clearly also the bodyguard of a noble inside the carriage. With leather breastplate and armoured greaves, the woman looked well equipped to take on any person who may cause offence. Sionan started as she recognised the driver was Hirae

Sionan willed herself not to call out, but she had to do something to make Hirae see her. When the guards gave her a swift nudge to keep moving, she took the opportunity to sprawl to the floor, letting out a piercing shriek in feigned pain as she landed on cold cobbles.

'Crow's blood!' the captain said in exasperation. 'Get her up and keep her moving!'

Sionan looked surreptitiously towards the Great Hall. Hirae's eyes locked on hers and she gave a barely perceptible nod of the head before turning back to the carriage, opening the door and standing back to bow as the nobleman gracefully exited. Sionan watched furtively as, almost unrecognisable without his stained clothes and baldric of knives, Chancer stepped from the wagon.

Sionan dipped her head to hide the delight on her face behind her curtain of brown hair as she saw them walk towards the banquet. She and Kayton were not alone.

Chancer and Hirae were in the castle! Suddenly everything seemed possible.

The tower now loomed before her as the guards came to a stop. Where there had previously been an open archway that she had escaped through, there was now a large, heavy oak door with a solid iron lock. Before, there had been only two guards outside the gateway. There were now four, each standing to attention with pikestaff held to the side. As Sionan approached, the door opened to reveal Gelanson standing inside. The captain bowed to his duke, and escorted Sionan into the tower. They walked down a small corridor, past the tower stairs that spiralled upwards on their right, and through a door.

'Thank you, Captain,' said Gelanson. 'That will be all. We are not to be disturbed.'

'Yes, my lord,' the captain responded, giving Sionan a pointed look of warning. He bowed to the duke and exited.

Books and scrolls lined shelving on the walls, the smell of must hung in the air. It was the odour that only volumes of aged books and ancient papers could bring to a closed space. Apart from some locked trunks which looked out of place in the small room, there were no ominous signs in what appeared to be Gelanson's private study. In fact, the room was cosy, with two large comfortable leather chairs facing a small fire. The fire was not lit, instead the light in the room was provided by a series of candles in beautiful cut-glass lantern covers creating crystalline patterns as the flames danced. On the wall opposite the fire, a large tapestry hung with lanterns either side, lighting an embroidered scene.

Gelanson pushed the door closed and locked it behind the

departing guards. Sionan felt a shiver run over her skin as the duke crossed the small room towards her. Silence fell on the room. Gelanson stood in clothes finer than any her family could afford in a lifetime. A fur-trimmed, black evening jacket over a bright yellow silk shirt. Soft, black leather boots encased silk trousers. The richness of his evening clothes emphasised his thin, scholarly frame. All knew the duke disdained wearing a sword, and his only jewellery was his Chain of Office with the precious amethyst gemstone dazzling in the candlelight. Sionan looked at him with contempt. She no longer felt fear of his station. Her anger rose like a white-hot fire in her gut, lighting her courage. She would not stand on ceremony to this man.

'Your men murdered my father!'

'Indeed,' Gelanson calmly replied. 'A disastrous accident that really could have been avoided had you not run off in the night. Really, child, what were you thinking? After your accident, I merely wanted to assure your care and safety. What is it you think is happening here?'

Sionan looked at him in astonishment. This was not the response she had expected. Denial or dismissiveness, certainly, but not this calm agreement that her father should still be alive. How could he believe *she* was responsible for this? Her eyes narrowed with hate. She had seen Leetha and the wrongness this man was capable of.

'Your lies mean nothing, I will speak on the stand at Justice Day. The townsfolk will hear what Leetha told me! I saw her die before my eyes.'

Gelanson's eyes flickered at the mention of the dead girl, and sighed with apparent distaste. 'An intelligent person such as yourself surely is not listening to ghost stories created by disgruntled townsfolk who do not want to pay their taxes.'

'Lies!' she hissed at the duke, stepping forwards, her hands clenched.

'I can see I have made a miscalculation,' Gelanson continued. 'There is no reasoning with you now that fool guard has killed your father. The lack of gratitude you people demonstrate despite the daily improvements I bring to your tiny lives is a source of continual grief to me. You do not even wish to assist me with my studies.'

Sionan was stunned into silence. Gelanson continued to speak, his words dripping with distaste. 'Clearly my complex work is too great an intellectual challenge for uneducated people to understand.' He paced the room with his hands crossed behind his back, appearing to reach a decision. 'You have suffered a loss, but when you understand the nature of the important work I am doing here, you will feel comforted.'

Gelanson walked to the right of the fireplace and lifted the beautiful tapestry. It was a depiction of a large eagle on a mountain, the wise overseer surveying its lands below. The luxurious wall hanging had intricate detail, and the eagle had ice-blue eyes, matching the duke's.

Gelanson pulled the ornate, iron candleholder to the left of the tapestry. With an eerie quiet, the stone behind the tapestry opened to form a small doorway into another room. An unpleasant odour drifted from the opening into the study.

'Aren't secret rooms in castles delightful?' he remarked companionably, ushering Sionan forwards. 'Come along. You are quite honoured to view my world of science.' He lifted a small lamp from one of the shelves and stooped to walk through the opening into the room.

Sionan hesitated, gauging the distance to the exit, but if she really wanted to discover what Gelanson was doing, she would have to go in, she reasoned.

The sickening stench increased as she stepped over the threshold. The air hung heavy, the sour smell stronger. A stink of decay permeated the air. Sionan's eyes adjusted, and she noted there were no windows in the stone room and the only light shone from the lamp Gelanson was holding. He crossed the room to light two large candles above the fireplace.

Sionan felt icy shock through her veins at the scene before her. From the comfortable, cosy study, she was now in a stark chamber of horror. Her eyes fixed on the workbench in the centre of the room. Her mind rebelled against what was resting on the table. The smell hanging in the room was clearly emanating from it.

'That's an arm,' she said, her voice trembling.

The arm was lying palm-up, with the skin cut along the forearm. Tongs had peeled back the skin, exposing the white muscle and red tissue beneath. As Sionan processed what she was seeing, her heart hammering in her chest, she felt herself struggling for breath. She recognised the calloused hand at the end of that arm. Years of stitching clothes to earn enough to keep his family warm and well fed meant her father's left hand was covered in rough skin built up over years of work. It was the hand that had held hers as a child and kept her safe.

She could feel wetness on her cheek as tears of anguish fell unchecked.

'That's my *father's* arm,' Sionan whispered in horror.

'Well, of course,' Gelanson warmly replied. 'To move on

in this modern world we must study human anatomy. A fresh corpse must always be utilised. Come in, come in, don't stand in the doorway gawping. Really, it's just an arm, there's no need to be so alarmed just because it is no longer attached to its owner.'

As Gelanson chuckled to himself, Sionan released with dread that there could be no reasoning with the duke on any level. His reactions were jarringly discordant with those of a normal person.

'So, child, you wished to know what I do: I study, learn, and share my knowledge for the benefit of my people.' Gelanson idly poked an implement at the arm. 'Has the town not prospered since I became its duke? Are the people not happier with their lot in life as we improve our processes of farming and medicine? We are in a new age of peace, and have the freedom to truly flourish if we are brave enough to embrace all forms of knowledge that exist in the world.'

'People didn't mysteriously die or have their arms removed before you were duke,' Sionan spat back.

'Really?' Gelanson raised his eyebrows. 'One person assists with my work per season, only one. Do you know how many more than that died of dysentery in the town before I revolutionised the wastage system? Are you really telling me that one sacrifice does not outweigh the advances? It is always such a disappointment when people do not understand the importance of advancing science. They always seem to think the dark arts are some sort of ancient magic consigned to the pages of history, but I am returning them to the light.' Gelanson looked at her with a self-satisfied smile.

'You are evil,' Sionan responded shakily. 'People will learn the truth and turn against you.'

Gelanson's smile faded. 'You townspeople just do not have the capability to appreciate the advances I am making, and my patience is wearing thin.'

'You're insane. The Overlord will serve justice on you!' Sionan threatened. Backing to the doorway, she readied herself to flee at the first opportunity.

'Enough!' Gelanson shouted, slamming his hand down on the workbench. 'I have wasted enough time with this stupid discussion. I should be with my guests. I can see you are as dull-witted as that other girl!' Gelanson moved towards the fireplace. 'Her heart gave out, but you, you underwent *three* transferences before your selfish escape attempt. Now, I do not have the time nor inclination to make the refinements necessary to protect your life, not after the way you have repaid my generous care. I'm sure someone who is willing to assist can be found, but unfortunately that will not be you.'

Sionan saw Gelanson's reflection in an oval mirror as he lifted a small wooden box from the mantlepiece above the fireplace. The box had designs and patterns engraved in the darkest, black wood Sionan had ever seen. She saw his thin lips move, but could not make out his whispered words as he held his hand over the box.

The noise of the box lid popping open echoed ominously around the room. Gelanson reverently lifted out a small, green, star-shaped stone. It was the exact size of the fading bruise on Sionan's arms and the horrific sores the baker's daughter had on her arms.

Gelanson, chanting softly, walked determinedly towards her. As he spoke, a soft mist emanated from his mouth.

Sionan turned to run, but her legs no longer obeyed her as tendrils of the ominous fog wrapped around her ankles. She struggled as the mist crawled up her skin, immobilising her lower body.

Gelanson smiled coldly as he drew level with her. Sionan's breath came in panicked gasps as her body froze in position, the icy cold touch of the mist cocooning her. She struggled to breathe as the fog rose to envelop her face and knew with certainty she would die in this room. She could only watch in terror, her body stuck like a statue, completely entrapped. She gasped for small breaths, able only to move her eyes wildly in terror.

'See, my child, it really does not need to be like this. All this fear and distress could so easily be avoided.' Gelanson moved her arm gently and raised the palm of her hand. As he held the star-stone to her palm, she looked into his eyes, searching in vain for some form of humanity. All she could see was a glimmer of academic interest. As Gelanson stopped chanting, the mist began to dissipate and she took a gulp of air. Desperately swivelling her head and twisting her shoulders, she tried to free the rest of her body from the vapour still enshrouding her lower half. The moment she felt movement in her shoulders, she tried to wrest her arm away from Gelanson, but he grabbed her hand.

Holding the stone firmly in place, Gelanson started a new incantation. Sionan could hear the words clearly, but did not recognise the language, with its strange guttural notes and cadences. Even listening was uncomfortable, as though the words themselves were hideous, their twisting forms burrowing into her head. She felt an abhorrent tingling in her hand.

At first, Sionan could not quite define it. There was no pain, only an unpleasant digging feeling as though the stone was alive and trying to delve into her skin. She struggled to tear her hand away. The sensation grew with intensity until it became unbearable.

The amethyst amulet Gelanson wore pulsed grotesquely like a discordant heartbeat. Exhaustion flooded Sionan's body as the amulet changed to a sickly green. The last of the mist dissolved and Sionan tried again to pull away, but her strength deserted her. Gelanson completed the incantation and released her hand. Then, like a puppet whose strings had been cut, Sionan crumpled to the floor.

Fear fell away to confusion when she tried to rise, her hair falling in front of her face. She lifted a shaking hand to push her hair away and froze when she saw heavy streaks of grey mixed into in its previously rich brown. She stared at the ends of her hair and wrinkled hands, knowing with dread that this was what had happened to Leetha. Gelanson had somehow stolen their youth. She felt as though she had aged twenty years in a matter of moments.

As she looked up in shock, Gelanson loomed over her. He looked younger, the wrinkles on his forehead gone and his face plumped out with youth.

'And so, you see,' he gently informed her. He turned away from Sionan to look in the oval mirror. 'Ah, a little too young, I think. We can't have our revered guests questioning my sudden change of appearance.'

With effort, Sionan turned her exhausted head to watch Gelanson walk over to the workbench. He placed the star-stone on the severed limb and chanted in the same language, although the cadences were different. Gelanson spoke only briefly while the green star-stone and the amulet he wore pulsed with unnatural light. Suddenly, the arm twitched and the fingers curled up. Gelanson laughed with glee.

'Marvellous! See how close I am. The sacrifice of a few will lead to the saving of so many. A spark of my youth transferred to bring life returned to what was once dead! Ah, but these are exciting times!' He hesitated by the workbench, clearly wishing to do more experimentation, then turned and placed the star-stone back in the box. 'No, this will wait. I must attend to my guests. Do not fear, my dear, I will return later to finish our work.' He strode towards the door, the vigour of youth apparent in his walk, despite the light wrinkles now returned to his eyes. 'Imagine what the future will hold. We can have a justice system with no distasteful waste of feeding criminals in cells. I will simply transfer the criminal's life to the person who had suffered the crime. Those with sickness that I deem worthy can be healed. It will be marvellous!'

He interrupted his musings to look at the collapsed form of Sionan on the floor.

'What to do with you until I can return?' He leant over her, peering down at Sionan.

She could see only emptiness in the duke's eyes. They looked at her as a person might look at an unwelcome insect that had encroached into a home. She tried to stand, but found a shocking weakness in her limbs, like a newborn foal trying to find its feet for the first time. She managed only to bring herself to a sitting position, and pushed herself as far away from Gelanson as she could.

'Get away from me!' Her voice sounded different: weaker, throatier. When she spoke, she could hear her mother's voice after a long exhausting day at the shop. Unprepared for the sudden reminder of her happy home life from only weeks before, tears sprang to her eyes unbidden as she hoped with all her being that her mother was already far from here, travelling to Sahjashorn as Chancer had instructed.

'Honestly, my dear, we can't leave you on the floor like this, can we? That would really not do.' Gelanson bent forwards and gently helped her to stand. The sympathetic and benevolent look he gave Sionan chilled her more than the coldly calculating stare of moments before. Hating the weakness in her limbs, she tried to pull away but had no strength to resist. Sionan had no choice but to allow her weight to lean on him as she shuffled in small steps through the stone doorway. They entered the study, and Sionan felt a small measure of relief at being out of that room of horrors.

Walking her slowly to one of the comfortable chairs in front of the fireplace, Gelanson gently helped her to sit. 'I will send Onway for you, he will be able to assist you to your room in the tower. Obviously, you must understand, I cannot allow you to leave.' He leaned in earnestly as if by speaking more closely he could compel her to understand.

Sionan sank as far into the chair as she could. Her skin crawled to be away from him.

'Rest assured,' he said, 'your life will go to a greater purpose.'

He patted her aged hand and then adjusted the light fitting on the wall by the tapestry. The door to the workroom swung closed. Gelanson shook the tapestry back into place. Satisfied all was as it should be, he left without a backward glance.

Sionan heard the study door close behind her and the duke's steps fade away along the corridor. There was no mistaking the sound of the lock as the door to the tower closed behind him. Shaking, Sionan made to rise, but had no strength in her limbs. She tried to lever herself up using the arms of the chair, but fell forward to land sprawling on her face.

Dizziness swamped her as her head banged on the unforgiving stone floor. The fatigue in her mind and body had left her with no resilience. She felt herself slip into unconsciousness, her last thought to hope Hirae and Chancer would come for her before what remained of her life was ripped from her body.

CHAPTER THIRTEEN

Onway waited at the entrance to the Great Hall to welcome the last of the guests. Exhaustion weighed heavily on him this evening; his despondency exacerbated by the richness of the banquet. The event was a crowning success for Gelanson, his influence and alliances with the noble houses growing ever stronger. As the duke's power grew, Onway's sense of disquiet grew proportionally. Recently he had wondered how he had become so trapped and embroiled in Gelanson's deceits, but with hindsight, it was easy to see the path he had trodden. The path that had been planned by the duke.

Onway had been adrift in the world, his grief consuming him after his wife and child died from dysentery. He had been powerless to stop them fading from him each day as they became sicker and weaker. Impotent anger at their unnecessary deaths alienated him from friends who kept telling him to accept what couldn't be changed and move on with his life.

The young duke had recently taken the Seat of the Manor and had heard of Onway's previous experience as one of the Overlord's quartermasters during the Ascalion campaign. Gelanson had personally approached Onway with the offer of the role of steward. Onway was confident that running a castle was no greater a challenge than the organisation of campaign logistics and supplies. He also understood that the duke's offer was a great honour. However, he had hesitated about moving on without his beloved family. Then Gelanson had shown him the books of science. He illustrated to Onway how engineering a clean water and sewerage system would reduce dysentery. This golden discovery that the illness was preventable gave Onway purpose; he'd accepted the role of steward, confident he could support the duke to make a real difference to people's lives.

Onway's aching sadness transformed into a single-minded loyalty and devotion to the duke. When the request for one person to humanely experiment on had come, the duke had been able to convince Onway that the sacrifice of one was a price worth paying when it would save so many. In Onway's broken mind this had seemed a rational balance at the time.

However, as the years passed, Gelanson's experiments had started to trouble him more and more. Strangely, it was not in the quiet of night or moments of peace during the day that doubts crept up, but frenetic times, like the arrival of guests for the banquet now, when he could see the respect and awe the people held for the duke.

Over the last year, he had seen Gelanson's fascination with transferring the spirit of life become all-consuming. The baker's daughter dying had been the final moment for Onway, when he admitted to himself that he was a party to murder. There was now a mother and father grieving, just as he had grieved for his family. Onway suspected that the duke was aware of his growing reticence and knew his own life would be forfeit. Thinking of the immoral actions he had faithfully completed, he was not convinced his own life was worth anything now anyway.

His heart sank as he heard a woman laughing gaily from the hall. No, there would be no support from the nobles if he tried to stop the duke.

Onway forced himself to remain straight-faced as he saw the final carriage draw up to the entrance of the Great Hall. Clearly it was a minor noble with little money, because there was only one driver, who seemed to serve as a guard as well. As the carriage drew parallel with the entrance, Onway watched the woman jump easily from the driver's seat to the ground and open the carriage door. Onway looked away from the driver when he heard the unfortunate commotion of the girl arrested today falling en route to the tower. He knew from the moment she had escaped that she would not live to see another season.

Murderer, his conscience whispered.

He gave himself a subconscious shake as he saw the nobleman approaching. Onway looked blankly at the man, struggling to recognise him. The noble stood in his fine blue silk shirt and black boots, looking pointedly at Onway. The man's clothes looked a little tight. Clearly, he did not have the sort of wealth to buy new clothes for a new-season banquet.

The nobleman raised his eyebrows in impatience. When there was still no response from the steward, he spoke in a haughty voice.

'You may announce Sir Dennier,' the noble instructed Onway as he swept through into the banquet hall.

'Of course, Sir Dennier,' Onway replied, performing a sweeping bow as low as his prematurely aged frame would take him. His mind skittered through all the nobles expected at the banquet. Lord Dennier was a minor noble, so the carriage and one guard looked correct. However, Onway was certain Lord Dennier was a young, unmarried man, more famed for gambling than hunting or physical sports. That did not fit with the large, muscular, middle-aged man in front of him. Onway had deliberately placed Lord Dennier next to the young ladies from the House of Sates as they were of equal status, age, and intellect. The man in front of him would not enjoy that seating position at all. Onway righted himself and watched the broad shoulders of the departing man. He could recognise a soldier's walk with ease. The person who had just entered the hall was a trained fighting man.

A small frown crossed Onway's face as he considered whether or not to call the guards. Maybe it was the despondency he had been feeling that caused him not to act, or maybe he was feeling a faint glimmer of hope that this person might be here to expose Gelanson. Either way, Onway made a split-second decision not to expose the imposter and wait to see how things played out.

As the woman made to follow, Onway stepped in front of her to block her way.

'I'm sorry, only nobility in the banquet hall. All other guards and servants must retire to the mess hall in the castle yard.' He gestured to the right of the hall, where there was an archway large enough for carriages to pass through to the stables beyond the castle square.

Bowing to acknowledge the instruction, the driver remounted the carriage and followed his directions through the archway. Onway watched thoughtfully as the woman disappeared from view towards the mess hall.

The banquet progressed smoothly, with jugglers and acrobats delighting the guests as the evening drew in. Onway had little opportunity to worry about the supposed Lord Dennier with the myriad of minor problems and issues he was constantly called on to resolve. Having just calmed the cook after a squabble between the kitchen and serving staff, Onway was making his way back to the great hall when he spotted the "lord" quietly exiting the banquet hall. The steward followed and noted the man meet the driver from the carriage near the tower. The driver showed no deference to Dennier, which further piqued Onway's interest.

'Can I help you, Lord Dennier?' Onway asked. 'Is the banquet not to your liking?'

'All is quite perfect, steward,' replied the nobleman. 'I am merely taking some air to reflect on the duke's speech before the next entertainments. Quite inspiring.' The nobleman moved away, appearing to dismiss the steward as any self-important minor noble would, and moved nonchalantly along the walkway.

Onway's eyes narrowed thoughtfully as he watched the two walk away. Having seen them talking, he knew the familiarity between them was more than one would expect between a noble and his paid guard. Onway's instinct that something was afoot was right. He could either call the guards to arrest them or take this chance to try and help them. He had seen them looking over towards the tower where the girl was held. He would bet his life that was who they were here for. The question was, would he allow another innocent person to die, with his silence making him complicit?

He made a decision, and called to a servant. 'Bring a tray with food for one, immediately.'

Onway waited. Only he and the duke had a key to the tower. Whilst he couldn't do anything about the guards without arousing suspicion, he could at least leave the way open for the pair. Onway felt his palms sweating as he envisaged the duke sucking the life from him with his dark and foul spells. He would pay the ultimate price if he was caught.

Just as his resolve started to waver, the servant returned with a tray of food.

'Would you like me to deliver this to someone, sir?'

'Thank you, no, that will be all.'

Striding determinedly to the tower, Onway could feel the eyes of the mock Lord Dennier and driver on him. As he reached the tower door, he juggled the tray on one hand whilst unlocking the heavy door with the other. Ignoring the guards who stood to attention as he entered, he closed the door behind him and headed straight to the study. He knew that Gelanson would not have been able to resist absorbing some of the young girl's life-force. Even so, he was shocked to see grey streaks in the hair of the woman lying prone on the floor. He placed the tray of meats, pastries, and bread on the table and carefully roused the woman. Her eyes opened slowly, confusion clearing from her face in order to be replaced with open hatred.

Onway helped her into the closest seat, despite her protestations not to come near her. 'Eat and gather your strength,' he said. 'You are not alone.'

The woman made no reply and Onway quickly exited.

Closing the study door behind him, Onway felt himself shaking as he walked back down the corridor to the tower door. All he had to do was forget to lock it. Who could blame him on a busy night like tonight when the steward was needed everywhere to resolve imaginary discourtesies and smooth over upsets?

With shaking hands, he opened the tower door and closed it behind him. Without looking at the guards, he walked briskly away, expecting a call at any moment to remind him to lock the door. He did not slow his pace until he was back in the banquet hall, where he decided to remain for the duration of the evening. He had done what he could. The rest was up to the fake lord and driver.

Outside on the walkway, Chancer and Hirae waited until the steward was out of hearing before speaking again.

'Could be a trap?' Hirae suggested, having observed the door remaining unlocked.

'A lucky break too good to be true,' Chancer responded. 'But I'm not sure what other choices we have.' Seeing the straight-backed steward disappear into the banquet hall, Chancer stopped his aimless walking and turned to Hirae. 'What are your thoughts?'

'I think if we're going to do this, we need to do it now whilst that awful racket is still in full swing. I'll take the two on the left.'

Without waiting for Chancer's response, Hirae moved into action.

Chancer swiftly followed behind. 'I guess I'll take the ones on the right, then,' he muttered. He marched past Hirae, giving her a none too gentle nudge to remind her he was supposed to be the noble in charge, and the tower guards looked at him blankly as he approached.

'Look at these good men, standing to attention and missing all the fun of the banquet!' Chancer jovially wrapped his arm around the shoulder of one of the guards.

The guard tried to disentangle himself, but Chancer gave him a sharp blow on the back of the neck. The guard dropped silently to the ground, breathing, but unconscious. The remaining three guards looked on with surprise, from their fellow in a heap on the floor to the previously assumed drunk noble now calmly brandishing the pikestaff.

Chancer struck the second guard between the legs with the end of the pike. As the unfortunate man doubled over in pain, Chancer used the butt of the staff to knock him senseless. He turned to aid Hirae, but saw the remaining two guards were already down. Killed with ruthless efficiency, one had a small throwing knife in the eye and the other had Hirae's hunting knife through the heart. Hirae had no reservations about killing when it came to survival. She cleaned the knives on the soldier's clothes and sheathed them.

'You better hope they don't wake up before we are clear,' she said, her disapproval with the risk Chancer was taking by not killing them evident. 'Move!' she hissed, seeing him looking at the dead guards. 'That's two less to come after us.'

Galvanised into action, Chancer opened the tower door and they pulled the four guards inside. Closing the door softly behind them, they paused to take stock of their surroundings.

There were no guards stationed inside, which made their lives easier, and there was a small corridor leading to a door at the end. Hirae peered up the turret stairs to the right.

'There are no candles or torches burning in the stairwell. I say we try the door at the end first,' she whispered, nodding to the candlelight they could see emanating from under the door.

Chancer nodded in response and took the lead, walking quietly on the balls of his feet to the door. As he reached the door, he gently lifted the latch and opened it a crack. All he could see was an empty fireplace and lamplight flickering on the walls. There was a tray of food on a small table. In one of two large chairs in front of the fireplace was a woman of similar age to him. She was clutching one of the knives from the food tray, and looked ready to use it.

The woman's face lit up with joy. For a moment, Chancer could not understand why, then as she dropped the knife he realised.

This woman was Sionan.

'You're here! You came!' Sionan cried.

Chancer stood, stunned into silence by the appearance of the woman. 'Sionan… what happened to you? Where is Kayton?'

'I'll explain, but we have to get out of here. Gelanson will be back,' Sionan said frantically. 'Come, see his evil, quickly, before he returns.'

She moved to the tapestry by the wall. Chancer sensed that her strength was leaving her quickly. What had *happened* to her? Sionan pushed the tapestry aside and pulled the lamp fitting to open a hidden door into the chamber beyond.

'Death's whore!' Chancer swore, the sweet smell of decay hitting his nostrils at the same time as he saw with horror an arm on the workbench. He could feel the malevolence hanging in the air.

Sionan headed straight for a box on the mantlepiece as Hirae and Chancer followed her into the room.

'We have to get this away from Gelanson.' Sionan pushed the box urgently into Hirae's hands. 'Whatever happens here, you must get this away.'

Hirae looked at the small wooden box. The darkness of the wood seemed to absorb the light around it, and the patterns carved into it seemed to have a life of their own, writhing like snakes.

'What wrongness does this contain?' Hirae asked.

'We have to run,' Sionan asserted. 'I will explain, but please, keep this away from Gelanson at all costs.'

'I will get this out of this castle,' she promised, giving Sionan the immediate reassurance she so clearly needed.

Sionan nodded in gratitude and fled the room, closely followed by her rescuers. Swiftly, she returned the lamp on the wall to its original position and smoothed the tapestry back into place.

'Sionan, where is Kayton?' Hirae asked.

'He's in the holding cells by the main entrance.'

'Did you see the guards? How many are there?' Chancer pressed for any information he could gain.

'Four or five, maybe. There was a group of them when they took me from my cell. Kayton's in a bad way. The guards beat him.' Sionan's voice shook with rage.

'We need to move,' Hirae cut in. 'Any minute now

someone is going to spot that the tower guards are missing.'

Chancer grunted in agreement and the trio left the study and moved towards the door. Chancer could see Sionan fading more rapidly. They were going to have to get her out of here quickly.

'Hirae, I'll go for Kayton,' he announced. 'You get Sionan out to the woods. We'll meet at last night's camp.'

'Be safe,' Hirae responded, nodding her agreement with the plan.

They quickly grasped arms before opening the tower door and setting out. Just as they were about to separate, they heard horses clattering into the main square.

'Stop! You there, stop!' came the distinct shout of a voice they recognised.

Captain Stegen came riding into the courtyard like a storm arriving, the soldiers they had left at the Gashon crossing cantering in close behind.

Chancer locked eyes with Stegen and knew they would have to fight their way out. The rasp of steel filled the air as he drew his sword and they ran for the postern gate. Just as they reached it, a guard rushed to block their way. More poured out of the Great Hall. At any moment, the trio would be overrun.

Chancer sprinted in front of Sionan and cut the guard down with a murderous swing, almost decapitating the man. Without pausing for breath, he wrenched his sword clear. 'Get to the horses!' he shouted as Hirae and Sionan passed through the gate.

Hirae ran to the nearest horses picketed in a line. They still had their reins tied to the wooden bar, but no saddles.

With no time to stop, she grabbed Sionan and pushed her up onto a brown mare. The girl struggled to lever herself up on to the horse's back.

'Quickly!' Hirae urged her. 'Grab the mane here, hold on, and whatever you do, don't look back or let go!'

She forcibly closed Sionan's hands around large clumps of the horse's mane. The horse, already skittish with the noise, threw its head up and down in disgust, nearly dismounting Sionan before they had even moved. Hirae smoothly vaulted on to a chestnut mare, grabbing the reins of a night-black mare tied next to it. She thumped her heels into the flank of her horse, using its body to guide Sionan's horse along the path towards the outer wall.

'Chancer!' Hirae warned as the guards converged on the postern gate. Chancer turned to make a run for it, but there wasn't enough space, he wouldn't make it.

With a smooth throw, Hirae cut down the leading guard, the needle-sharp throwing knife arcing through the air to land in the man's chest. As the guard collapsed, Chancer sprinted through the sudden gap and leapt on to the black horse, grabbing the reins from Hirae.

Hirae let out a blood-curdling yell, urging the horses forwards into a canter. The smell of fresh blood in the air coupled with her shout was all the encouragement the horses needed. They leapt towards the gate, charging down the soldiers who were spilling out of the mess hall to see what the commotion was.

Hirae, Chancer, and Sionan passed at a frenzied canter, riding directly at the soldiers stationed at the gateway. The guards threw themselves to the side to save themselves from being trampled. Shouts from the castle resonated around the stone walls. Risking a glance over her shoulder, Hirae saw that Captain Stegen and four of her men were already giving chase.

As the trio thundered down the road, Stegen exited the castle, only a breath behind. They galloped at breakneck speed along the road. Realising that Sionan was hanging on for grim death, Hirae bent low over her own steed to urge on Sionan's mount. As Hirae took the lead, she lifted her head to the wind and let out a long, high-pitched whistle. There was a glint of steel as Captain Stegen, face twisted into a snarl of hate, was almost upon them.

Suddenly, a dark streak appeared from the woods up ahead, racing back across the flat towards the galloping horses. In the near dark, the animal looked like a mythical beast in the moonlight, and the horses' eyes widened with terror. Hirae whistled, a short, shrill, ear-aching sound, and the large hound ran in an arc past the escaping trio towards the guards who were an arm's length from striking them.

'At them, Scase, at them!' Hirae shouted to her faithful friend. The hound changed direction so quickly his back legs slid from under him, but then he was on his paws again, bounding directly towards the oncoming guards' horses. The dog barked furiously, flashing massive white fangs as he ran towards the lead horse. The horse reared and whinnied in terror, knocking the horse next to it as it twisted away from the dangerous flesh-rending teeth. Both guards were sent flying, landing with a thud on the ground as the horses ran from the beast.

The remaining horses balked at the ferocity of the

monstrous hound with frothing jaws. Another guardsman lost control and his horse went careering back towards the castle. He wrenched on the reins to try and turn the petrified animal, but to no avail, his actions only serving to terrify the frightened animal even further.

Stegen aimed a vicious swipe of her sword at the hound. It narrowly missed Scase's snout as he harried the two remaining horses. As one reared, the guard lost her seat and was dragged along the ground with her foot caught in one stirrup. Stegen urged her horse at the dog, turning to the side to deliver a killing blow, but Scase was faster, locking his bite to hold onto her boot.

Stegen could feel the crushing jaws scraping the bones in her leg. The weight of the massive dog dragged her from the horse and she fell with a bone-jarring crash. A seasoned veteran, Stegen lifted her other leg to kick the dog free. She kicked down with all her might but before the blow could land, the dog was gone, racing to catch up with the fleeing traitors.

Swearing violently, Stegen pushed herself on to her hands and knees, carefully testing the weight on her bitten foot. Her boots had protected her from the worst of the damage, and she was able to stand. She turned, her eyes following the dog streaking across the flats alongside the horses of the murderous rebels. She shouted her frustration into the night sky as they disappeared into the forest.

'Get up, you useless imbeciles! Up!' she shouted at the guards, who were slowly bringing their horses back under control. 'Back to the castle for reinforcements,' she commanded.

Stegen's rage was unmeasurable as she smarted with the knowledge that the traitors had bested her. Since finding the body of her younger brother on the opposite shore of the Gashon crossing, she had been consumed with the need for vengeance. Her brother had been the only family she'd had left, and all her thoughts were focused on revenge.

After days of searching the surrounding area at the ferry crossing, she had accepted they needed to return to the castle for a tracker. To find the traitors here in her own Manor – in her own duke's castle no less, and perpetuating more violence on her people – was more than she could bear. She shook with rage at the knowledge that she had lost them.

Stegen turned her horse and angrily kicked it into a gallop back towards the castle. This time they would not escape. The duke's soldiers would search every inch of that forest if they had to.

Stegen would see those murderers on the gallows before the week was out.

CHAPTER FOURTEEN

Within moments of reaching the woods, the darkness and dense undergrowth made it impossible for the escapees to continue on horseback. Chancer and Hirae jumped from their mounts to land lightly on the ground. They slapped the horses on the rumps to send them galloping back down the trail.

After the harried flight, Sionan was unable to even will her hands to release the horse's mane. Chancer gently prised her fingers open and pulled her towards him. She was helpless to assist as her exhausted body refused to follow commands.

Chancer carefully pulled her from the horse's back, took her weight, and brought her to a rest on the soft earth of the forest floor. The feel of the ground under her aching muscles was as welcome as her own bed. She lay down on her side and closed her eyes, listening to the sounds of the night. Soft calls of nocturnal creatures and the rustle of leaves brought comfort to her tortured mind.

'Have you still got it?' she asked Hirae.

Hirae tapped her breastplate, where the box was safely hidden. 'It's here.'

Sionan felt a pang of jealousy: Hirae showed no signs of tiredness or the frantic terror that was lurking at the edge of her own consciousness. Hirae always seemed to exist in a confident, untroubled state.

Sionan watched as the woodswoman sent the remaining horse back down the trail after the other two. The muffled thudding of hooves on the earthen ground quickly faded into the distance.

'And what of Kayton now?' Chancer asked.

A heavy silence settled on the group. Their faces were known in the castle and everyone would be searching for them. There would be no more rescue attempts there.

'We're not out of trouble ourselves yet,' Hirae said, pragmatic as ever, moving to pull Sionan to her feet.

'Have you no heart?' Sionan said, pushing Hirae's arms from her in disgust. 'They'll kill him, and you know it.'

Hirae looked her in the eye for a long, steady time before turning and walking deeper into the forest without a word, Scase close at her heels. Sionan knew she had been unjust to lash out, but her emotional and physical state was stretched to breaking point, and her pride would not let her call Hirae back. She pushed herself onto her knees with a sigh, her legs tingling and cramping with pain.

'Hirae cares,' Chancer said after a moment. 'She cares more deeply than you know. She just doesn't show it in the way you and I do. We need to get you to safety and find out what in crow's blood is in that box.' He helped Sionan to stand, she nodded in resignation. She could not trust her voice to speak. She desperately fought the inner turmoil that was threatening to overwhelm her again.

Slowly moving along the trail, they followed Hirae, Chancer with his arm around Sionan to support her weight.

Sionan flinched as she caught sight of the streaked grey hair falling across her face. She honestly did not know if the aching in her limbs was from the physical and emotional toll of all she had suffered or if this was how your body felt when you grew older. Despite her resolve not to cry, the tears slid down her cheeks and she wept for her lost youth. They trudged along the trail, each step feeling like an eternity to her.

'Stay strong, Sionan,' Chancer said kindly. 'Just a short while further and we will rest for the night.'

Like an apparition, Hirae appeared silently before them and led them from the trail to a small outcropping of rock with a narrow cave. The group silently went inside, where Sionan collapsed gratefully to the floor.

'Rest now, we will talk when you awake,' Chancer said.

'They will find us,' Sionan replied fearfully as she saw Hirae leaving the cave.

'Not yet, they won't,' Hirae replied confidently, and moved out into the night and back down the trail.

Sionan felt like her mind was too stretched with fear to ever allow her to sleep. She watched as Chancer sat down, leaned his back against the cave wall, and stared out into the night. Next to him sat Scase, watching his mistress disappear down the trail, but ever faithfully following her command to stay and protect them. Comforted by their presence, exhaustion took over, Sionan's heavy eyelids dropped and she fell into a fitful sleep.

The night had reached its deepest point when Hirae finally

returned to the cave. She had spent hours obscuring their trail and laying false leads. She knew the duke was likely to have excellent trackers in his employ. All of them would be out on their trail by morning, if they weren't already searching through the darkness of the night. Hirae had therefore taken her time to carefully disguise their passage and leave dummy trails to fool any scent-hounds they may bring. She obscured the front of the cave with branches and saw Chancer sitting, awaiting her return.

As she bent down to enter the cave, she could see from the set of his shoulders how his gnawing worry for Kayton was grinding him down. They had all been aware of the potential risks when taking on this madness, but she knew Chancer. He would feel solely responsible for any misfortune that befell Kayton in the castle.

'I'll take first watch,' he said.

'Thanks,' said Hirae as she lay down on the cave floor. The numbing rock and damp, cool air was not the most conducive setting for a good night's rest, but Hirae had slept in a lot worse. Until they were a long way from Clasterne, there would be no fires, and only a meagre breakfast of the spring fruits that Hirae had collected on her way back. At least the small cave, with its raised vantage point, was relatively safe. Whoever was on watch could view anyone approaching through the screen of branches, but it would be difficult for an onlooker to discern there was a cave here.

As Hirae gazed up at the ceiling, she felt Scase's warm body nestle in next to hers. The dog lay down full-length beside her and laid his head on her shoulder. Absent-mindedly, she tousled his ears as she thought about the almost completely botched rescue attempt today. Without Scase's bravery, they would not have made it.

She knew from his silence that Chancer's mind was ticking over strategies to free Kayton.

'We're going to try and rescue him, I take it,' she said quietly.

'Of course,' Chancer responded, with a self-mocking smile. 'What sort of hero would I be if we didn't? The boy came looking for the legendary Captain Chancer. Let's just hope I still have the same luck.'

Hirae muffled a laugh. 'And what daring strategy will we try this time?' Her thoughts turned to the bittersweet memories of friends she had lost in the Ascalion rebellion. That too had started from small seeds, with folk protesting about the Duke of Ascalion abusing his power. Hirae longed for the day when the people would be governed by someone of their own choice rather than by those who felt it was their birthright.

'We're not going to get in the castle again,' said Chancer. 'I dread to think what might have befallen the lad after Sionan's escape… and the betrayal he must feel at being left behind.'

'It's sickening,' Hirae agreed. 'But we aren't done yet.'

She saw Chancer's eyes narrow, knowing he was analysing all possible scenarios to create the best strategy for freeing Kayton even as they spoke.

His voice cut across her thoughts. 'Our only chance will be when they move Kayton for Justice Day. It's only one more night, and I reckon the duke is going to want to make an example of the boy because we interrupted his banquet.'

'Agreed. What about this?' Hirae pulled the box out from

her breastplate. 'Whatever is in it is clearly important.' She tried without success to prise open the lid. Turning the box in her hands, she could find no hidden catches. How the box opened was a mystery to her.

'Hide it somewhere,' said Chancer. 'Don't tell Sionan or me where. If we get captured, we can't reveal where it is if we don't know.'

'And what if *I* get captured?' Hirae asked with mock seriousness.

'You and Scase could fight your way out even if there was a whole battalion surrounding you!' Chancer laughed. 'Your ability to survive is legendary. Without you, I would never have made it out of the mountains all those years ago. It was *you* who pulled me from the inns the first time I was so soaked in booze that I no longer ate or thought coherently. *You* took me into your home, sobered me up, and fed me until some health and muscle was restored. It was *me* that fell off the path again. You have more iron in you than all Gelanson's guards put together!'

'Thanks for the confidence boost,' Hirae said. 'Seriously, though, what do you think has happened to Sionan?' Hirae turned her head to look at the sleeping form. In slumber, with the fear gone from Sionan's eyes and the lines on her face softened, she almost appeared to be young again.

'I don't know,' Chancer replied. 'Nothing good, I'll warrant. Get some sleep and we can plan in the morning, after we find out everything that's happened.'

'Wake me for the next watch,' Hirae replied, tucking the small box back away and settling down for sleep. Her mind dwelled on how Kayton must be feeling, knowing as the second night fell, that his rescue had failed.

Gentle morning light filtering into the cold cave woke Hirae from her slumber. Chancer looked like a stone statue on guard at the cave mouth.

'You didn't wake me,' Hirae said accusingly, embarrassed she had not taken her turn on watch.

'I couldn't sleep,' Chancer responded, standing and stretching. 'All I can think is that we need more manpower to rescue Kayton, and I don't know how we're going to get it in Clasterne.'

'Me and Scase will have to do, then,' Hirae replied, rolling her head from side to side as she tried to work out the kinks in her neck from sleeping on the floor. She left the cave to complete her morning ablutions. When she came back, Sionan was slowly waking.

Last night in the moonlit forest, Sionan had appeared like an anguished ethereal fairy, greying hair caught in the gentle breeze. This morning her face was bone-white in the sunlight. Hirae was concerned about how much more Sionan could cope with.

Hirae emptied out the meagre contents of her hunting bag and shared the berries and plants she had gathered, passing round her waterskin that she had refilled during her night's expedition to cover their trail. Scase sniffed at the fare with disgust before loping out of the cave to find his own breakfast. Hirae let him go. The dog would do better hunting alone than with them all in their weary state, crashing through the undergrowth.

'How are you feeling?' she asked Sionan. 'Are you ready to tell us what happened?'

Between mouthfuls of breakfast, Sionan recounted all that had occurred. Hirae and Chancer listened silently as she spoke of the cells and Kayton's beating. She visibly trembled as she described the disbelief at seeing her father's arm on Gelanson's worktable. Horror reflected in her voice when she spoke of the mist wrapping around her body and immobilising her. Hirae and Chancer's eyebrows rose in astonishment, but they did not interrupt, or question whether she had been mistaken, even though the tale sounded outlandish and unbelievable.

'…When he completed the second incantation, I could feel my energy dropping – no, it was more fundamental than that – it was as though my life was being drawn through the green stone he held to my hand. As I aged, the duke looked as though he was getting younger.'

'The duke is a sorcerer?' Hirae remarked in disbelief. 'How is that possible? I thought they only existed in children's tales.'

'And what's worse,' Chancer said. 'Is that if he has the power to transfer people's life energy into other things, even dead limbs, what does that make him? A deity? This is a corruption of the natural order. In all my travels across the four Manors of the Principality, I have never seen nor heard of any real sorcery.'

Hirae leaned back on the wall and looked at her two companions. She could see the fear in Sionan's eyes. The aging process that had been inflicted on her made her look more delicate in the early morning light, as though already more spirit than living being. Hirae knew that if they were to have any chance of success at rescuing Kayton, they needed to keep Sionan hidden, she looked as though she could shatter into tiny pieces at any moment. Chancer, on the other hand, looked focused. The strategist deep down within him was rising to this challenge. The excitement of facing an unknown foe was making him more alive than he had been for years.

'So, how do we stop a sorcerer?' Hirae asked.

'We have the star-shaped-stone as evidence,' Sionan said. 'We could take it to the Overlord and petition for justice. Where is the box?'

'Hidden,' replied Hirae cagily. 'If we are caught, at least the duke will not have it back.' She frowned. 'I'm not sure about going to the crown, who's going to believe us in court? I'm having trouble believing it myself, and I can see with my own eyes what has happened to you.'

'I can use some old connections to at least gain an audience,' Chancer replied. 'I don't see that we have any other choice. I can lead you into battle against a legion of soldiers, but I have no idea how to combat a magician. If that's even the right word for his evil.'

Hirae shook her head, mentally rejecting the idea but unable to think of another viable option. She hated to think of travelling into the Overlord's domain, not least because she did not wish to travel to the city of Atipac. Its densely packed houses and thousands of people rushing around like ants made her feel suffocated. Forests were her natural habitat, and thus far they had stayed relatively safe due to her woodlore and ability to make people invisible, like ghosts passing through the trees. They would be completely exposed in the city, with nowhere to hide.

'Going to Atipac is going into the viper's nest. Let's just kill the duke and be done with it.'

'And what of the lives of the townsfolk when the Overlord hears the duke has been murdered?' Sionan asked.

'Martial law will be inflicted on them,' Chancer replied. 'We need to try to get justice from the Overlord first. Unless you have a better idea, Hirae? One that *doesn't* involve killing the duke?' he continued, despite Hirae opening her mouth to speak. 'Any magical friends hiding in the depths of the Ascalion forest we can call upon?'

Hirae looked at Chancer with disdain. 'I live in a forest, not a children's story. But no, unfortunately, I have no better ideas. At least we will be putting some distance between ourselves and the duke if we are travelling to Atipac.'

'Justice Day is tomorrow,' said Chancer. 'Hirae and I will get Kayton back when they move him for trial. As soon as we have him, we'll make directly for the Overlord. Sionan, you need to remain hidden and safe. Without your testimony to the Overlord, we have no chance. Our only benefit will be that I don't think Gelanson will expect us to be bold enough to go to Atipac.'

'We need more than just a green stone in a box and my tale,' Sionan replied. 'If I can reach Leetha's parents at the bakery and tell them our plans, I'm sure they would help us. They know what's happening, and are as alone and scared as I am now. If they make it to the Overlord too, surely with their sworn testimony as well as mine the crown will have to investigate?'

Hirae and Chancer looked at each other. It was a thin strategy at best, but it was all they had to work with for now.

'Okay,' Chancer said. 'We keep to the woods as far as possible.'

I'll take care of our trail and keep watch.' Hirae stated, 'They'll be searching every nook of this area now that it is first light. We try for the bakery first and then watch and wait for our best opportunity to free Kayton. Sionan, you'll need to stay here,' Hirae continued. 'You've neither the physicality nor skills to help with getting Kayton out right now, and before you object, remember you are still getting used to whatever Gelanson has inflicted on you. We need to move fast and fight to free him if needed. We need to be fully focused on Kayton.'

'Fine,' Sionan agreed. 'I will trust you to rescue Kayton.' She stood slowly, which added weight to Hirae's argument, before continuing pointedly. 'But I will need to go to the bakery. They won't trust strangers after all that has befallen them.'

Hirae caught Chancer's look of admiration as he saw Sionan willing herself onwards. Hirae sighed; she could see more complications coming. Chancer was always a fool to his heart. There would be no warning her old friend, who was now following Sionan out of the cave and telling her one of his lively stories to lift the girl's mood.

Hirae collected her bag and left the pair to wend their way down from the cave into the woods. Chancer's heart getting bruised would be the least of their troubles with the way things were developing. Hirae took a moment to sweep over the cave floor and remove any evidence of occupation. She had spotted a small ledge at the back of the cave when lying down to sleep last night. Seeing Chancer and Sionan disappear into the trees, she walked back into the depths. Stooping as the ceiling of the cave lowered, Hirae crawled to the very back and carefully placed the box on the ledge, pushed it as far back as she could, and then wriggled back out. Hidden there, the box would be protected from the elements and she could easily retrieve it when the time came.

Hirae carefully moved round the cave, checking to see if the box could be seen from any angle. Satisfied it was safely hidden, she left their safe haven, the morning sunlight bright in her eyes as she stepped out.

Setting off after the others, she gave Scase three short, high-pitched whistles to let him know they were on the move. Her hound would rejoin them after a more robust breakfast than they had enjoyed. As she followed Chancer and Sionan into the woods, she obscured the trail behind her. Listening vaguely to Chancer's hushed storytelling, and a small laugh breaking free from Sionan, her spirit lifted.

Hirae strode down to catch up with Chancer and Sionan, hoping the sun shining down on them was a good omen. Yesterday, they had rescued Sionan. Today they would go for Kayton. Hirae knew that by nightfall it would all be over. Either they would have Kayton free, or be in irons themselves.

CHAPTER FIFTEEN

Gelanson stood in the Great Hall looking at the vestiges of last night's celebrations. The cherry blossom that had fragrantly filled the room the evening before and the brightly coloured spring flowers were wilted and dying. Petals that had fallen to the floor had been crushed under foot by revellers making a speedy exit after the bloodshed at the tower. Months of planning to elevate his status as head of the most influential Manor in the Principality had been destroyed by that girl and her rescuers. Flies, disturbed by the first servants entering to start the clean-up, were already buzzing around food scraps left on the floor as the sun crept over the horizon.

Gelanson's fury was a cold, white blade, sharp enough to cut anyone who dared to trouble him this morning. When he had accessed his hidden research room and discovered the star-stone was gone, his rage was incandescent with volcanic heat. He took some comfort in the fact that the thieves would not know how to use the stone and it was useless to them, but without it Gelanson felt dangerously exposed. Suddenly everything was a threat to his life and health. Panic threatened to engulf him at the realisation he could not regenerate himself anytime he needed to.

He pinched the bridge of his nose between his thumb

and forefinger, and forced himself to breathe slowly and deeply. His mistake had been not killing the girl when she had first been in the tower. These pathetic people would never understand the generosity of spirit he had shown them. With their limited intellect how could they grasp the honour he bestowed in allowing them to be subjects of his experimentation?

After the castle guards were overcome by the escaping criminals, there had been no reassuring the nobility of their safety. Some shrieked in terror, whilst other pompous fools loudly bragged that such a thing would never occur in their abodes. No amount of reassurance from Onway or Duke Gelanson had worked. Like a herd of sheep, once one noble decided to make his way home, the rest followed. Some of the aristocrats took great pleasure in this disastrous turn of events. They resembled crows picking over a dead animal's bones as they dissected all that had happened. Nobles who had been seeking favour with the rising star of Duke Gelanson now smelt blood in the air. Each individual house would use any leverage they could to climb the perilous ladder towards the Overlord's favour. Some, who still wished to show their allegiance to the duke, offered to stay and assist him in hunting down the offenders. Gelanson, however, politely and firmly declined. Things had already spiralled dangerously out of his careful control, his activities did not need to come under further scrutiny.

Within an hour all the carriages had left with their departing guests. Empty promises to return for a summer banquet were made with little desire to revisit the event.

As the final carriage clattered out of the main entrance,

Captain Stegen returned, calling for reinforcements to search through the night for the escapees. The duke stepped into the castle square and called her to him.

Stegen bowed to the duke, her face red and voice winded, she spoke of the battle and breakneck ride back to the castle.

'My lord, the intruders have made it into the woodland. I am confident, with your tracker and a full complement of soldiers, we can find them this very night and bring them to justice.'

'And how exactly did they make it that far with my best guard detail on their tail?' Gelanson asked with an icy glare.

'Their hound attacked the horses and unseated us. I'm sorry, my lord, it will not occur again.'

'You are quite correct, Captain Stegen, it won't occur again, or you will be gone from my employ.' Gelanson watched Stegen blanch white at the threat. Gelanson knew well that the captain had no family. Without the castle barracks, she would effectively be homeless until he chose to allow her back into his good graces. 'You may take one complement of guards to patrol the edge of the forest, but no more. I want the rest of the barracks alerted here to oversee our remaining prisoner. There can be no more escapes. It is imperative that judgement be made on Justice Day. How could we do that if there were no one to sentence?'

'Oh,' Gelanson added. 'And see if you can't find the *real* Lord Dennier whilst you are out along the road – I recall that he is a young, supercilious man without a grey hair in sight.'

Stegen bowed to his departing figure.

Gelanson strode across the castle square to the cells, where the sergeant stood to attention, and waited to be addressed.

'And what exactly occurred at the tower, Sergeant?'

In a gruff voice the sergeant recounted how the four tower guards had been either incapacitated or killed. 'Entry was gained to the tower without a key, sir. The door must have been unlocked, but there'll be no escape for the other murderous savage.' The sergeant nodded his head in the general direction of Kayton's cell. 'All guards have been roused from their sleep and will be on duty in double shifts through to Justice Day.'

'Very good, Sergeant. Ensure the men who were bested at the tower and are still alive are given their marching orders. We have only the very best of soldiers in Clasterne Castle.'

'Yes, my lord.' The sergeant bowed and moved off to the infirmary to inform the unlucky survivors that they were no longer in the service of the duke.

Gelanson continued to pick over, piece by piece, all that had occurred in the night. He had been foolish not to kill the girl outright but his excitement at reanimating the dead limb had momentarily blinded his usually calm and analytical mind. He ruefully realised that, even on the precipice of an amazing scientific discovery, he could get carried away with enthusiasm.

The duke was certain he had locked the door after leaving the girl. As only he and Onway had a key to the tower, that meant that it was the steward who must have left the door unlocked.

The remnants of the dinner tray in the study was evidence enough that Onway had entered the tower after the duke had left. The steward had been fanatically loyal to the duke for so many years that Gelanson had not paid close attention to his servant's current state of mind. Gelanson could not reconcile the possibility that now their righteous mission was reaching fruition Onway may be turning on him. The steward's steady explanation that, with the business of the banquet, it must have slipped his mind to lock the door may have been the truth, but the niggling doubt remined.

What of Onway's mistake with Lord Dennier? Allowing an imposter into the banquet was treasonous. The steward would need to be watched. Although, maybe it was the fault of the aging state of the man, rather than any betrayal. The elderly *did* suffer with lapses of memory, the duke considered. The steward may be reaching the end of his useful service, and Gelanson had failed to spot it.

Gelanson summoned Onway and stared into his Steward's eyes as though observing an insect for dissection. The duke's eyes were cold as he searched the man's face for any lie or weakness of spirit.

'You do believe in our cause here, don't you, Onway?'

'Of course, my lord. It will be a medical revolution when you refine your powers.'

Gelanson watched Onway carefully, searching for any trace of subterfuge or doubt in the steward's mind. Seeing none, he nodded to the man.

'Very good, Onway. I realise I have taken much from you. When the girl is found, I will ensure that your years are returned. I hold myself responsible for your errors, I have relied too heavily upon you without maintaining your youth. I see that now, and that will be corrected. I have refined the art of transferring the energy from one vessel to another without difficulty. Do not worry, man, we will ensure you are back to your usual efficient self in no time.'

Onway bowed deeply, his expression unreadable.

'Now, Onway, we must prepare for Justice Day tomorrow. Send a barrel of ale to the town for folk who attend and distribute any leftover food from the banquet. We want to ensure they are in a positive frame of mind for the judgement tomorrow.' Gelanson dismissed the steward with a gesture, missing the gleam of cautious hope that appeared on the Steward's usually sombre face with news of the girl's escape.

The noise of another contingent of guards arriving in preparation to escort the town lad to his hearing echoed around the castle courtyard. Gelanson would leave nothing to chance this Justice Day. The townspeople would be made to see the treachery lurking in their midst.

The boy would be judged.

CHAPTER SIXTEEN

Kayton awoke from a fitful sleep, shivering in the cold, dark cell. He had no way of knowing how much time had passed. In his dreams, he had seen Sionan standing in the distance on a hill, calling his name. He was running to her as fast as he could. She was entrancing with her rosy, sun-warmed skin and hair waving in the breeze. She smiled lovingly and called to him, but as he got closer, her hair started to streak with grey. She was aging before his eyes and screaming for his help. Kayton ran with all his might, his lungs heaving with exertion and legs on fire, but every time he tried to reach her, to envelop her in his arms and tell her she was safe, he would suddenly appear back at the bottom of the hill. The nightmare would loop back to the beginning, again and again.

Kayton rubbed his gritty eyes with the back of his hands, trying to wipe away the vestiges of the disturbing dream. He slowly stood and shuffled to the furthest corner of the cell to relieve himself. The bruising on his torso from the beating felt raw today, exacerbated by the cold stone floor he had fallen asleep on. He was still alive, though, and whilst he had breath in his body, he would stand against Gelanson.

Kayton peered through the grate in the cell door into darkness. He ached to see Sionan's face, but also hoped she was free. He called out to her but there was no response. The dream felt like a portent of doom. He paced carefully in the small confines of his cell, favouring his left side where the pain flared strongest. Kayton tried to think of something useful he could do, but the isolation and dank darkness chipped away at his optimism until he realised he had no choice but to follow the course of events as they unfolded.

His best hope was to speak on Justice Day. There would be people there who had known him from birth, and he could trust them to do what was right. His slow pacing stumbled to a halt as the sharp pain of his injuries forced him to lean on the wall and catch his breath. He flinched as he heard the door at the end of the corridor unlock. Anger rose within him at how quickly he had come to fear the noise of approaching guards. He squared his shoulders, determined to stand tall against his tormentors.

'Right, then. Time to get moving. Justice Day for you.'

Kayton looked into the impassive face of the sergeant who had beaten him two – or was it three – days ago. If it was Justice Day today it must be three. If Sionan was not in the cells, could it possibly mean she was free? Kayton's heart surged at the thought she had made it out.

The sergeant unlocked the cell door and roughly gestured for Kayton to follow. He led him into the main guard room, where Kayton was surprised to see a full contingent of six armed guards. Three faced the exit and three faced him, eyeing him suspiciously.

'Where's Sionan?' he asked the sergeant.

'As if you don't know,' the sergeant retorted with bitterness. 'Well, she'll get her comeuppance, you'll see. Captain Stegen's out looking for them now and Stegen's the best. They'll be no escaping her. Then you can all swing from the hangman's noose together.'

Kayton felt a glorious sense of relief wash over him as he realised Sionan had escaped. The alleviation of the fear he had felt for her safety was so great, he swayed and clutched the table in front of him for support. His joy was intermingled with dismay that Chancer and Hirae had not freed him as well, but at least he could comfort himself knowing that Sionan had escaped.

The sergeant opened a side door that led to a small, windowless room with a tub of water and a clean set of clothes on a chair. Kayton looked at the sergeant quizzically.

'The duke says you're to be clean and presentable for the town later, and clean you will be, even if I have to dunk you in there myself.'

Kayton ignored the threat and walked into the room. As he tried to close the door behind him, a foot jammed it open.

'No chance. You'll be under watch of a contingent of guards all the way from here to your execution.'

'To my *trial*, you mean,' Kayton responded. 'Maybe I'll walk free when the people hear what I have to say.' His fighting spirit was returning now that he knew Sionan was out of danger.

The sergeant ignored Kayton's response and nodded at the tub. Kayton turned his back and tried to ignore the gnawing worry in his belly. He toyed with the idea of refusing to bathe so the townsfolk could see the filth and squalor he had been kept in, but his instinct was to be free of the muck and the stench of his own sweat and the vileness of the cells was too strong.

Removing his stinking clothes, he stepped into the tub, only mildly surprised to find it was full of cold, rather than hot, water. Heating water for a criminal to bathe in was not the guards' priority. Normally the cold water would have shocked his system, but after a night in the cells, it felt warm by comparison. Kayton climbed into the tub, feeling his limbs thawing out. He grabbed a bar of lye soap and scrubbed his body and hair, the water quickly turning a murky grey, and used the jug next to the tub to rinse himself. As he gingerly stepped out, he saw the deep purple and black bruising across his torso in all its colourful glory. He rubbed himself dry with a rough cloth, taking care with his damaged torso.

Kayton dressed in the linen shirt and plain trousers that had been left for him, and donned his own shoes. He was not surprised to find the clothes fit perfectly. He felt more and more that he was being dressed up like a prized sacrificial lamb for the crowd to witness.

Seeing Kayton dressed, the sergeant stepped into the room and placed iron manacles around his prisoner's wrists. They were locked shut with a click that had a horrifying finality about it. Kayton felt a sickening rise of bile in his throat as the spectre of the gallows became more real. The manacles had a long iron chain fastened to them, which the sergeant hooked on to his own belt.

'That's your last meal.' The sergeant pointed to a cup of watered wine and a small, hard bread roll on the table.

Kayton sat to eat without speaking, adjusting to the uncomfortable feeling of the weight of metal on his wrists. He slowly ate the roll and drank the wine, reserving all his energy for thoughts of escape and what he would say when he was on the Justice Day platform.

Despite being orphaned at a young age, he had grown up as a happy, friendly lad and was well known throughout the town. He was sure at least someone would vouch for him against Gelanson's lies. The food disappeared all too quickly, but the sustenance revived his flagging spirits.

The sergeant pulled on the chain to signify it was time to leave. Kayton dutifully stood and followed him out of the door. The other six guards spread out, eyes constantly scanning for signs of trouble.

The prison carriage awaited Kayton in the centre of the castle square. There were another six armed guards already mounted surrounding the carriage. As Kayton walked across the square, he felt the eyes of servants and workers upon him. A hush fell over the usual hubbub. Everyone paused in their work to watch the young man walk with quiet dignity to the carriage.

Kayton's eyes scanned the servants, hoping to see a friendly face and some compassion in the crowd, but saw only cold hard stares or dark curiosity. He felt the weight of those looks as much as the manacles, which the sergeant pulled on to hurry him along. The creeping dread that normal, everyday people might believe Gelanson rose in him. Kayton climbed carefully into the carriage, relieved when the door closed on the hostility of those faces. He reasoned with himself that the castle folk did not know him, so they were bound to believe whatever intricate lies they had been told by their duke. They were, after all, beholden to Gelanson for their livelihoods. The carriage pulled away slowly, surrounded by the sergeant, his troop and the other mounted guards.

It will be different in town, he thought, as the swaying carriage left the castle. *That is where I grew up, they know me, they will know the truth.*

Whilst Kayton's prison carriage was rolling along the road into town, Sionan left the cover of the trees and made her way towards the bakery. After their escape, the trio had made quick time, heading directly through the forest to the outskirts of Clasterne, relying on the hope that no one would be expecting them to return. The familiar sounds drifting on the breeze from the busy town felt so unfamiliar to Sionan now. As she walked purposefully towards the smell of baking bread, she could not understand how people could not see what had happened to her. She felt it was screaming out of every pore of her being, and everyone must know. Her heart leapt into her mouth when she passed one of her neighbours, feeling sure the woman would stop and exclaim at the sight of her, but the neighbour's eyes skated past her as she continued on her way.

Why would people recognise me now? she thought. *No one could have expected me to return looking as old as my mother.*

Chancer's instructions echoed in her ears. "If you act as though you should be there, no one will notice you. You've aged years in a matter of days. Don't look around, don't check behind you. Only people with something to hide search for people following them. All you are doing is going to buy a loaf of bread. Walk like you belong and no one will stop you." He had smiled encouragingly at her, and she had taken courage in his belief that she could do this.

It was helpful to Sionan that Justice Day was underway in the marketplace. The majority of people were already flowing there to get a good place in the crowd to watch the proceedings. One group's excited tones reached her across the steady din of voices as she approached the door of the shop. They talked of the banquet food, ale, and wine that was being handed out to the people, the sort of fare that most townsfolk would rarely have a chance to enjoy. Sionan felt nauseous as she realised people were treating this Justice Day more like one of the duke's festival days.

A group of girls passed by talking in rushed, elevated voices, thrilled at the intrigue as they spoke about the events.

'I always knew that Kayton was a wrong 'un,' one of the girls announced with certainty. 'The way he shined after the tailor's daughter wasn't normal. He was besotted with her, it's no wonder it came to bloodshed. Her poor father killed by that lovesick boy.'

Sionan clenched her mouth shut as she forced herself to walk by. *How could these people believe that someone with such a gentle, kind nature could commit murder? But then, why wouldn't people believe it? Didn't I pity the baker's husband when he was sent to serve time in prison for dissent?* Not for one moment had Sionan considered his protestations could be true. People would always choose to believe a basic lie rather than a radical truth, and with Gelanson's gifts of food and drink distributed, people were already kindly disposed to whatever ruling the duke would make.

Sionan tasted blood in her mouth and forced her jaw to unclench. Kayton had no hope of justice today; only escape with Chancer and Hirae.

As she entered the bakery, a small bell tinkled above the door. Unsurprisingly, she was the only customer in the shop. She had banked on the family not attending the hearing. They were still grieving for Leetha and would not want to be in Gelanson's presence at the hearing.

'What can I get you, dearie?' the baker asked in a flat, tired voice.

Sionan looked the woman directly in the face, willing her to recognise her. 'I need your help.'

The baker's eyes widened in recognition at the soft tones of Sionan's voice.

'Oh, my child, what has he done to you?' The baker rushed from behind the counter to wrap Sionan in her arms. The unexpected empathy and warmth of the embrace was too much for Sionan, who felt close to shattering and she gently disengaged herself from the woman's arms.

The baker, seeing the desperation in Sionan's eyes, locked the bakery door and turned the painted sign in the window from "open" to "closed". She led Sionan into the back room, where her husband was sitting quietly in a chair. His time in prison had clearly not been easy; he was thin to the point of emaciation. He regarded the two women with seriousness.

Sionan sat whilst the man poured a hot tisane for her, then she recounted everything that had happened. When she came to talk about her life being stolen from her and the sorcery involved, Leetha's mother turned a sickly white and placed a hand over her mouth. The final understanding of how their daughter had died in the terror of dark magic was too much to bear. The husband put his thin arm around his wife's shoulders, Sionan could see from his expression that her news was reinforcing what the man had already believed. It was not a shock to him. The obvious grief and sadness bowing his shoulders spoke volumes.

When Sionan came to talk of the plan to go to the Overlord and beg for the crown to intervene, the man's eyes glittered with savage conviction.

'You are right, of course. We should have done that immediately instead of relying on justice from within the Manor.' The spirit of hope was returning to his voice. His thin frame belied the strength still in his limbs as he pulled his wife to her feet. 'We must set off immediately. We must be there when the next Atipac Justice Day occurs. Then Gelanson will see true justice.'

'How do we explain closing the bakery?' his wife asked. 'That will make people suspicious.'

'It doesn't matter. Everyone's caught up in the hearing today. No one will notice until they come to buy their bread tomorrow. By then, we'll be gone.'

Sionan was amazed at the couple's resilience. She had anticipated having to convince them to travel to Atipac, not that they would be out the door before she'd even finished speaking.

The couple leapt into a flurry of activity, finally having a direction where they could expend their frustration and anger. They halted only when Sionan begged for some food supplies and a cloak, having nothing save what she had ridden out in during the previous night's harried flight from the castle. She waited quietly while the couple hurried from the room, calling to each other as they packed a trunk of clothes.

The husband was already talking of hitching the horse to the wagon that they usually used to collect the flour from the town mill. Travelling by cart, they could get to Atipac more quickly.

Sionan felt gratitude and relief that they were willing to put their own lives at risk to support her. But then, what parents wouldn't do all they could to bring their daughter's killer to account?

The baker rushed over to wrap Sionan in one of her daughter's cloaks. 'You must come with us,' the woman said. 'We can travel now, together.'

'I need to meet my companions,' Sionan replied. 'They will fear for me if I am not there, and you must make best use of people's distraction with Justice Day.'

The woman smiled her understanding and handed Sionan a sack containing bread, hard cheese, and meat.

'This will last you for a few days,' she said. 'We will be at the Overlord's court on the next Atipac Justice Day, and every day until we can gain time for our grievance to be heard.'

Sionan grasped the baker's hands. 'We will find you, I promise. Be careful who you speak to, we cannot know how many friends Gelanson has in the Overlord's court.'

The women shared a fierce hug, before the baker ushered Sionan to the back of the shop.

'Stay safe, child,' the baker said, before returning to her hurried packing.

Sionan stepped back out into the daylight and walked towards the wood line, a determined spring in her step at successfully mobilising their only allies against Gelanson. Now she was to follow Hirae's instructions exactly and move on to their identified meeting point. She turned to wave at the couple; her last glimpse was of the husband standing in the doorway, his hand raised in a solemn farewell.

Making her way carefully into the woods along a deer trail, she tried to remember all of Hirae's brief tuition about not leaving any easily visible signs for a tracker. She walked lightly, taking care not to disturb the low-level branches and brambles. Despite her promise to remain hidden, she skirted along the woodlands to her old home. Her heart ached as she came upon the back of the house where she had grown up. She sat inside the tree line watching her home with the melancholy of longing for days gone by, an indulgence she knew she should not be entertaining, but her heart yearned for. A part of her wished she had not been burdened with the truth and knowledge about Gelanson. Let him do as he wanted as long as her family were safe, but as fleetingly as the thought came, her conscience chased it away at the memory of Leetha.

Sighing, Sionan knew that sitting on the tree line watching her old home was not only feeding her sadness, but also increasing her risk of capture. She eased herself back into the woods to make her way to the agreed meeting point, her heart aching for her family who by now should be far from danger on the road south to Sahjashorn.

As though thinking of them brought them into being, Sionan froze, unable to believe her eyes as she saw the back door to her home open and her mother bring out dishwater to pour on the kitchen garden. Sionan could see the toll her father's death had taken on her mother. Normally a fastidiously clean and tidy woman, her hair looked lank and unkempt and her skin a pale grey. Grief for her husband lay like a heavy shroud over her body. Sionan started forward with no conscious thought other than to comfort her mother, when a guard appeared from the inside of the house and leant on the door frame.

'It's time to go, Widow Hellard,' the guard said. 'Don't you worry, now, there's nothing to fear. Just tell everyone the truth of things and all will be well.'

Sionan saw her mother's head hanging in defeat as she walked slowly into the house.

'I must see to my girls,' she said to the guard. 'They'll be frightened without their mother.'

'Don't worry about them,' the guard replied. 'They'll be just fine. Gelanson's sent the best servant from the castle to watch over them. You just get your coat and let's move along, so you can do your duty for the duke.'

Sionan watched the exchange with bewilderment. What duty could the duke possibly require from her mother? Something was very wrong here. Dread crept up Sionan's arms, raising the hairs on her neck with foreboding. Struggling to decide how to proceed, she decided she could not wait in the woods. She had to know where they were taking her mother.

Like a shadow, she flitted through the edge of the wood to follow the back streets of the town as two soldiers walked her mother towards the market square. Sionan pulled her cloak over her head, following at a distance, and lost herself in the busy crowd that gathered in front of the Justice Day review platform.

The platform was a sturdy structure built from oak. It had stood in the town square for as long as Sionan could remember and served as an ever-present reminder that judgement would be passed on anyone who committed wrongdoing under the Overlord's law. Sionan watched as her mother was seated on a small bench by the side of the platform, and waited to see what would develop. She willed her mother to know she was there, as if she could communicate across the crowded space to offer comfort and support. Her mother looked defeated and haggard, her shoulders slumped forwards and her brown eyes red-rimmed from crying.

Sionan started to ease her way towards her, desperate to offer words of comfort, when suddenly, the crowd surged to the left of the platform. The townsfolk were eager to see the arrival of the criminal as the jangling of the carriage and clop of horses' hooves announced his approach.

Further into the depths of the steadily growing crowd, a man in a filthy, hooded cloak was jostled as he worked his way closer to the platform. Anyone who looked closely at him quickly moved away in disgust as the pervading smell of rot and horse manure assaulted their senses.

Sionan was pulled inexorably away from her mother as the black carriage drew alongside the platform. She allowed herself to be moved with the ebb of the crowd; she had no wish to draw attention to herself, and resolved to wait for a better opportunity to speak with her mother. She watched the dark, heavily guarded carriage draw up and soldiers dismount to surround it. Sionan held her breath, waiting with trepidation for the occupant to step out, desperately hoping anyone other than Kayton would emerge.

CHAPTER SEVENTEEN

A hush fell over the gathered townsfolk as the sergeant opened the carriage door to allow the accused to step out into the sunshine. Kayton, squinting from the brightness of the fine day, looked around the square before him, searching the crowd for friendly faces. Moving carefully out of the carriage to protect his injuries, he reserved his strength for the rescue he hoped would come.

Captain Stegen strode forwards from the platform and took control of the prisoner. Firmly grasping the chain, she led Kayton back up the steps to stand before the crowd. The platform resonated with the sound of each step Stegen took with her heavy boots. Leading Kayton to the centre, the captain stood watching the crowd for any sign of trouble. Whatever judgement the duke passed, it would undoubtably be actioned.

To the far side of the platform, a raised dais stood holding the Seat of Hearing: a large wooden chair with velvet cushions. Guards stood to attention, armed with staves which they appeared more than ready to use. Kayton's eyes were drawn with morbid fascination, past the dais, to the scaffold at the back of the platform. The rope swung gently in the light breeze, hypnotising those who had come for judgement. In all Kayton's life, he had never actually seen a noose hanging from the wooden framework. Previous Justice Days had seen sentences of confiscation of land, fines, or time in the cells. Often the duke was lauded for his generous nature in allowing forced labour as reparation for serious wrongdoing. Terror crashed through Kayton's body as the noose taunted him. He felt a weakening of his bladder, and forced himself to tear his gaze away from the petrifying sight. He looked around the crowd, hoping to see his friends, Chancer, or at least one kindly disposed face. All he could see was people furtively looking away, trying not to make eye contact, or staring aggressively at him with open hostility. He ducked just in time as someone threw an unidentifiable piece of rotten food and shouted an obscenity.

The remaining guards from the convoy filed out in front of the platform to push the crowd back amidst calls of "Hang him!" and "Murderer!". Kayton stood in stunned silence, watching the ugliness evolve. His mind was unable to reconcile how the people of his own community could turn against him so readily. Loathing rose from the mob like a heavy fog, suffocating him with its intensity. Kayton's blood thundered through his ears as the rushing anguish of isolation and fear swamped him.

Silence fell as the duke's carriage approached. Decorated with gold filigree, the expertly crafted coach stood out in stark contrast to the black prison carriage nearby. A young boy leapt from the stand plate before the white horses, resplendent in their purple livery. The boy opened the door for the duke and stood smartly to attention, proud of his role in these important events of the day. The duke stepped from the carriage and cut an imposing figure in his full-length judicial grey robe, the traditional dress of the nobility when conducting hearings.

The robe was adorned with the finest silver thread around the cuffs and hem. In Gelanson's hand was a golden sceptre, the mark of office presented by the Overlord to those deemed worthy to oversee the law in their Manor. The golden rod was beautifully embossed at the top with emeralds.

Gelanson stood smiling benignly at the crowd, the sunlight catching the sceptre and bouncing off the intricately placed jewels. The golden Chain of Office was, as usual, the only jewellery the duke wore. The crowd was silent, in awe, as Gelanson stood, looking regal and powerful – a man in absolute control of his Manor.

After a suitable pause to allow the townsfolk to view him, the duke walked in a stately fashion towards the hearing platform. His face reflected the sombre gravity required by this occasion.

By now, the crowd was in full swing for the hearing, having heavily imbibed from the barrels of ale and wine sent from the castle. The audience was peppered with trusted servants, given the day off and primed with intimate knowledge of the case to be heard. Or rather, Onway had circulated the version of events that the duke wished the crowd to know. Gossip would spread the news more effectively than a town crier. The duke had also taken the precaution of sending a pair of guards to each of the houses where the boy Kayton was reputed to have friends who could be troublesome allies. A gentle request from two town guards on the doorstep generally stopped all but the most foolhardy supporter from venturing forwards.

Kayton stood trembling as the duke approached, shaking his head sadly at him, like a father who has been sorely let down by a wayward son. Gelanson's face showed a wealth of compassion and sorrow for the judgement about to be made. Turning, the duke walked sombrely to the Seat of Hearing and sat observing the crowd.

Having watched the duke's theatrical arrival, Kayton no longer held any illusion there would be justice. His impending execution was a foregone conclusion for everyone in the market square. He jumped, heart thumping, as he heard Captain Stegen command the attention of the crowd to read out the charges before him.

'Kayton Stratton, you are charged with the murder of Stanton Hellard seven days ago. You wilfully sought his death and stabbed the unarmed man, seeking his death. When the castle guard attempted to arrest you, as was their right by the Overlord's law upon these lands, you killed them without remorse. On this Justice Day, the sixteenth day of spring, you are brought before the Duke of Clasterne to make your case and receive his judgement.'

Captain Stegen looked to the duke, who nodded for the case to proceed.

'Kayton Stratton,' she continued. 'Do you have anything you wish to say in your defence of these charges?'

Kayton stood with his mouth hanging ajar. He gulped air into his lungs, feeling as though he was drowning in hopelessness. Who here was going to believe him? None of his friends nor neighbours were here, he could not even see Hirae or Chancer in the crowd. He was facing his death utterly alone.

Resolving to tell the townsfolk the truth, he gave himself a mental shake and stood taller, the chain to his manacles rattling as he shifted. He would not die without speaking, and could only hope that the truth would start a small spark of questions about the duke, even if he was not alive to fan the flames of protest. He was as surprised as Captain Stegen appeared to be when his voice rose calmly, addressing the crowd.

'I do wish to speak and share a true accounting of events. I will speak only the truth on this day, though others may not wish it to be heard.' He stood tall and straight, took a breath, and turned to face Gelanson, intent on ensuring the duke did not have the satisfaction of triumphing over his spirit. 'Three days ago, I returned from seeking the aid of comrades to free Sionan Hellard. You all know there is something amiss at the castle. You have all heard about the deaths. Today, I stand before you, condemned for my wish to protect Sionan, one of our own, and expose the evils of the duke.'

The crowd booed and hissed in response. Shouts of "Liar!" filled the air.

Kayton plunged on, raising his voice over the cacophony of the crowd.

'I did not kill Sionan's father. He was killed by one of the duke's guards when they were trying to drag Sionan back to the castle against her will.' Raising his manacled arms in supplication, he appealed to the crowd. 'How can you not see what he is doing to you all? You *know* me!' Kayton emphasised, voice rising in his desire to be believed. 'I am not a murderer! The duke is killing your sons and daughters, and you are pretending not to see. Even if I die this day, know that

I have spoken no falsehoods. You all have the power to stop this evil continuing! Stand togeth—'

Kayton's impassioned speech was cut short as a piece of decayed fruit hit him squarely in the face. His cheeks burned as laughter rippled across the square.

The duke imperiously raised a hand to address the crowd. Silence fell immediately, everyone straining to hear the response to these accusations.

'You have had your chance to speak, Kayton Stratton.' He turned to the crowd and addressed them. 'You all know that Justice Day embodies honesty, equality, and fairness in all its rulings. For this reason, the accused was provided the opportunity to speak. I now present to you a true witness of the events, so all can know that there is no dark conspiracy, as this young man alludes to.'

Captain Stegen nodded to the sergeant, who supported a woman to walk up the platform steps. Kayton felt a brief moment of joy seeing Sionan's mother ascending to speak on his behalf. He rejoiced with the heady sensation that all would hear the truth now. The tailors were well respected throughout the town. When the crowd heard her speak, things would change.

Sionan's mother turned to Kayton with a beseeching look. His mind struggled to understand what she was trying to communicate as Stegen addressed her.

'Widow Hellard,' said Captain Stegen. 'Please enlighten us with what happened at your house that day.'

The crowd collectively held its breath.

'I can't do this,' Sionan's mother said so quietly that only Kayton and Stegen heard.

'Think of your children, Widow Hellard,' Stegen prompted.

Sionan's mother froze, her face a mask of grief. A murmur ran through the crowd as the duke rose and walked towards her. Her whole body tensed as Gelanson placed what appeared to be a comforting arm around her shoulders. 'We understand how distressing this is for you, Widow Hellard. We want to make this as painless as possible. Please just tell the crowd what you saw.' The warm melodic tones of the duke's voice carried over the crowd.

Sionan's mother looked at Kayton; he couldn't understand why her eyes were begging him for forgiveness. Then the world lurched with sickening realignment as, at the same moment she spoke, Kayton realised what was going to happen.

'I saw Kayton kill my husband and the guards.' As the words came trembling out of her mouth, she started sobbing uncontrollably.

The crowd erupted into righteous fury. The sergeant quickly ascended the platform and led the woman away. The last thing Kayton saw of her was the desperate plea in her eyes for understanding. He felt icy dread whisper across his skin. He had done his best, spoken the truth, but no one would believe anything he said in the face of the widow's testimony.

The duke held the sceptre aloft as he stood in front of Kayton, commanding the crowd's attention.

'We have heard from the prisoner and we have heard a true account of events from the brave widow of Stanton Hellard. I therefore make the final ruling on this day that Kayton Stratton is guilty. To serve as clear and present warning to any who hold murderous thoughts in their heart, the punishment will be the severest allowed under the Overlord's law.'

The duke looked straight at Kayton as he pronounced judgement.

'Kayton Stratton. On this sixteenth day of spring, you will be hung by the neck until all life has fled your guilty body. May you find forgiveness in the River of Death.'

As the duke lowered the sceptre, Kayton knew his life was over. Shock immobilised him. His face drained of colour as the sceptre came down. The words of his sentence echoed around his mind, a bleak betrayal of his hopes and dreams for the future.

The crowd cheered at the pronouncement. A pack of wolves baying at the scent of blood, they called in excitement and fascination for his execution, and awaited the horrifying display of death. The duke returned to the Seat of Hearing and the roar of the crowd marked Gelanson's triumph over the boy's attempted rebellion. Turning to acknowledge the crowd's approval, the duke missed a step and stumbled slightly on the platform.

In that instant, chaos erupted.

Gelanson righted himself as the guard behind him fell silently to the floor, a feather-tipped arrow planted squarely in her chest. Red blood pooled out across purple livery as the guard's sightless eyes stared at the duke. Gelanson recoiled from the danger, quickly surrounded by two more guards utilising their bodies as shields. Another arrow thunked into the platform as Stegen, immediately taking charge, shouted for the sergeant to escort the duke back to the castle. Stegen allocated guards from the platform to usher the duke towards the safety of his carriage. The previously excited pageboy stood in terror, watching arrows sailing down around him. A guard wrenched the carriage door open, urging the duke to climb in quickly.

Whilst all attention was diverted to the duke, the man in the crowd threw off his filthy hooded cloak, and drew his sword.

Stegen's eyes focused on the sudden movement, recognition dawning on her face as Chancer exploded into action.

'Stop him!' she commanded.

The pikemen moved swiftly into their ready position, sharp points of the pikes facing out to the crowd. Chancer reached the men and launched into a frenzied sword attack, trying to find a way onto the platform, but his sword was no match for the length of the pikes, and the guards were easily able to keep him at bay, jabbing as he danced and twisted to avoid getting skewered. Chancer battled to reach Kayton whilst Hirae's arrows rained down from the window of a nearby inn. But for every arrow that thudded home into an unprotected leg, another guard stood in to maintain the impenetrable barrier between them and Kayton.

Stegen wasted no time joining the defence; using the guards on the platform for cover, she pulled Kayton towards the hangman's noose. Kayton fought with desperation, but the hardened warrior was more than a match for his manacled arms. He kicked out at her and lost his footing, falling to the platform with a hard thump, the wind crushed from his ribs. Stegen followed him down with a swift punch to his face.

His head striking the floor, pinpricks of light danced before Kayton's eyes. He felt his body being dragged unceremoniously across the platform, and he renewed his thrashing, trying to punch at Stegen with his manacled hands and use the heavy iron as a weapon. The blows he landed seemed only to enrage the soldier more. With one hand, she pulled him to his feet, keeping the shield in front of her body. She forced the hangman's noose over Kayton's neck as arrows thudded a hair's breadth from her.

'This is for my brother,' Stegen hissed.

Kayton twisted like an animal caught in a snare to try and release himself. The coarse rope chafed and rubbed against his neck as Stegen tightened the noose in one swift, brutal movement. Kayton's urgent gaze raked the crowd, and he saw Chancer's desperate attempts to reach him. Kayton struggled, panic bringing new strength to his limbs. Looking around for anything he could use to aid his escape, his eyes suddenly focused on the most beautiful face he had ever seen. A vision of the future he had hoped to share.

Time slowed.

The deep hazel eyes that he had loved since the day he had first seen them connected with his. All of his dreams of their future together shattered with the tightening of the rough hemp rope around his neck. Sionan's eyes never left his as she pushed to get through the crowd and reach him.

Then, as quickly as he had seen her, she was gone, and his life fell away beneath his feet.

Sionan screamed as Kayton's body dropped through the trap door. One moment his eyes had been looking into hers, and the next he had plummeted away.

Her body jolted with emotional shock, her eyes flashing from hazel to a deep emerald green. Like lightning coursing through her body, something writhed to be free as her anguish crushed all remaining belief of goodness in the world. The horror in her scream of rejection was matched by the deafening cheer of the crowd, delighted that Stegen had delivered the hanging.

The pain of loss brought her to her knees. A keening noise rose from Sionan's throat. Her body trembled in denial and she felt like she could no longer control herself as her mind spiralled in horror, rejecting the knowledge that the young man who had been Sionan's friend since they could both walk now swayed at the end of the rope, lifeless.

CHAPTER EIGHTEEN

Chancer had felt rather than heard the snap of Kayton's neck when Stegen released the trapdoor lever, sending the boy's body falling into the yawning gap. Stunned, he barely managed to parry a lunging pike that ripped through the clothing on his left side, slashing open a gash on his torso.

The rescue attempt had failed. It was over for Kayton. A red-hot rage swept down over Chancer. His voice screamed incoherently, aching anger at his inability to save the young life of another who had looked to him for leadership. His searing wrath poured into a frenzied attack on the remaining pikemen, who briefly fell back from the assault, buying Chancer a few seconds of space. Taking the opportunity, knowing there was no life left to save, he fled into an alley.

He felt the whoosh of air as a pike went sailing past, only just missing him. He doubled his efforts, pumping his arms and legs to sprint round a turning. Chancer ran down what appeared to be a blind bend and had to use precious seconds to climb a wooden trellis on the side of a house.

Following the escape route he'd planned in the first light of the morning, he did not stop to look back as he moved onto the roofs of the tightly packed houses to make his escape. He heard shouts as soldiers flooded the area to search for him. He bent low to move swiftly and unseen along the rooftops. Keeping to the edge where the joists were strongest, he moved as silently and swiftly as he could. Every second he expected to hear a shout of recognition as someone spotted him from below. He kept moving, but knew there would be no immediate escape. Rather than making his way to the edge of town, he stayed in the central area. Reaching a more affluent area, where the houses were taller and roofs higher, he climbed to the highest point and hunkered down. Catching his breath, he lay flat on the roof, heart pounding in his chest, ears straining, waiting to hear a cry of discovery. He tensed as he heard Stegen's voice cutting across the noise of the town, directing troops to keep searching house to house.

Chancer stamped down the overwhelming urge to take vengeance for Kayton's death there and then.

As the afternoon passed into evening, he waited. The vision of Kayton's body falling, and the lad's expression of desperation when his neck snapped, played over and over in Chancer's mind. He questioned every decision, tortured himself with every violent detail. Perhaps if they had attacked sooner – or later – or attacked the carriage…

He slipped into despair as night began to fall. Sounds of revelry in a nearby inn taunted him. Chancer was overwhelmed with the need for comfort. At that moment, he didn't care if he lived or died, he just needed to drink. As the feeling consumed him, an image of Kayton's clear, blue eyes looking at him with disappointment filled his mind. Kayton had expected Chancer to bring the duke to justice, he'd believed it so strongly that he had travelled across the Principality to find him. How could Chancer let him down a second time?

He felt the steel of resolve tightening in himself. From his campaign days, he still had ears in the Overlord's court. He would use every favour he could call in to get time with the Overlord on an Atipac Justice Day.

Chancer waited with the grim patience and determination of a man who had resolved to give his life for one cause. The darkening sky marked the passage of time. As the first stars appeared, he made a solemn promise to Kayton.

If he could not bring justice to Gelanson by the Overlord's law, then he would bring justice with the end of his sword.

CHAPTER NINETEEN

Hirae sat at the cave mouth, watching the trails, remembering her shock at seeing Sionan in the crowd. The girl should not have been there at all, but she knew she had to get her to safety. Hirae had moved, wraith-like, from her vantage point in the inn down into the street with Scase following closely at his mistress's heels.

Sliding through the animated crowd she quickly caught up with Sionan and reached down to help her stand. Hirae had been momentarily taken aback by Sionan's frenzied green eyes looking back at her, the girl's gaze feverishly bright, as though lit from within by cold starlight. Wrapping Sionan's cloak more tightly around her, Hirae had deliberately averted her eyes from the intense green stare and the madness she saw lurking there.

Guiding Sionan along, they had blended in with the surging townsfolk, who were trying to either move away from Chancer's desperate battle near the platform or get closer to watch the drama unfold. The crowd buzzed, alive with the excitement of the attempted rescue and the hanging, laughing about the brutality of the morning's events.

'Did you see his face when he was condemned? Like a gasping fish!' one man laughed to his friend.

'Well, the duke certainly always provides a good show. I bet they catch those idiots who tried to rescue the boy.'

Hirae cursed herself again for missing the duke with her first arrow. Despite her apparent agreement to go to the Overlord for justice, she had quietly decided to kill Gelanson. When her first shot had missed, she knew there would not be a second chance. Unfortunately, she and Chancer had not banked on Stegen being more fixated on killing Kayton than getting the duke away from the danger of arrows raining down. They had rationalised that when the arrows started flying, they could free Kayton because the soldiers would be focused on trying to protect the duke. The cold reality was that the rescue had failed, with fatal consequences.

Hirae had moved into the back streets of the town, steadily heading out towards the woodland. With her head bowed she had dragged Sionan's silent, stumbling form along with her. She willed Chancer to freedom, but had known if she tried to help him, it would only sacrifice Sionan, who, in her state of shock, would be lost.

They had reached the edge of town and looked to the trees for salvation. When Hirae was as certain as she could be that they were not being watched, she had led Sionan across the intervening meadow lands towards the woods. The sight of Kayton's body swaying at the end of the rope burned into her mind as they sought safety in the trees.

For two nights they hid in the forest with Hirae's woodlore keeping them safe from searching eyes. Sionan appeared trapped inside her own mind, mute to all questions and conversation. After their initial flight from the town, the girl's eyes had faded from their intense, cold emerald green. As the light had dimmed from her eyes, so to, it appeared, had Sionan's will to live.

Unwilling to give up hope on Chancer, Hirae had taken Sionan back to the cave to wait. For the first day, they had remained hidden, Hirae watching carefully as Sionan's eyes returned to their natural brown, although unusual flecks of green, like shards of glass, remained. Scase did not leave the girl's side. Each day the dog sat, gently leaning his solid form on Sionan, offering silent comfort.

Hirae wondered if Sionan had succumbed to some strange madness born of the dark magic inflicted by Gelanson. The girl ate mechanically when food was placed in her hand, and drank when the cup was raised to her lips. For all intents and purposes, she appeared absent from her own body. Hirae had deliberated at length about whether it was safe to leave Sionan alone, but as the girl's near comatose state continued, Hirae knew there was no other option.

Hirae left their hiding place on the second day to ensure that their trail was covered, and to leave false trails to make it look as though they were heading directly for Ascalion. They needed more food for their travel to Atipac, and currently Sionan did not have the ability to move through the woodland. Leaving Scase to guard the girl, Hirae went to hunt rabbits and gather berries and tubers so they would at least eat well during the first part of their journey.

During her hunting foray Hirae found the privacy for her own grief for Kayton; she had never been one to show emotion in front of others. On the second afternoon, she had sat in a glade, watching the river rolling by. The woods provided a gentle balm on her soul, her solace always coming from the peace provided by the nature around her. Hirae wondered if truly they would be better off disappearing back into the forests to live their lives and treasure the time they had spent with Kayton, but she knew, whilst it might kill them all, they would all see this through to the end.

Hirae returned to the cave, hoping yet again that Chancer had arrived. She moved through the entrance to find Sionan sitting exactly where she had left her some hours ago. Hirae knew that if the girl did not return to her mind soon, there was a risk she would never find her way, having seen this level of shock in her comrades during the war. Only time and kindness could bring her back.

As Hirae moved silently across the cave mouth, she spotted a flash of purple. Dropping to the ground, she crawled out into the undergrowth and down the hillside. She watched a troop of soldiers moving through the bush. A man dressed in forest greens was leading them, reading the trail ahead. Hirae lay perfectly still, barely even breathing as she watched the tracker. He knelt to carefully scrutinise the ground, taking long moments to read the signs he saw there, then beckoned the soldiers to follow him down a side trail.

Hirae breathed a sigh of relief as she watched the troop move off along one of her dummy trails. She lay still until the sun dipped on the horizon. Having made certain they had gone, she cautiously made her way back into the cave.

After two nights of waiting for Chancer, she knew their time was running out. The soldiers were combing the woods around Clasterne. It would take only one small slip, a broken branch or some crushed leaves, for the tracker to guess their direction and hiding place. Hirae resolved with a heavy heart that they could wait only one more day. Without Chancer, she did not hold out much hope of successfully receiving any audience with the Overlord or navigating the foreign ways of the Atipac, but they would try.

As she climbed towards the cave, she spotted a man's boot print in the soil. Quietly drawing out her large hunting knife, she edged towards the entrance, hugging the wall as approached. She could not hear any growling from Scase, and peered around the opening carefully. Her shoulders dropped with relief at the sight of Chancer. However, her joy at seeing her old friend did not cloud her judgement, and she swiftly returned down the slope to obscure his boot print. Hirae then worked her way back down his trail, erasing signs of his passage as best she could. Whilst Chancer may know all the intrigue and etiquette of Atipac, the woods were her domain, and she would ensure they stayed safe. Hirae scouted the perimeter, checking for any other tell-tale signs. Satisfied she had found none, she returned to the cave.

Pushing the brush aside, Scase padded towards her, tail wagging in welcome. Hirae saw Chancer's arm around Sionan in comfort. He looked over to Hirae and nodded in welcome. She could see blood on his left side where a weapon had scored him, but, for now, she did not disturb them.

Chancer's eyes were red-rimmed, whether from lack of sleep or weeping for a life lost, Hirae did not know. As he knelt beside Sionan, he held her hand and said only two words.

'I'm sorry.'

Chancer's obvious anguish appeared to trigger the release of Sionan's own grief. Hirae watched the girl weep for the young man whose dream of freedom for her had led to his own death. She carefully replaced the brush screen and turned away from witnessing their shared pain. Sionan wept quietly, Chancer folding his arms around her to offer comfort.

Hirae busied herself preparing food until a hand touched her shoulder, and she looked up to see Sionan looking at her. This was the first time since Kayton's death that the girl had shown any awareness of Hirae at all. The young woman enveloped her in a crushing hug, conveying with actions what she had not yet the voice to say – Hirae had saved her life.

Hirae patted the girl awkwardly on the back, never entirely comfortable with open displays of affection. She had always envied Chancer's ease with people. She knew that sometimes she appeared unapproachable with her controlled manner, always more at ease with her dog. Hirae felt she should say something consoling, but as usual could not think of the right thing to say. She patted the girl awkwardly on the back once more and hoped that was enough.

'We should eat and then move,' she eventually said, looking over Sionan's shoulder to Chancer. 'I've seen one tracker heading off in the forest, but I don't think he'll be alone, and we've been here too long already.' Gently, she disentangled from Sionan and gestured her to sit.

'Let me see that wound,' Hirae said to Chancer, beckoning him to move into the light of the cave entrance.

Removing his shirt carefully, Chancer winced as the fabric came free from the matted blood. Using water from a canteen, Hirae cleaned the wound, poking mercilessly to check for any signs of infection or material caught in the gash.

'Is that really necessary?' Chancer asked through clenched

teeth. 'It feels like you're opening it back up.'

'Stop being a child,' she admonished him. The wound looked clean, but would best be stitched to keep it closed as they travelled. She pulled out her healer's kit; a hangover from the days of the rebellion, she never travelled without it. Within the kit were strips of clean cloth, needle and thread, willow bark, and thin tongs to remove foreign debris. It wasn't much of a medicine bag to save someone's life, but its contents had done the job many a time. She handed Chancer a small bit of willow bark. 'Eat this, it will help fight infection.'

Chancer dutifully complied. 'It tastes disgusting.'

'Well, it's nicer brewed with hot water, but as we can't light a fire, you'll just have to make do.' Hirae started to thread the needle, angling the eye towards the light to better see.

'Let me,' Sionan said. Hirae handed the girl the items with her eyebrows raised in question. 'I'm sure it's no different from sewing leather,' Sionan answered the unasked question. 'I may not be able to contribute much to this group, but I can sew in a good, straight line.'
Chancer sat and leant back on the wall, raising his arm so it was clear of the wound.

Sionan knelt beside him and, as gently as she could, coaxed the two angry pieces of flesh together. 'My mother always joked that my father taught me to sew before I could walk,' Sionan said, distracting herself from the grisly task. For all her confidence in her sewing ability, the feeling of the needle pulling through the flesh of a person made her feel slightly nauseous. Setting her mind to focus on keeping the stitching straight, she finished as quickly as she could. She tied off the end of the thread and borrowed Hirae's knife to cut it free.

Hirae tipped more water onto the wound to clear the trickling blood away.

'Once it's dry, we'll bandage you up. It will be close to nightfall, then, and we'll make our move.'

'To Atipac,' Chancer confirmed. 'I don't think we have any other option than to go to the Overlord.'

'And if we can't get an audience or if we're dismissed as truth slayers?' Sionan asked.

'We kill Gelanson,' Hirae said.

'What of my mother?' asked Sionan.

'There is nothing you can do for your mother,' Hirae responded. 'She has fulfilled Gelanson's demands by giving witness against Kayton. We have to hope that means she will be left alone. The duke should have no more use for her.'

Sionan stared at the floor in defeat, knowing that Hirae's harsh words were true, but wanting desperately to provide some argument against it.

Chancer gently gripped Sionan by the shoulders. 'Even if we managed to make it back to your mother and persuade her to leave, travelling across the Manor would be dangerous for her and your siblings. They are safer where they are now, where Gelanson feels he has control of the situation.'

Sionan saw certainty in his grey eyes. She nodded in response, then, feeling uncomfortable with his closeness whilst his shirt was removed, she quickly stepped away and sat in the shadows of the cave. She watched Chancer gazing out from the cave, raising his arm to let the gentle breeze help dry his wound.

'We travel at night,' Chancer said to Hirae. 'We'll take the stone to show the Overlord. Can you still locate it?'

'Easily,' Hirae responded. Walking to the back of the cave, she stooped, and continued into the shadows. When the ceiling of the cave was too low, she crawled through to the back. Sionan watched, intrigued, as Hirae reached out with her arm and felt along the ledge. Hirae squeezed in slightly further, extending her arm as far as she could, and Sionan heard her breathe a sigh of thankfulness as she crawled back the way she had come, bringing a box with her.

Hirae handed the box to Sionan. 'You keep this safe, so you can tell the Overlord all that has happened. We'll keep *you* safe so that you can do it.'

'We will succeed,' Chancer said to Sionan with conviction. 'Kayton deserves this much from us. He believed that justice would prevail, and so it shall.'

'What's the plan, strategist?' Hirae asked.

'We head straight for Atipac as quickly as possible. We'll strike east and buy some horses on the way. Sionan, you will need to be armed and know how to defend yourself. It's unlikely we will make it safely to the city without needing to fight at some point.'

Chancer removed the baldric of throwing knives and handed it to Sionan. He helped Sionan belt the knives around her waist and gave her brief instruction on how to handle them until he was satisfied she wouldn't cut herself rather than an enemy.

'What of Scase?' he asked Hirae.

'I'll not risk him in Atipac,' she answered. 'He knows nothing of cities and their dangers. He will travel with us until the outskirts, but when we leave the forest, we will be on our own.'

Chancer nodded in response. 'We'll think about our back story and disguise for entering Atipac. Stegen and the duke's guards recognised us, but our faces aren't known to the Overlord's guards. We will keep a low profile. I still have connections, so we can at least request an audience during Atipac Justice Day. Let's take some rest now, the moon will be full tonight, it will give us enough light to travel by. We head east, directly across country. If we keep our pace up, that will be faster and safer than following the road.'

Chancer took up a sentry position, looking out of the cave, as Sionan and Hirae readied themselves for the journey ahead. Sionan looked at the deadly weapons she now had strapped to her waist and wondered if she would ever have the courage to kill someone. Images of her father's blood soaking the ground and Kayton plunging to his death leapt into her mind, and she realised that she had changed. She could kill now. The town girl had been crushed from her, leaving a woman, aged before her time, who would willingly take a life to right wrongs.

Kayton's death would not be for naught.

CHAPTER TWENTY

For two days Gelanson lay in his chamber attempting to float above the pain of his excruciating headache. Well-wishers sent gifts to the castle after the vicious attempt on his life at Justice Day. The only positive outcome he could hold onto was that the attack seemed to have solidified the townsfolk's loyalty to him. He heard the servants quietly talking as they passed his chamber. An attempt on their duke's life was an affront to their own person and not to be borne. Every person was watching out for the girl and her comrades, and the threats of violence he heard some of the servants make towards the traitors pleased him greatly.

No one seemed to remember the tailor's daughter, or that idiot boy with affection anymore. The fickleness of human nature provided Gelanson with all the loyalty he needed.

A servant pulled the drapes across the rare blue and green stained-glass windows, which were creating beautiful patterns of light as the sun blazed through. The sunlit display was lost on Gelanson as he welcomed the relief of a darkened room. The sumptuous bed, covered with exotic silks from Sahjashorn, filled half the room. Gelanson always enjoyed the very finest of things, seeing the beauty in a carefully spun silk coverlet, but unable to recognise the beauty in the people around him. Today though, Gelanson was immune to the decorative opulence of his chamber. Since the horrifying attempt on his life, his head felt like it was being split in two, an unseen axeman splicing his skull like wood for the fire.

Onway had, of course, been carefully tending to his master as expected. The steward fussed with the drapes the servant had already closed to ensure not even a tiny crack of sunlight entered the room.

The pain of the headache was infuriatingly debilitating and without the star-stone, the duke had no ability to treat it. He sent a healer away in disgust after the man poked and prodded at him before announcing that bleeding by leeches was required. Gelanson tolerated only forward-thinking people who practised the science of medicine, not outdated traditionalists. Once he was feeling better, he resolved to send the "healer" away from his Manor.

Onway had been his saviour, bringing him strong tea sweetened with honey and with small amounts of foxglove to control the pain. Gelanson slowly sipped from the cup. The relief was like a blessed breeze on a hot and still summer's day. Slowly, the agony receded, leaving him weak and nauseous, but at least able to think coherently. Maybe he had made an error in questioning the loyalty of Onway, whose care and attention to the duke since the attack was without reproach.

The only good news was Stegen's report that the boy had been hung. Tomorrow, when the duke's headache had passed, he would travel to view the body. As required under the Overlord's law, the corpse would remain hanging in the town square for a week and would then be placed in an unmarked grave. The duke felt some measure of satisfaction that one of this troublesome band was dead. All would see the boy's body bloat and rot, and the crows would peck at his eyes and entrails. Generally, Gelanson did not agree with such barbaric displays of power, but unfortunately he knew he had reached a tipping point with the townsfolk and he had to ensure any dissent was firmly crushed.

There were reports that the girl and the two fighters were still at large. He knew these two warriors were the key; without them the boy and girl would have amounted to nothing and would have been easily dealt with. The other two were highly skilled in fighting and evading capture. Professional fighters, he concluded, wondering from which land they had travelled. The woman fighter, with her dark curly hair and green eyes, certainly did not have the look of this Manor, but without further information any ideas were just speculation. He had set one of his captains the task of hunting them down, assigning him four guards. Stegen, he had assigned to another task of importance.

Sighing with frustration, Gelanson knew he urgently needed to understand what the rebels would do next. Whilst hanging the boy had, of course, been the correct course of action, he rued that his only possible source of information was now dead.

'Onway, I would appreciate your thoughts on the present situation. What is your analysis of the events? The rebels have stolen my star-stone. Where do you think they will strike next?'

The steward stood in his purple doublet looking weary, even beyond his unnaturally advanced years.

'I am not sure what these dissenters can do next, my lord.

After Widow Hellard's testimony, no one will believe that the boy was innocent, and the girl will be tainted by association. There is the added complexity of her aged appearance, but this can easily be explained as the wasting disease.' Onway rubbed his forehead. 'I do not see what other actions the rebels can take, apart from another attempt on your life, my lord. There is no one they can appeal to in the Manor.' Onway paused. 'I would propose we double the guard on your chambers and ensure you always maintain your personal bodyguard with you when you travel, my lord.'

'It is such a disaster, Onway.' Gelanson let out a heavy sigh. 'I was so close to triumph with my experiments. We should have killed that boy as soon as he started spouting rubbish and trying to incite the townsfolk to rise up.'

'My lord, you could not have known the depths of evil that boy would sink to.'

'True, Onway. Please take whatever precautions you think are necessary to maintain my safety.'

Gelanson waved a hand at the steward, dismissing him. The duke relaxed back into the pillows as Onway left the room. He knew he needed more information, and without the star-stone he felt the steady march of time against him. Living like this was intolerable, knowing his life was ticking away with each moment the sun passed lower into the sky.

Gelanson slept for a time, his inability to cope with pain taking its toll. He awoke when the moon was high and bright in the sky. The headache had receded to a dull throb, and was soothed by the cold moonlight.

Gelanson had focused all of his research, in the ancient scrolls and books, on life transference and immobilisation of subjects, but there were reams of information available that he had not yet studied. Another vital reason why he needed to maintain his youth. Sitting up in the bed, the duke moved slowly and carefully; he did not want to reawaken the pain. He pulled the cord by the bed and made his way to the garderobe. Once he had finished, he found a servant waiting in the room. Gelanson ordered food and wash water to be brought immediately. The people of the town needed to see him, and he needed to find a way to locate the missing three before more damage could be done. He would spend the remainder of the night searching through the scrolls for any incantations that would help him, and then he would ride into town to view the disgusting corpse.

Three servants filed into the room bringing two buckets of warm water, which they poured into a large, round, and beautiful earthenware bowl. The bowl was delicately decorated with leaping fish, and as the water touched the pattern and splashed in the bowl it looked as though they were swimming in circles. The tray of food and a small flagon of wine was a simple repast for this late at night.

'That will be all, thank you,' the duke said. 'Rest and seek your beds. I will not need you again this night.'

The servants smiled with gratitude as they left the room. Gelanson was always intrigued at how pathetically grateful these people were when you offered them the tiniest of courtesies. He dismissed them, not because he was concerned for their sleep, but because he wanted to be alone with his thoughts. The duke stripped from his sleeping garments of cotton, retaining only the thin silver necklace with the key to the tower around his neck. This key never left his person, and he was still debating with himself as to whether Onway, in his decaying state, should still be trusted with the second key.

Age was such a cruelty.

The duke washed fastidiously, never having been able to abide dirt or grime. He felt his head clearing as he dunked it in the scented water and cleaned his face and torso. After drying himself he donned a simple, clean tunic of soft, sky-blue wool. There was still the cold edge of winter in the air at night during these early weeks of spring. In his fragile state, he had no desire to take a chill.

Once dressed, his hair combed through, he thoughtfully ate his repast, ruminating on which scrolls to start with. As he sipped the full-bodied wine, which he guessed was from the vineyards of Atipac, he decided the best way was merely to start with the oldest scrolls he had not yet fully investigated.

He moved to the large mahogany cabinet at the end of the room where an intricately carved wooden stand rested. On the stand was one of his most important possessions, his amethyst Chain of Office. He put it on, feeling its reassuring weight as he caressed the stone. Whilst the rebels may have the star-stone, he was not devoid of power. This stone was sister-stone to the one the traitors had stolen. Naturally jade-green in appearance it was disguised by a small simple incantation to appear amethyst in colour, matching the original amethyst that had been in the Chain of Office bestowed upon him by the crown. The duke felt a tingle of power as the chain settled on his chest.

Gelanson left his chamber, heading through the corridors towards the tower. He was aware of two guards carefully shadowing him and was pleased to observe how unobtrusive they were. As he descended the stone steps, he enjoyed the peace of the castle at this time of night. He always found these early hours before the sun rose the perfect time to work. He reached for the key around his neck, and unlocked the heavy tower door.

'Wait here,' he informed his guards.

The two guards snapped their feet to attention and took up watches next to the four pikemen who were always stationed at the tower door.

Lifting a small flaming torch from the outer wall, Gelanson entered the tower, locked the door behind him, and walked down the small corridor to his study. He then moved the tapestry of the eagle to activate the latch to his research room. As the stone door swung open, the first thing that assailed his nostrils was the smell of rot and decay. On his workbench the corpse arm remained, a putrid mess. Gelanson utilised tongs from the fire to lift the disgusting, rotting stump and placed it in the fireplace. Annoyance flashed through his mind that the limb had perished without further experimentation. He put his torch into the fireplace, lighting the wood neatly stacked there, and as the wood caught, the arm burnt, creating a smell not unlike roasting pig. Waiting to ensure the fire was burning well, the duke placed more logs on it and berated himself for not waking Onway, this was really something the steward should have dealt with.

Again, Gelanson questioned the wisdom of keeping Onway alive after his errors of leaving the tower door unlocked and not recognising Lord Dennier as an imposter. However, the duke realised with intellectual interest that he seemed to have some level of attachment towards the steward.

The idea of Onway not being around anymore elicited an uncomfortable sensation – perhaps sadness, or distress. He wasn't sure how to label the feeling, having never experienced a sense of potential loss before. His curiosity peaked by this unusual feeling, Gelanson decided to allow things to continue as they were for a little longer. He could afford to be generous to Onway after his loyalty over the years.

Opening one of the heavy black trunks, Gelanson selected an armful of scrolls, and returned to his study. Closing the door behind him he sniffed the air, thankful that only a small amount of the dreadful smell had escaped from the research room. Tomorrow he would have Onway fully air the chambers and hang scented plants from the rafters. Gelanson particularly liked lavender, and as spring marched on it was coming into bloom.

Settling himself into the comfortable chair closest to the lamp, Gelanson opened the first scroll and started to read. He paid large sums of money to merchants to gather unusual scrolls from far-flung places. He believed he now had the largest hoard of knowledge in the Principality. He had discreetly collected knowledge over the years, not wishing to be seen to pose any possible threat to the Overlord.

Gelanson felt a pleasing anticipation at the reading ahead. From a young age the duke had found solace in the pure and unmeasured joy of learning. As the hours ticked by and night passed into dawn, he immersed himself in the research, confident he would find what he needed.

Stiff from sitting for so long, Gelanson jumped at a gentle tapping on the study door. How had he not heard the main tower door opening? Looking to the small window he realised it was full daylight outside. During his reading he had set aside three scrolls he deemed to be of importance, each with partial information about the ancient art of scrying, allowing the unseen to be revealed. At first annoyed at the disruption of his thoughts, he then realised that only Onway would disturb him, and bade him to enter.

Onway deftly opened the door and entered with a tray laden with sausage, soft bread, and a glass of water fresh from the castle's spring. Placing the tray on the table by the chair, Onway awaited further instruction from the duke.

'The best of news, Onway,' Gelanson shared with pleasure. 'I have found the means necessary to locate the missing rebels.'

'Congratulations, my lord. What assistance can I provide to allow this search to occur?'

'We will need to focus on the girl, Sonni? Sinoa?'

'Sionan Hellard, my lord.'

Gelanson eyed Onway for a time. He thought for a moment he detected a hint of criticism in the response, but the dull ache from the head pain still lingered, and perhaps this was making him see a slight where there was none. The duke sat watching Onway for a time, the steward's face remaining impassive under his lord's scrutiny.

'Yes, that girl,' Gelanson finally replied. 'Thankfully I have located a longsight creation that we can use to find her.'

'Very good, my lord,' Onway replied, with his impassive stance.

'I do not have time to refine the traditional incantation, so we will have to complete it using the old methods of blood sacrifice. We will need someone of the same bloodline to complete this process.'

'Sir?'

'The family has brought this upon themselves, Onway. Instead of sacrificing just one child for the greater good, they shall now lose two.'

'My lord, there is only the mother and two young children, just twelve and six. I do not think they will be able to assist you in searching for their sister.'

Gelanson laughed. 'Do not worry, Onway. It will be far beyond you to understand the intricacies of this. Bring me the middle child. I have read that mothers have a strong affinity with their youngest, so leave the small one for her comfort. I am sure the widow will be most grateful that we take away one of those demanding mouths. Children are always so relentless in their capacity for food.'

'My lord, you wish the twelve-year-old brought to this tower? A child?'

'Yes. Is there an issue with that?' Gelanson questioned, detecting what sounded like criticism coming from his steward.

After a pause, Onway responded. 'My lord, you are always most generous to those who assist in your studies. May we offer a purse as well to help the mother with the young one?'

'Ah, so that is what is troubling you, Onway. Of course we must! You are ever the one to remind me of my responsibilities to these poor folk. Supply a generous stipend to the mother, so she knows she need have no further worries in life.' The duke smiled at his own generosity, comforted in the fact that he was assisting the woman by taking one of her children away.

'Thank you, my lord,' Onway replied with a flat voice. '

'Return to me by nightfall with the girl,' Gelanson continued. 'I will take some rest now and then have a tour around the town to mingle with the common folk.'

'Very good, my lord.' Bowing, the steward left the tower.

Closing the tower door behind him, Onway walked away. Crossing the castle square he carefully kept his stride measured to his usual calm and sedate pace, although he felt like running from this hideous place. The steward had teetered on the brink of explaining what was clearly very wrong with the duke's request. Never had Gelanson extended his research to include children. Onway had now reached a line that he would not cross. Remembering his own beautiful child, he could not force that grief onto another.

Onway had known he needed to cover his seeming lack of enthusiasm for the idea when questioned by Gelanson. The request for a purse was a quick solution that would also be valuable for the plan growing in his mind. His own death would be imminent once the duke discovered the betrayal he was about to commit, but he could not leave a child to become a blood sacrifice. He would never be able to compensate for the lives he had already aided Gelanson to take, but in this one moment he would try to prevent further evil.

Calmness settled on him as his plan solidified, he called for a guard, instructing the man to have four horses prepared to escort the duke to town, and then headed to the kitchen.

Entering its clamorous noise and heat, the steward saw the cook stirring a large pot over the fireplace. Wonderful aromas drifted through the room that was the true heart of the castle.

'Morning, steward. How is our duke today?' the cook called over the noise of the busy kitchen. 'Did he enjoy the breakfast? I know how delicately he likes the meats spiced. Were the sausages up to standard?' the cook chattered on.

'Quite perfect,' Onway replied to the kind cook. The woman had been in the castle since the previous duke was in power. She set great store by the way the son was now running things. She beamed with pleasure to hear Onway's remark. He did not have the heart to tell her that the duke had never and would never comment on something as mundane as food. 'The duke will travel to town today. Please can you parcel up four bags of food supplies? You know how generous our duke is.'

'At once, steward!' the cook exclaimed in delight.

Onway thanked her and made his way from the kitchens to his chamber. He changed into a sturdy set of travelling clothes. A warm woollen cloak with waxed outer would allow the rain to drip to the ground. All his clothes were of the finest quality as befitted the status of a steward of such an important duke. He paused to look round the room he had called home for the last ten years. The chamber was nondescript, with nothing that shared anything personal about the occupant. The only item that could create some interest was a small child's toy in the shape of a rabbit and a shell necklace looped around it.

Onway bent and picked up the last precious mementoes of his wife and child and wondered what Jale would have thought of him now. His hands brushed against the small shells. His wife and children had never seen the sea. Jale had been fascinated by the necklaces on sale in the market. He had bought one for her and the toy rabbit for his daughter as a surprise for the summer festival. He remembered with a joy that cut him now, sharp as a knife, Jale and his daughter's delight at their gifts.

Onway carefully looped the shell necklace over his head and tucked it inside his tunic. He wrapped the rabbit tenderly in his blanket and packed it into his travel bag. Unsure if Widow Hellard would have any suitable travel clothes, he placed another set of clothes in the bag. He unlocked a small trunk under his bed. Within was a pouch containing his lifetime savings and he hefted the weight of it, wondering how far it would get them.

Taking one final look around the austere room, Onway closed the door firmly behind him and closed the gate on the man he had been.

Taking the narrow servants' stairs, he entered Gelanson's main study, removing enough coin for one purse only to prevent suspicion, and made his way back to the kitchen. He paused frequently to let the servants dash about their morning duties. As he reached the kitchen, he saw four bags of supplies and grabbed them, thanking the cook for her time. He quickly made his way to the stables and saw the stable hand already had four chestnut mares saddled. The one with a white patch on her snout whickered in greeting as Onway attached a bag of food to each saddle. He mounted the horse, and the stable hand placed the reins of the remaining three horses in Onway's hands. The servant may have wondered why the steward was leaving ahead of the duke, but Onway knew that servant would not dare to question someone above his station. He left without fuss, walking the horses calmly through the postern gate. As soon as he felt he was far enough from the castle to avoid attracting suspicion, he kicked his horse into a gallop, and the three other horses lengthened their stride to catch the leader.

Galloping towards town, he did not see the large black stallion and rider leaving the postern gate to follow his trail.

CHAPTER TWENTY-ONE

Onway made good time riding to town. Whilst not a dedicated horseman, he was an adequate rider. The spring flowers bursting forth along the verges mirrored his escape from the stifling confines of the duke's constant threat.

The steward rode directly through town to the tailor's shop. Discretion would not serve him any benefit; speed was his only ally. He tied the horses to the hitching post outside and rapped smartly on the door. He was greeted by a soldier in purple livery. He could not remember the man's name, but nodded to him in recognition of his service. The soldier stood quickly to attention.

'You are all to return to the castle for new duties,' Onway briskly informed him.

Confusion at hearing these new orders was evident on the soldier's features, but the steward had ten years' experience of ensuring the castle ran smoothly. Everyone followed his directives. He paused and raised his eyebrows at the soldier, who dropped his gaze to the ground in embarrassment. Onway entered the house, and walking through to the parlour at the back of the house, he spotted the remaining guard lazing around as though in his own front room. The man sat in a comfortable chair with his feet up on a delicate table designed to hold teacups, not filthy boots. Onway was enraged at the guard's arrogance in the widow's home, and treated him with the disdain he deserved.

'Get up!' he snapped. 'Show some decorum when you are on duty. You are to return to the castle immediately. The duke shall hear about this laziness on my return!' Onway's voice whipped the soldier to his feet and drove him out of the door.

Onway returned to the entrance of the shop and opened the front door pointedly, not uttering another word as both soldiers retreated sheepishly. He judged he had maybe an hour before they reached the castle on foot and their return was questioned.

Quickly he searched the downstairs of the house. He found the widow and her two girls in the sewing room, surrounded by unfinished work. He could see tension and fear in their shoulders as he entered the room. As the most trusted aid of the duke, he could only be bringing more strife into their home. He paused in the doorway, wondering how to begin. How could he convince this family that he was leading them to safety and not into a trap? Onway realised there was nothing he could do but try and hope that they believed him.

'Widow Teina Hellard,' he began. 'May we speak privately for one moment?'

'I am not inclined to be separated from my daughters for even one moment after everything the duke has ordered!' the widow spat with venom at Onway. 'You know they made me provide false testimony against Kayton, and I will carry that guilt to my grave to protect my girls. You will not renege on the duke's promise. They are to remain safely with me now.'

Teina pushed her needle and thread into the lapel of the coat she had been trying to work on and looked with loathing at Onway. 'My husband is dead, my eldest daughter missing. That captain – Stegen – stopped us leaving when the guard murdered my husband. Forced me to bear witness against Kayton. She placed me under no illusions as to the level of evil you people are capable of. Whatever dreadful request you wish to impart, my girls remain with me.'

Onway cleared his throat, unsure what to say next.

'My daughters remain with *me*,' the widow repeated. 'We will not be separated.' She lifted her chin in defiance, daring him to challenge her.

'Very well.' Onway took a breath and plunged on. 'I'm sorry, but another of your children is in danger.'

'When are we *not* in danger from the *beloved* duke?' she asked angrily.

'The duke wishes to find your eldest daughter urgently,' Onway responded. 'To do this he must know where she travels.'

'I don't know where she is,' Teina interrupted. 'I haven't seen my daughter since you killed her father.' The bitterness of her hatred filled the air between them. 'At least now I know she is still free of your vengeance.'

'Widow Hellard, the duke does not require your knowledge.' Onway paused, looking at the two daughters, not wishing to terrify them but at a loss how to explain and ensure they understood the gravity of the situation. Feeling the steady march of time turning against them, Onway continued. 'The duke would use a blood sacrifice ritual on your middle child to locate Sionan.' Onway realised he sounded like a madman, but instead of shock or denial from the mother, he saw her absorb the words.

'And you are here to take my children?' she asked, looking around urgently.

Onway saw her eyes focus on the sharp scissors used to cut the finest of cloth. 'No, Widow Hellard, I am here to help you flee.'

Teina halted, looking with disbelief at Onway.

'I have horses and supplies outside but we must go *now*,' Onway insisted. 'We have only moments before the duke knows something is awry.'

The widow made no response other than immediately guiding her girls out of the workroom. Onway breathed through his nose as he wracked his brain for what to try next to convince her, and convince her he must before the soldiers were upon them. He followed the widow from the room, and stared in amazement when he saw that she was already ushering the girls into cloaks and boots.

'Under my bed upstairs is a traveller sack. Please grab it for me,' Teina asked Onway.

The steward nodded with relief, not pausing to question why she had accepted his words. He ran up the stairs and opened the first door. Seeing two small children's beds inside, he blundered across the hall to try another door. Time was not on their side. He flung the door open, saw a large bed, and rushed to look under it. Onway pulled out a leather sack, slung it over his shoulder, and ran downstairs to face the widow again. His urgency and desperation must have cast away any of her fears that this was an elaborate trap.

'We will flee with you,' Teina said. 'But if you play me

false, you will be sorry.' Stepping forwards, she pulled the bag from his shoulder, placed it securely on her own, and thrust her tailor's scissors into her belt.

As they left the front of the shop, the two girls in tow, Onway watched the widow take a moment to look at the home that, before recent events, had brought the family happiness. She looked as though she was yearning for a life that had been ripped away.

As Teina closed the shop door for the last time, the steward was already lifting the two girls on to the chestnut mares, adjusting their stirrups and reins. The girls were bone-white with fear but said nothing as their eyes followed their mother's every movement. Once they were settled in their saddles, Onway looped his hands together to offer Teina a boost up. Accepting his help, she climbed on to the horse.

'Can you guide the horse?' Onway asked.

'We can all ride well enough,' Teina assured him.

The steward nodded in response and turned them to take the trail towards the main river. He had no real idea of where they were headed, just away from this Manor.

'We go to Sahjashorn,' Teina stated. 'Hamden village.'

Onway looked at her, about to question the destination, but instead, seeing the determined set of her features, he nodded. 'I will get you there,' he promised.

Any place that was not this Manor was as good as any other to him. His promise echoed with the fickle ring of fate as they rode away along the trail to the river.

Behind him he heard a horse break into a gallop. Turning his head, he almost fell from his horse in shock to see Stegen closing the gap between them.

'Flee!' Onway shouted as Stegen's large black stallion quickly gained ground.

The family needed no encouragement, their horses careening off the trail, taking the road for speed they sped out of the town to shouts of protest from people on the street as the horses thundered past. But when the road became wider, Stegen's stallion easily reeled in their small lead. Onway had never been a fighting man and had not even thought to arm himself, swallowing the bitter taste of disappointment and resignation, he turned his horse to challenge Stegen and at least block her path.

Suddenly, Teina dropped from the saddle and fell to the ground. Onway's horse reared as an arrow protruded from the widow's back. Blood frothed from her lips.

'Go! Save my children!' she spluttered, staggering to her feet and gesturing to Onway to take the travel sack off her shoulder. Her eyes pleaded with him. The steward knew with sickening certainty that she could ride no further. If he tried to save her, the children would be captured. He quickly reached down, removed the travel sack and hoisted it on his shoulder, then screamed in desperation at the horse to run.

Stegen was almost upon them. Onway's horse leapt forwards, almost unseating him as it chased after the fleeing mares. The children had not seen their mother fall, their horses galloping ahead out of control, racing with panic. Onway looked back to see Stegen rein in and jump down beside Teina. He hoped with every fibre of his being that her end would be swift. Fool that he was, he had not thought to end her life when he took her travel sack. Now she was in Stegen's hands.

Knowing it was too late to change this awful mistake, Onway let the horse take the bit and followed the children as they continued their headlong flight away from the Manor.

'Well, it's not ideal, but you'll do,' Stegen said, nudging the prone woman with a boot. 'Better patch you up as best we can.' She removed her bow and arrows and attached them to the pommel of her saddle. She ripped the widow's cloak into strips to plug the wound, left the arrow embedded in it, and wrapped more strips tightly around the injury to stem further bleeding.

Hearing a wet wheeze from the widow, Stegen realised that she did not have long to get her to the castle. She looked with avarice at the road Onway had fled down, wanting nothing more than to hunt down and kill that betrayer, but the duke had been clear, they required someone of Sionan's bloodline to aid with finding the rebels, and the woman lying at her feet could fulfil that role. At least the duke had evidence now of the steward's disloyalty. Stegen had suspected it for some time, noting the stories that Onway had stopped the guards when they were beating the boy Kayton.

Why should they not beat him? Their comrades, including my brother, died because of him.

The woman coughed up blood and tried to crawl away from Stegen. The captain sighed.

Can she not see how pointless her shambling crawl for freedom is?

Stegen lifted her and dumped her unceremoniously over

the saddle of the bay mare, then leapt smoothly onto her own stallion and led the other horse back to the castle. She hummed to herself while the cadence of horses' hooves on the compact earth and the tortured breathing of the injured woman provided percussion to her contented song.

CHAPTER TWENTY-TWO

Gelanson stood at his worktable, looking critically at the widow lying on the large slab. The arrow wound meant she was closer to death than life now. He had no time to waste. Clucking his tongue, the duke unrolled the three scrolls of interest. He caressed the amethyst stone on his chest and reviewed the information again. This would be a difficult incantation. He was going to combine the blood-creation and longsight search craft to try and produce something entirely new. Normally, he would have prepared methodically for his first foray into a new area, although it was certainly a thrill to be moving forwards at this heady pace. He took a moment to ensure all thoughts and actions were detailed in his ledger. However, the strained whistle that escaped from the widow's body every time she breathed out told him time was running out.

Gelanson had felt a mild sense of disappointment when learning from Stegen that he was right in his suspicions of Onway. The fool had taken the widow's remaining children when he fled. That would make it easier to find them. The blood-creation could be cast twice to find both Sionan and her sisters. All previous affection he had imagined he felt for the steward melted away like ice in the morning sun, leaving a dull sense of irritation. However, the loss of Onway's organisational skills was a problem. Stegen seemed a reliable sort, in a martial way, but he would have to elevate one of the current house staff to the role of steward. Yes, he resolved, Stegen could help him adequately with the more private matters. The new steward had no need to be a party to his research.

On her return, Stegen had been rewarded handsomely with a promotion to Head of Household Guard. Gelanson had scrutinised her closely when he opened the secret research room and instructed her to carry the woman to the worktable. The circumspect soldier had held her tongue. She had efficiently snapped the arrow shaft, left the point buried in the bleeding widow, and laid her flat on the worktable.

As Stegen departed the room, Gelanson felt comfortable that the captain's own ambition, combined with her personal hatred of the rebels, would keep the duke's secrets safe.

The widow's eyes watched Gelanson as he moved across the workroom. Through bloodstained lips she spluttered only three words with vehemence.

'*I curse you.*'

Gelanson looked with mild amusement at the backward-thinking woman. Words were only words unless backed up with science and artefacts of power such as he had. However, her look of intense hatred made it difficult for him to concentrate on his vital work. Despite the widow's grievous injury, there was murder in her eyes. Gelanson wondered if he should blindfold her, but in her current state of anger, she may try to bite him like a rabid dog.

The duke took the first scroll and began the incantation

in the ancient language of the dark arts, the strange guttural words filling the chamber. He lifted two statues of small-winged rooks with emeralds for eyes. He had perused all animals available in his stunning collection before deciding that winged creatures were the fastest and therefore the obvious choice to complete the search. Whilst it was a sad loss to his collection, he was willing to sacrifice the delicate pieces for the sake of what he was about to create.

He deepened his voice as the chanting increased in timbre and tempo. The strange language washed over Teina. She was close to death, but her eyes never left Gelanson's while he carefully placed the two statues on her abdomen and circled his hands. The statues started vibrating imperceptibly. As the duke brought his hands down onto her front, she writhed in obvious pain, opened her mouth to scream, and fell into unconsciousness.

The duke watched the rooks shatter into dust. He frowned at the silence that fell, and waited as the dust of the statues gently swirled in the breeze coming through the chimney. Not even the emerald eyes remained of the figurines. Grabbing a small mirror from his tools, he held it to the woman's face. She was still breathing, but only just.

Why have the statues not come to life?

Irritation flared in him as he grabbed the third scroll and re-read the words. They clearly denoted that the statues would come to life. He was sure his addition to the incantation, in order to target the rooks on blood-kin of the sacrifice, was accurate. Gelanson knew from experience that all actions must be completed precisely to ensure success.

Was my pronunciation of the words incorrect... or too hasty?

Throwing the scroll on the floor in disgust he stalked towards the fireplace, then marched frustratedly back to the workbench to stare into the woman's face. Without the star-stone, he had no options available to extend her life.

Is there time to try one more incantation before she dies?

Suddenly, the widow's eyes opened, appearing to stare straight through him. The duke jumped back in alarm at the feral madness he saw there. Any humanity in her eyes was gone. A strange shrieking, unlike anything he had ever heard, came from her mouth. Had he not seen it emanating from the body in front of him he would have thought some hideous beast was screaming its defiance at mankind. He felt the hairs on his neck stand on end as the noise intensified, reverberating off the walls. He covered his ears with his hands, desperately trying to block out the piercing sound.

Then, as quickly as it started, the sound ended. The woman was dead, and an ominous silence fell.

A small scraping noise started, quietly, quietly, like a cat scratching at a door. Then it became a tearing sound, like a wet sail ripping in a storm. As the sound increased in volume, the woman's abdomen split open and a black beak appeared, glistening red with blood and entrails. The beak pecked at the sides of the gash, and its talons clawed until it had pulled itself free.

Green eyes glittered with an unnatural intelligence. The rook scrabbled free and shook its black feathers, droplets of gore splattering across the room. As the bird preened itself, a second rook emerged, ripping its way clear of the body. Gelanson watched in admiration of his work as the two birds preened and flapped their wings to dry themselves.

'Aren't you beautiful?' he murmured to the creatures. Stepping forward cautiously, he placed a hand on each rook's head. Gelanson spoke the word of summoning – '*Tukanan!*' – and felt a thrill of power as the birds cawed and flapped, then launched themselves from the table to fly a circuit of the room before gliding to land on his shoulders. He gestured for the birds to move onto his outstretched arm so that he could view his magnificent work more carefully. One flapped to alight on his arm whilst the second hopped down from his shoulder onto his forearm. The duke drank in every detail, analysing each one carefully, turning over in his mind the exact inflection of the incantation, and storing every detail in his memory to be recorded in his ledger.

Although delighted with his success, he realised he did not know how long these blood-creations would survive. Whilst he dearly wished to study them in detail, he could not lose any precious time. Touching each one on the head, the duke spoke the blood-kin search words. The stone in his golden chain flared with power after each incantation. When he finished, the rooks rose, screeching and circling the room once more, before flying up the chimney and out into the world.

Now all Gelanson had to do was wait, and be patient.

Well, that is no issue, he thought, as he looked at the eviscerated body on his workbench. It was always interesting to dissect a fresh cadaver. The mechanical workings of a human body were fascinating.

A smile of satisfaction danced across Gelanson's lips as he sought his scalpels and tongs, and set to work.

CHAPTER TWENTY-THREE

Scase scouted ahead in the moonlight each night, criss-crossing the woods, scenting for danger. Hirae covered more ground than any of them, constantly doubling back to lay false trails and check for pursuers. So far they had been lucky. They travelled carefully by night and rested each day. Any outcropping of rock or overhang where they could screen themselves from searching soldiers provided their respite.

As the days passed, Sionan's strength slowly grew, her resolve not to slow the group down forcing her drained limbs to keep moving. Her stamina increased, but she still looked older than her years. Each day when they replenished their water skins in any clear brook, Sionan would stare at her reflection. It was not through vanity; she was trying to learn the new lines on her face and specks of green in her eyes. Her grey hair held only strands of autumnal brown now. Over time, she came to know the face that stared back at her. She was unable to answer any questions about her change in eye colour or the strange feeling that had thrummed through her body when she saw Kayton hanging by the noose. Chancer had questioned her at length, but she had no answers to give. That moment of anguish had unleashed something that now felt dormant again.

During the nights of travel, Sionan found peace with her lost youth. When she realised how close she and her mother were in appearance now, she drew comfort from her reflection. Sometimes she felt as though her mother was gazing back at her. She wished she had some way of letting her know that she was safe, and dreamed nightly of her family and Kayton. Every day she awoke with a start, followed by a hollow feeling of loss.

During their travel, Chancer, Hirae, and Sionan talked of Kayton and how he had struck out on his own to seek help. Sionan was astounded to hear of Kayton's journey across the Manors to search for aid from the fabled Captain Chancer. Kayton's unwavering belief in the importance of what he was doing had somehow protected him like a talisman from harm on the road. Bitter was the knowledge to Sionan that the worst danger had come when he returned to his own Manor.

Chancer and Hirae talked with affection of their travel with Kayton from Ascalion to Clasterne. They laughed as they recalled his first sword lesson when he had landed in an ungainly heap, and when he'd tried to catch his first rabbit, trapping his own foot in the snare. Sionan shared tales of when they grew up together. As they talked, the wound of loss became less angry and raw, like an infection that had been lanced, but the deep pain of the injury remained.

The trio also talked in detail about their plans to go to the Overlord. Sionan, never having left her town, listened in fascination to Chancer's recounting of the glory of Atipac and its festivities on every street. She was not foolish enough to believe there was no danger, but was grateful for the respite from fear that Chancer's descriptions provided. Atipac was a centre of learning, peace and prosperity. If any of them doubted their mission to go to the crown, none of them voiced their concern openly.

Sionan used their resting time during the day well. She learned to sharpen and throw knives, practising diligently until each one thunked solidly into the chosen target. Chancer spent time teaching her to fight without knives, how to free herself from an attacker and defend herself with only her fists and elbows if the need arose.

They had made good distance over the last five nights, finding themselves at the border already. Tomorrow they would cross into the Manor of Hatlerna, where Atipac was located. For the remainder of today they would camp in preparation for what tomorrow may bring.

Chancer and Sionan launched into another mock battle as Hirae sat on an outcrop of rock with Scase who was stretched out, clearly enjoying the warmth of the spring sunshine. Chancer launched an attack, grabbing Sionan by the hair to pull her to the ground. She wasted no time in resisting the hold, twisting her body under his arm, tapping the points of her fingers to his throat and eyes as fast as a snake striking. Chancer laughingly released her, bowing at her improved defensive skills.

'We're going to hunt,' Hirae called down to them as Chancer and Sionan circled each other warily, searching for an opening to attack. Chancer mumbled in acknowledgement, not wishing to take his eyes off Sionan as she waited to pounce like a cat. Sionan waved to acknowledge Hirae moving off into the woods, Scase ranging ahead for potential kills. The next moment, the floor rose up to meet Sionan. Chancer had taken the opportunity of her distraction to throw her to the ground like a sack of flour. She jumped up and lunged for an attack, but Chancer made a simple sidestep and swept her legs from under her. A solid whoomph of air knocked out of Sionan was swiftly followed by his laugh.

Sionan levered herself up on one elbow, looking at Chancer, who was now sitting on a log with a stupid grin on his face. She was irritated, but knew Chancer was employing his most charming smile to disarm her. Despite her fall from grace, Sionan's smile mirrored his as she struggled up to a seated position.

'Next time!' she promised.

'Up you come, then,' Chancer said, offering an arm to help her stand.

As she grabbed it, he pulled her up firmly. Off balance, she bumped against his chest. Sionan had noticed a growing physical awareness between them over the last few days, but did not want to add any further complication to their day-by-day existence. Her life had already spiralled out of control.

Gently disentangling herself, she stepped back out of his arms, and out of the embrace that she could feel he wanted him to provide. 'How far do we have to go?' Sionan asked, looking to divert their thoughts from each other.

'Two more days to Atipac,' Chancer replied.

'I hope the bakers made it safely,' said Sionan, sitting on the soft grass by their weapons as her breathing slowly returned to normal. The belt of throwing knives Chancer had gifted her was carefully placed, ready to be strapped back on as soon as their practice session was complete. Sionan never liked to be further than arm's length from her knives now.

Trauma and grief had battered her into someone that she barely recognised when she thought of the uncomplicated life she previously had as a tailor's daughter only a few weeks ago.

Sionan's hand wandered to the box that contained the star-stone, the square shape of it showing through her travel sack. She had told Chancer of her strange premonition, that since Kayton's death, she would be able to open the secured container. It was a premonition that she was not yet ready to test.

'The safest thing we can do now is to keep our distance until Atipac Justice Day,' Chancer said, watching her patting the travel bag. 'When we reach the city, I know of a quiet place on the outskirts where we can stay whilst I try and contact some old friends. It's not going to be easy getting an audience with the Overlord, but at least in Atipac we are away from Gelanson's control. We need to be smart and quiet, but we should be safe.'

Sionan suddenly tensed, her whole body taut like a coiled spring. Chancer placed his hands on hers.

'Are you well?' he asked anxiously.

Her eyes flashed green, like lightning in a stormy sky as she turned to the trees. 'We are being watched,' she whispered fearfully.

Chancer leapt to his feet, drew his sword, and searched the trees and undergrowth for any flicker of colour or movement.

'I see nothing,' he responded quietly. 'What did you see?' he asked, as he moved his body in front to shield her. She raised an arm high to point up into the trees, Chancer followed her line of sight.

'What do you see?' he repeated urgently. 'I see only trees

and a bird.'

'Gelanson's evil…' Sionan replied.

The rook cocked its head to one side and appeared to regard them as closely as they warily observed it. There was something unnatural about the creature. No rook she had ever seen had green eyes. Before Chancer could react, Sionan drew a knife from her belt and threw it with vehemence at the creature. The knife thudded into the trunk, startling the bird into flight, its green eyes glittering in the sunlight. It circled up and broke free of the leafy canopy. Gaining height, the bird banked to fly away west. Sionan launched another knife at the bird, but it had no hope of reaching its target. The rook flapped away with a *caw* of disdain.

'What in the curses of night was that?' Chancer asked.

Sionan watched the bird wing its way to the west. 'We need to run,' she replied. 'There is no time left. Gelanson will know all our plans.'

Chancer studied Sionan, as if weighing up the truth of her words. Cursing, he grabbed Hirae's pack and lifted it on to his back. 'I have no idea how you came by this conclusion,' he said. 'But I know that you speak the truth.'

'We take the road now,' Sionan replied while they swiftly packed up their meagre camp. 'Haste is more important than hiding. He knows we're going to the Overlord.' Her voice resonated with certainty.

'How does he know?' Chancer asked.

'That bird was not natural. It will show Gelanson everything it has observed.'

'How do you know this?' Chancer repeated carefully, not wishing to anger her but clearly struggling to understand. 'If

Gelanson truly knows we are headed for the Overlord, this will jeopardise everything. We have to present our case before Gelanson can intervene. If he knows, and has his way, we will be unlikely to even receive a platform to speak.'

'How *do* I know?' Sionan paused, rubbing her head to drive an ice like pain away. 'I knew nothing of the dark arts until Gelanson inflicted them on me. Something has changed in me. Today, as my eyes sought and found the rook, I knew its purpose as soon as its emerald eyes connected with mine. When the creation was near us, I could feel it calling. There's a wrongness to it, the bird. It only needed to find me to impart its discovery back to the duke.' Her shoulders sagged as she frowned. 'What is happening to me?'

'I don't know,' Chancer replied gently. 'But I will take care of you, whatever the future brings.'

Sionan could hear the ring of Kayton's own promises in Chancer's words. When he stepped forward to offer her comfort, she backed away out of his reach and squared her shoulders to the challenge. Sionan strapped on the baldric of knives, retrieved the two thrown at the rook, and hoisted her pack.

'We have to go, now,' she repeated. Her long grey hair gently moved in the breeze as she strode off with determination.

Chancer followed closely, clearly intent on demonstrating his commitment to keeping her safe. He deliberately snapped a small branch as they left the clearing. With Hirae's tracking skills, she would be able to follow them as clearly as if they had left a written sign. Hirae would read the haste in their passage and would hurry to catch up.

While Sionan headed towards the road and Atipac, she

wondered if they had anything to fear from the changes being wrought within her, as she felt the writhing connection with the rook slowly fade.

The duke stared thoughtfully into the fire in his chamber, the remains of his evening repast on a tray. The cook had provided a delicately flavoured fish pie with spring greens and a delightful pastry filled with sweet strawberries. All carefully cooked for the duke out of concern for his health.

He drummed his fingers on the arm of the chair, a beautiful creation of oak with heavy scrolling carved into the arms. Gelanson felt comforted by the luxury of the cushion filled with goose down. Since he had been unable to maintain his health and youth with the star-stone, he had noticed the cold creeping in, despite the spring air warming for summer. The servant had attempted to mask his surprise when Gelanson requested the fire lit. His people obviously thought he was ailing.

He watched the flames as he schemed. The loss of Onway was a blow, but he was not a fighter. The duke had no fear that his former steward would return to the town looking for revenge. Gelanson would dispatch a squad to kill him when the blood-creation located the fleeing children.

The prime concern was the girl, Sionan, who had obviously taken the star-stone. Gelanson felt a nagging dread without it. His vulnerability coloured each day with grey. All resources must be devoted to capturing the girl and returning the stone.

As the evening ticked away, his planning ground to a halt.

This was a rare and frustrating occurrence for the duke. Given his superior intellect, he was always able to pre-empt anyone's next move. However, right now all he could do was wait.

Finally, the duke heard the sound he had been hoping for – a tapping on the window. Looking through the pane of glass he saw green jewel-eyes looking back at him. He opened the window, allowing the creation to hop onto his shoulder. Already some of its feathers were missing, as though the rook was slowly disassembling. He had to hope the second rook would return soon before it too started to disintegrate. He marked this information with interest.

Perhaps the length of animation the blood creation has is dependent on the amount of life left in the subject sacrificed, he reflected, *and the widow had been close to death…* Gelanson packaged away for another day the exciting idea of attempting a further creation with someone who was in their physical prime.

Leaving his chamber, the duke walked along the west corridor, heading straight for his research room. The rook perched quietly on his shoulder as he made his way through the castle. The new steward, Janter, if he recalled the name correctly, knew that only Stegen was allowed to disturb the duke when in the tower.

Gelanson descended the wide stone steps, barely noticing the servants bobbing with respect as he passed. If anyone thought it strange the duke was walking about the castle with a rook perched on his shoulder, no one would dare to mention anything. Withdrawing the key from his tunic, he walked to the tower door. Four pikemen stood to attention at the entrance. Since Stegen's recent promotion, Gelanson had seen a pleasing increase in the alertness of the guards. Clearly Stegen meant to prove how invaluable she was, and thus far, the duke was impressed.

Unlocking the door, he swiftly entered, locked it behind him, and made directly for his research room. He was delighted to see that the body of the widow had been removed.

Yes, he thought, *Stegen is exactly the person I need. No squeamishness or doubt lurking in that one.* When Stegen had seen the corpse, she'd made some comment about the Hellards being responsible for the death of her brother. Gelanson had not paid close attention, whilst thinking of more important matters, but he noted Stegen's obsession with bringing the warriors to justice along with the town girl and her family. That level of fanatical hatred was exactly the sort of passion Gelanson could use.

He lifted the creation from his shoulder and placed it in a large, silver scrying bowl. The bird filled the bowl, the tips of its feathers poking over the side.

Gelanson spoke the word of release, '*Hakashameren!*'

Green gore leaked from the emerald eyes and beak filling the bowl. The duke lifted the creature by its claws, and waited patiently until the dripping of viscous liquid had stopped. Once the last drop had fallen, the bird crumpled in on itself, becoming smaller and smaller, until everything fell into dust apart from the emerald eye stones that dropped onto the table. Gelanson carefully lifted the stones and placed them to one side. He would see if he could commission a new statuette, perhaps something larger next time. An eagle would be an interesting option.

Turning his attention to the gore in the bowl, he chanted

to exhume the knowledge from the liquid. He focused his concentration on the scrying bowl. For a moment, Gelanson suffered a strange sense of vertigo as he looked down on his own castle receding in the distance as the bird had started on its journey. He could tell from the position of the sun during its flight that the fugitives had headed north-east.

'Intriguing,' he murmured. The rebels had entered his lands from the Gashon crossing, therefore he had thought they would flee to Ascalion, not to the north-east. As the bird's wings covered the leagues, the duke recognised the road to the Atipac.

Surely, they are not seeking to hide there? Gelanson was not without influence in the Overlord's domain. He swayed abruptly, feeling as though the stone floor was rushing up to meet him, as he saw the bird landing on a tree. The rook focused on a clearing, where the images showed Sionan and the man talking.

Leaning into the bowl, Gelanson listened intently. Their voices were faint amidst the noise of leaves rustling and branches swaying. Gelanson strained to make out their speech which was no louder than a whisper through the noise of the trees. He rocked back on his heels, aghast, when he heard them speak of their plan to petition the Overlord. All his work would be in jeopardy, all his careful planning challenged! Years of ingratiating himself in the Overlord's favour were threatened. He would have to get to the Overlord first.

Gelanson ground his teeth in displeasure. The Overlord did not like to get involved in local Manor difficulties. If a duke could not adequately resolve things internally through the mandated Justice Days, then they may call into question his ability to govern.

Gelanson would have to leave for Atipac immediately.

He was about to call Stegen to organise their travel when he stopped in amazement. He bent lower over the bowl – so close his face was almost touching the green gore – unable to believe his eyes. He watched the woman's eyes turn to green, a flashing contrast to her greying hair. He grabbed the worktable in dizzying disbelief as the world twisted around him. The duke had read about this phenomenon in some of his scrolls, not daring to believe these people even existed, but the change of eye colour and the power radiating from the girl's vision could only mean one thing.

The girl was an Instinctual.

Gelanson's mind raced furiously.

Why was this not evident during the initial experiments? Could the star-stone have awakened this power in her?

Gelanson's body shook with barely contained excitement. A girl born with the innate ability to practise the dark arts! Jealousy and excitement tore through him. If only he had been born with such power, not having to rely on artefacts gathered from across the seas, he would be unstoppable. However, alongside this resentment was also the fascination that he had discovered a living Instinctual. And she was almost within his grasp! The girl would have no idea how to use her power. He had only to capture her, and the heady wonder of studying a living being with arcane powers would stretch out before him enticingly.

Nearly falling over his own feet in his haste to exit the workroom, he burst from the tower. Pikemen immediately rushed to his aid.

'Call for Stegen and ready my carriage!' the duke shouted. 'And send the steward to me!' he called over his shoulder as he set off at a run for his chambers.

Gelanson did not spare his lack of decorum a second thought, his mind already planning what he would need: artefacts to capture an Instinctual and gifts for the Overlord. Nothing would stop him from taking the girl, not even the Overlord. This chance was too monumental to miss. He would need some special token of his deep esteem to show his loyalty to the crown and that all his work was for the good of the Manors. His mind clicked and whirred through an array of possibilities.

Duke Gelanson would have his day of reckoning.

CHAPTER TWENTY-FOUR

Sionan was weary beyond words as evening fell. She had started at a brisk walk as soon as they had connected to the main road that would lead to Atipac. Chancer had encouraged her to slow down. The seasoned veteran knew that it was better to sustain a steady-paced walk than burn up energy at a fast pace, but Sionan felt compelled to keep going, as though she could walk away from the unnerving thrumming inside her veins.

Chancer had reminded her that they were still another ten leagues from Atipac, two days' travel. She wished now she had listened to him and slowed down. Her lower back ached abominably, she had blisters on her feet, and the sun shining down felt like it had leeched all remaining strength from her body.

Rounding a corner in the dusty road, Sionan barely had time to steady herself when Scase suddenly appeared in front of her, jumping up on his hind legs and launching himself up to lick every part of her face. Pushing the dog off in a mixture of disgust and joy at seeing him, she wiped her face with the back of her hand and knelt to stroke his back. Scase looked as though he was smiling as he panted with his mouth wide open. Sauntering after him came Hirae, looking every bit as relaxed and in control as always. Sionan felt a momentary pang of envy.

Just once can't the woman look exhausted or worried? Sionan knew her tiredness was making her scratchy towards someone who had put her own life on the line to help her. To make up for her unworthy thoughts she smiled a welcome at Hirae, who stopped and stared at her.

'Your eyes are completely green,' Hirae said in surprise. 'I mean, really green… like emeralds.'

Sionan turned to Chancer, who nodded in agreement whilst wincing slightly at Hirae's usual forthrightness.

'Why didn't you tell me?' Sionan asked Chancer accusingly, glowering at him in annoyance. 'I didn't know they were *all* green,' she said to Hirae, and shared what had happened with the rook and why they were on the road, travelling as quickly as they could.

'Well, that's great news,' Hirae said emphatically.

'Is it?' Sionan queried.

'Yes, it means you have magic of your own.' The tone of Hirae's voice clearly suggested that should have been obvious.

Sionan couldn't think of a suitable response. Shakily, she realised this was another change to her body that she did not understand and could not control. She wondered if her mother and sisters would even recognise her when they were finally reunited.

The three travellers continued along the road, lost in their own thoughts as to what Sionan's new-found power could mean for their plans. As they drew closer to Atipac, there was more passing traffic; people riding in to sell their wares or look for work. They had seen no patrols of soldiers wearing the bright yellow sash of the Overlord's own guards yet.

When Chancer saw a merchant with an empty wagon rolling along the hard-packed earth, he decided to take a risk and bartered to pay three coppers for a ride into the city. It was a pricey amount of money for sitting in a rickety wagon on its way to Atipac, but the driver pointed out he didn't much like the look of the vicious hound with them and nor did his horses – and the ride would therefore cost extra. The deal struck, the driver pulled on the brake and waited for them to climb aboard. Sionan struggled to pull herself up over the tailgate, but Chancer helped, almost lifting the exhausted woman, and left her leaning against the back of the wagon board. Sionan's eyes closed in relief.

Scase trotted along behind as the old wagon creaked and groaned along the road. It turned out the wagon driver was right about Scase unnerving the horses, although the horses made much better time with the large dog's shadow following them.

As night drew in, the driver directed his horses towards a wayside inn.

'That's as far as I am going for tonight. I'll be on my way again tomorrow if you want another ride. Three more coppers, mind.'

'Thanks, we'll make our own way tomorrow,' Chancer replied.

They walked away from the inn to find somewhere to camp for the night. Sionan looked longingly at the warm, welcoming lights of the tavern twinkling through the window and thought of the joy of a bath, but knew it was too risky.

At a suitable clearing they paused, and Sionan, practically

asleep on her feet, laid down where she stopped, not even having the energy to unravel a bedding roll and climb into it. Chancer looked at her sleeping form and gently laid his blankets over the top of her.

'Do you think what's happening to her is dangerous?' Hirae asked Chancer quietly, looking at the girl's delicate features as she slept in the moonlight.

'I have absolutely no idea,' he said. 'This is far beyond my understanding. Give me a battle any day, where you fight what you see with swords. This thing with her eyes, I don't know where it will lead. We need to get to Atipac fast. If Gelanson is riding behind us we've only got maybe two days' head start.'

'Can we purchase some horses? Buy ourselves a bit more time?'

'I'll try the inn. It won't hurt to have a quiet look around, anyway, see if anyone is asking questions about us.'

'Chancer, are you doing okay?' Hirae asked carefully.

Chancer was aware of what Hirae's loaded question implied, and he paused to assess how to respond. Despite everything, he found that when he thought carefully about it, he *was* okay. Maybe because of everything he knew, he could go into the inn without succumbing to temptation. Kayton's faith in him had been the first step to believing he could do something worthy with his life again. The growing affection he felt for Sionan was like a butterfly unfurling its wings for the first time, and he did not want to do anything to risk that, including taking a drink.

'I'm doing fine,' he said firmly.

They grasped hands and Chancer quickly disappeared

into the darkness.

Hirae remained in the clearing, keeping watch over Sionan's sleeping form as she had done during those early nights in the cave after Kayton's death. She sat with her back to a tree, whittling away on a piece of wood. Looking over at her dog lying beside Sionan, Hirae knew they would soon be reaching the point where she would have to leave Scase behind.

'Boy, I must leave you soon, but I will be back.'

The dog grumbled in response, aware from her tone that she was moving off into territory where she would not allow him to follow. He crawled along the floor in supplication, trying to show her that she should not leave. The hound knew they were safe in the woods. His sensitive nose had already picked up the scent of Atipac wafting along the spring breeze, and with an animal's instinct, he understood those places brought danger.

Hirae looked at the dog with love and stroked his big head.

'Tomorrow we will share the last of the rabbit. Then you will have to hunt alone, my old friend.'

The dog's ears pricked forwards at the word "rabbit" and he soon settled into sleep. Hirae rested, enjoying the presence of her faithful hound for one more evening.

The heavy stillness of night had settled when Scase's ears twitched, his nose snuffling the air as he looked across the glade. Hirae kept still and followed Scase's fixed stare. His hackles were not raised, so it did not appear there was any imminent danger, but something out there had stirred him. She waited, her eyes scanning the shadows. Then she picked up the soft fall of horses' hooves on the trail, and she could make out a different shade of grey moving out of the undergrowth – Chancer's silhouette.

Chancer dismounted and crouched by Hirae. She could smell no alcohol on him. His gait was steady and his eyes clear, though tired.

'Well, they won't win any races, but they'll get us to Atipac alright,' Chancer said.

'How much did they cost?' Hirae asked.

'More than they should, but it's better to invest in horses than get caught on the road on foot.'

'Do we continue now?' Hirae queried. There were dangers in travelling by horse at night, not least due to robbers and unseen holes in the road, but even if they moved slowly, it would mean they were gaining time.

Chancer looked at Sionan's sleeping form.

'I hate to wake her, but we don't know how quickly Gelanson will be on the move, and he'll have fresh horses at his disposal. We need to go now.'

Hirae nodded in agreement and rose to pack her things. Her eyes were gritty with exhaustion, but she reassured herself that once they had made it to Atipac, they could lose themselves in the throng of people, and hopefully have some rest.

Chancer gently woke Sionan and found himself staring into the most beautiful, crisp, forest-green eyes. He realised he was still expecting her eyes to be brown again, but each time he looked, they seemed greener. The gentle moonlight gave them a touch of luminescence. She was like an ethereal creature gazing back at him. She sat up and Chancer rocked back on his heels, giving her space to stretch and wake up.

The first words Sionan heard when she awoke were Chancer's, explaining the need to move on.

'If we get caught on the road it will mean our deaths,' he said. 'But when we get to Atipac, I can find a safe house where we can sleep and recover.'

Sionan bit the inside of her cheek to drive away the tears threatening to well up. She had been dreaming of simpler times when her father had been delighted at her first attempt to sew. The trousers she had made for him had one leg longer than the other, but he had been overjoyed. She had been basking in that warm, golden family love when Chancer had gently shaken her arm. Just seeing his drawn face with lines of concern bought everything crashing back onto her again.

'Should we check your stitches first?' she asked, her mind flitting to her more recent sewing work. Chancer lifted his jerkin.

Hirae walked over to take a look at the wound too. She sniffed it. 'It's not infected, and those stiches are holding nicely,' she said. 'You did a good job there, Sionan.'

Sionan smiled, glad to feel her skills from a previous life were not entirely wasted in this madness. 'When we get to Atipac we'll take the stitches out,' she said. '…Or we could use the stone to heal it,' she whispered, barely daring to utter the words.

Hirae and Chancer paused in astonishment.

'The stone is dangerous. None of us knows how to use it. You could create more damage than good, to yourself or Chancer,' Hirae responded. 'Besides, it's pointless to discuss it,' she added as she tied her bedding roll to the horse. 'We can't open the box. It's protected in some way. We've all tried.'

Turning to help Sionan onto her horse, she saw the girl sitting with the opened box in her hand. 'How did you…?'

'I don't know,' Sionan replied. 'It was after I saw that hideous bird-creature. I just knew how to open it, instinctively.' She groped for the right words to describe something she did not understand herself. 'I can only say that as the bird absorbed knowledge about us, it provided information for me. Perhaps the knowledge flows both ways?'

Hirae and Chancer leaned over, looking at the small star-stone. Rather than reflecting the moonlight, it seemed to absorb the light around it. Scase whined and paced around the perimeter of the clearing, not wishing to be any closer to the object.

'You don't know how to use it. You might kill Chancer, or yourself. It's too risky,' Hirae re-iterated.

'I agree,' chimed in Chancer. 'I don't want that thing anywhere near me after what you said it can do.'

Sionan looked at him, seeing the truth and conviction in his words. She gazed at the stone a moment longer. Her eyes were reflected in a searing green, as though the black of her pupils barely existed now. Her expression unreadable, she shut the box with a firm snap and replaced it in her travel sack.

'At least we can open the box to show the Overlord what's inside now,' she said. 'People won't think we're completely mad.'

Standing, Sionan walked to the horses and allowed Chancer to help her mount and adjust her stirrups. A gentle brown roan who appeared almost as tired as she was made no protest about the light passenger deposited on her back.

Sionan stroked the horse's neck, observing with sadness the scars from a previous owner who must have been too free and brutal with the use of a switch. The horse's ears pricked back, listening to her soft words. Whilst Sionan doubted she would ever be a comfortable or accomplished rider like Hirae and Chancer, she could at least befriend the animal who was going to labour to get her to the city.

Hirae, Chancer, and Sionan moved down the trail, back towards the road, Scase loping along next to them. All three were quiet, reflecting on what may come, as they started their last day of travel to the Atipac.

CHAPTER TWENTY-FIVE

One day behind, Gelanson's team pulled up to rest and refresh the horses overnight. The duke stamped down his frustration at the delay, although he understood the captain's explanation that it would be better to have fresh horses in the morning, and continue at a gallop, than exhaust the horses by pushing onwards when it would inevitably be slower going at night. They had covered leagues in the first day alone. If they maintained their speed, they would be in Atipac tomorrow.

The duke was sore throughout his body, his carriage jouncing and bouncing over every bump in the road, but every time the driver had suggested to slow down, the duke had ordered him on at speed. The discomfort of the journey was far more bearable than the idea that the Instinctual girl and her companions would reach the Overlord before him.

Stegen had instructed the team to stop at a farm to seek shelter. The farmer's eyes goggled at seeing the duke on his doorstep. He and his wife politely insisted that the duke utilise their home as his own. They quickly moved their own blankets into an outbuilding and scurried away from Stegen's stern countenance, hoping their important guests would not find their hosts wanting in any way.

Stegen housed the guards in the barn. She would sleep

on the floor in front of the fireplace. Gelanson closed the door on the living space and looked around the simple, rustic bedroom that the farmers had given up for him. The room contained only a bed, wardrobe, and trunk with a mirror and washbowl resting on it. He looked around with disdain. The bed had initials carved intricately into the frame, and small cushions stuffed with pleasant-smelling herbs were carefully arranged on the bed. All these small touches of homely love were lost on the duke.

Gelanson prepared for sleep, resigning himself to the awful lodging he would have to tolerate for one night. A tapping on the window drew his attention and he looked out to the kitchen garden. In amongst the plants, the second rook rested, feathers dropping from its body as it cocked his head to look at the duke. In dismay, Gelanson opened the window to allow the rook in. The bird was practically disintegrating in front of his eyes. The risk Gelanson had taken in hurrying directly to Atipac meant the second creature had travelled far longer to reach him. The bird hopped from the windowsill on to the clothes trunk, a trail of feathers littering the floor, each one crumbling to dust as it fell to the floor.

Gelanson grabbed the small earthenware washbowl off the trunk. He held the rook over the container. The word of release whispered through the room: '*Hakashameren!*'

Only a small amount of the viscous green gore dripped from the emerald eyes of the bird, barely enough to create a small circle of liquid in the bottom of the bowl. Gelanson dangled the creature by its feet, desperately waiting for any more drips to fall, but the bird had been gone too long. It no longer had any stolen life-essence to sustain its purpose. The rook slowly disintegrated into dust, leaving only the small emerald eye-stones that dropped towards the pot. The duke swiftly caught them before they could mar the small quantity of green gore. He gazed into the bowl, quietly whispering the exhumation chant. His nose almost touched the viscous liquid as he leaned in closer to gain any knowledge the flight of the bird could show him.

Again, he felt that wrenching vertigo. The room swayed around him as he viewed the world from the bird's eyes. He could see his castle receding into the distance. Clearly the bird was flying south, away from Clasterne. It was winging its way and following the main vein towards Sahjashorn. The hard-packed earthen road, looking like a brown serpent, stretched out across the land below. Gelanson watched avidly, but before he could see any sign of the Hellard girls and his treacherous steward, the view faded to nothing as the last of the energy was released from the liquid.

Gelanson sat on the bed, disappointed at the outcome. Nonetheless, ever the experimenter, he calculated how quickly the images had faded compared with the first rook. Frustratingly, he knew only that the children may be travelling south towards Sahjashorn, but whether they were still following that route and what their final destination would actually be, he was none the wiser.

Pulling open the door, he summoned Stegen to his room.

'Send back one guard to the castle. We need a unit on the road to Sahjashorn to search for Onway and the Hellard girls.'

'And what actions would you like taken when they are found, my lord?' Stegen asked.

Gelanson thought carefully. Things had spiralled out of control when he left Sionan alive after drawing on her life-force. His logic told him the children and Onway should be killed immediately, but although his soldiers were loyal, he would struggle to justify to them the killing of two children. There was also the matter of the leverage he could gain over the Instinctual if her two younger sisters were in his power… and what if these younger girls also had the innate powers of an Instinctual?

'Kill the steward with no trial,' he announced. 'The children will be returned to the castle, where they will remain at my sufferance.'

Stegen nodded in response, not questioning why this command had been given now, as night approached.

'Captain,' Gelanson added. 'This must be done discreetly. The peace between Sahjashorn and Clasterne must not be impacted by our searches within the Duke of Sahjashorn's territory. She is most particular about her borders and will be unhappy at our unannounced entrance to her Manor.'

'I understand, my lord,' Stegen replied. 'I have suitable guards in mind who can take care of this. With your approval they will be dressed as common mercenaries rather than in the purple livery.'

'Approved, Captain. Continue.'

Stegen sketched a small bow at the dismissal and turned to execute the orders.

Gelanson closed the door and lay down on the bed. Trying to block the roughness of his accommodation from his mind, he focused on the joy of knowing he would be playing the winning move tomorrow. He would reach Atipac and gain the Overlord's ear before the rebels. Although he had lost Onway to the winds, he was sure the steward was too fearful to return to Clasterne. If Stegen's squad were successful, then it would be helpful to have the children contained in the castle. However, he was not overly worried about the steward and the girls. In Gelanson's mind, Onway was like a frightened mouse, darting from one place to another to hide. He presented no real threat. The prize would be finding the Instinctual and returning her to his keep.

Gelanson lay in the bed wondering how long blood-creations from horse statuettes would last if he sacrificed a healthy human being to the incantation. *An interesting experiment for another day,* he thought, as he settled to his slumber.

CHAPTER TWENTY-SIX

Hirae, Chancer, and Sionan sat astride their horses looking at the sprawling mass of the city of Atipac on the horizon. They had ridden throughout the remainder of the night and following day, only stopping to rest the horses when necessary. Now, as late afternoon approached and the sun began to wane, they could finally see the destination they had pinned all their hopes to.

Sionan gazed upon the scene, longing for a return to her old life. She had never seen so many buildings in one place. She had thought Clasterne town was large, but realised it was minute in comparison to the seething mass of humanity before her. The Spire, the largest stone building in the centre of the mass, rose like a needle spearing through fabric. Sionan looked at it gleaming in the sun with pearlescent beauty. Constantly changing colour as the sun began to set, the Spire was a structure of immense splendour, of the approaching sunset gleaming from its high tower.

'That's the Overlord's palace,' Chancer explained. 'Within the Spire is where Atipac Justice Day is held each month. They say the colours of the Spire are to remind people of the beauty of truth and honesty, and to drive all thoughts of lies and deceit from their minds.'

'And how many lies and half-truths did the Overlord tell to get that Spire built from the sweat of good, honest people?' Hirae asked in disgust, turning her horse away and starting down the final descent to the city.

Hirae had nothing but distaste for Atipac. On the singular occasion she had ventured here before, she had remained on the outskirts, feeling compelled to watch the triumphant return of the Overlord and her victorious troops after they crushed the Ascalion rebellion. Hirae's mental anguish was like vinegar in an open wound as they had filed proudly past. Her bitterness at the defeat of the rebels was directly contrasted by the glittering splendour of the newly appointed Duke of Ascalion riding proudly behind the Overlord. For Hirae, Atipac embodied the worst traits of humankind, its endless buildings like a festering wound in the countryside.

When they were half a league from the outer dwellings, Hirae slid down from her saddle and patted her horse on the neck. Calling Scase to her, she gave his ears a strong, playful rumple, stopping to scratch him at the exact spot behind his left ear that he loved. The dog made a low grumble of appreciation before she stood and pointed at the woodlands to the east.

'Hide,' she commanded.

The dog whined as if he could feel her sadness and did not want to travel without his packmate. He barked once questioningly.

'No. Go hide,' Hirae said firmly, pointing again to the woods.

The dog loped off, ever obedient to her command, but his tail remained tucked between his legs. Hirae watched until he disappeared beyond the tree line, and then with a heavy heart, turned her horse to Atipac.

Chancer looked at Atipac with calm resolve. This was the city he had once called home. After the campaign he had revelled in the parades. Revered and adored by the crowds, he had felt untouchable. He remembered the cheers from then as part of the Overlord's parade, resplendent in his finely polished ceremonial breastplate. It had taken only a few months for everything to change. Unable to cope without the structure of army life and thrill of the campaign, he had made the taverns his new home. The good wishes of the nobility quickly disappeared and, with no war to fight, Chancer had struggled to find purpose, the alehouse patrons providing companionship and solace. Now that he was sober, he had to hope that in Atipac he still had some reliable comrades from the days of campaigning.

His horse moved forwards, naturally following Hirae's down the road, the sodden thump of hooves matching Chancer's apprehensive mood. The horses were all done in. The many rest stops could not compensate for the hard use they had received during their lives. Chancer would see them stabled well on the outskirts of town and grain-fed until they returned. That would give them the best chance to recover some strength in the event they were needed for an escape.

Listening to the clomp of tired hooves, Chancer realised they needed reshoeing as well. He thought with a smile that he certainly wouldn't come out of this venture financially better off than when he started, but at least he had recovered his purpose and had hope for the future. His wayward gaze drifted to Sionan again.

They rode into the city, the swell of noise rising like a wave over them. The din was almost unbearable after the peaceful solitude of horses' hooves and Scase's panting for company over the last day of travelling. Chancer watched Sionan feign nonchalance, obviously not wishing to appear like a wide-eyed child. He smiled at her encouragingly, delighted to see the fascination in her eyes. He laughed as her nose wrinkled at the stench of sewerage that assailed them as they entered the outskirts of town where the more squalid buildings nestled tightly on the outskirts.

Hawkers selling their wares shouted on street corners, and dogs ran through the streets stealing scraps of food. When Chancer glanced back at Hirae, he could see she was not managing well. A cold sheen of sweat had appeared on her forehead. Taking great gulps of air, she looked as though she was suffocating. Her body was as tense as a bowstring. The heavy press of people going about their business seemed to be more than Hirae could bear. Chancer knew if he tried to offer support he would get short shrift in response. Hirae was always a self-contained woman. Chancer had never known a time when she had not overcome any challenge, so he left her try to find her own balance as they slowly pressed on. Chancer had deliberately chosen the east entrance to the city where the majority of trade folk entered. Whilst the heaviness of the traffic would help disguise their entry, Chancer had not considered how overwhelming the press of people would be to Hirae.

Atipac had changed dramatically since Chancer had last seen it. Its size was the most obvious alteration; he did not recognise any of the outer streets. They continued to follow the flow of traffic along the main avenue and reached a large stone wall, over two storeys high, that Chancer remembered used to surround the city. When he had last been here, all the buildings had nestled comfortably within the fortification, but as the prosperity of Atipac had grown, more and more people had been attracted there to look for work. The populace could no longer be contained within.

Guards either side of large wrought-iron gates watched the daily traffic. In these times of peace there was no need, it appeared, for people to be challenged when they entered Atipac.

The trio passed quietly through the gate, waved through by a bored-looking guard. Almost immediately, the earthen streets gave way to cobbles. The stench of human excrement lifted as they moved into the city itself where the sewers ran. Although still vastly crowded, there was definitely more room to breathe once entering the city proper. Chancer could hear Hirae's breathing slowly start to calm. Before long, the streets changed from cobbles with wooden houses along the street to wider, tree-lined avenues. Chancer directed them off the main thoroughfare down one of the many side streets. He did not want to go too far into the centre, because the closer they were to the Spire, the closer to nobility they would be. Chancer did not want to risk any of Gelanson's supporters recognising them and stopping them from reaching the Overlord.

Sionan had not uttered a word since they entered the city.

She was completely absorbed by the teeming sea of people in all manner of clothing and guises. She felt a sharp pang knowing how much Kayton would have enjoyed these sights. The way the houses had been built up between each other were so intriguing; some so thin it looked like you could barely fit a bed in them. The dwellings were painted in a variety of colours, each seemingly brighter than the last, which gave Atipac its festive air, as though the colours of the Spire were reflected in the houses around it.

Looking around, Sionan noticed Hirae's tense state. Usually at ease in the saddle, she sat poker-straight, knuckles white as she gripped the horse's reins. She edged her horse closer to Hirae.

'Are you well?' she asked.

Hirae's eyes flickered to Sionan furtively. Sionan could see the woodswoman was far out of her comfort zone, and did not push for a response when no answer was forthcoming.

Moving along the side street, they came to a small non-descript inn. A faded board hung over the door entitling it "The Black Bear". They rode through a small gate to the side, where a stable hand waited to take their horses.

'Grain-feed them whilst they are here,' Chancer instructed the boy as he helped Sionan dismount and remove her travel pack. 'Have any of the horses stabled here been re-shoed recently?'

'Yes, sir,' the boy answered. 'Blue, in the second stall, saw the farrier today.'

'May I look at the quality of the work?' Chancer asked.

The boy nodded in response, ushering him to the stall.

Chancer carefully lifted each hoof, talking soothingly to

the horse. 'Please arrange for all three horses to see the farrier for reshoeing. Send the bill to my room, and this is for your trouble,' he told the boy, obviously satisfied with what he saw.

The boy caught the copper deftly in one hand, eyes widening with pleasure, and bobbed a quick bow. 'I'll see they receive the best grain and are reshod tomorrow. You can rely on me, sir.'

Chancer acknowledged the boy's response and entered the inn via the back door. Hirae and Sionan followed. The daylight barely seemed to penetrate the inside, causing a coolness in the air and a faint smell of damp.

'Afternoon, Reaser. Any rooms available?' Chancer asked the innkeeper, who was busy polishing tankards. The innkeeper turned, and Chancer ducked as a tankard sailed past the spot where his head had just been.

'You better have the three silvers you owe me or I'm going to rip that smiling head right from your shoulders!' the innkeeper growled and lifted a wicked-looking cudgel from behind the bar.

Chancer backed away, raising his hands in supplication. 'Now, Reaser, there's no need to be like that.'

Hirae watched the commotion with a sigh and turned to Sionan. 'Some things haven't changed with Chancer and inns,' she explained, then turned back to Reaser. 'Here.' She placed four silvers on the bar. 'I'm sure the noble Sir Dennier will not miss them,' she commented over her shoulder to Chancer before continuing, 'One extra for the trouble I have no doubt you suffered, having this reprobate under your roof.'

The innkeeper seemed mollified by Hirae's words and money. He looked at Chancer with an evil eye as the silvers swiftly disappeared from the counter.

'We need somewhere quiet to stay, Reaser,' continued Chancer. 'And I know you are a man to trust.'

'What nonsense are you caught up in this time?' Reaser asked.

'The less you know, the better,' Chancer responded.

The innkeeper gazed at Chancer with suspicion. 'On the battlefield I'd trust you with my life, Chancer, but in the city you're a liability. You'll not drink my profits and cost me customers again.'

'I won't cause you any problems, Reaser. I'm off the drink. We just need somewhere safe and discreet to stay.'

'All right,' Reaser responded after assessing Chancer was sober. 'This one time for an old comrade, but steer clear of my husband. He hasn't forgiven you for your escapades last time.'

'No problem,' Chancer readily agreed with a grin. 'The years haven't mellowed him, then?'

Reaser grunted in response to the question. 'As long as you're dry, you can stay, What sleeping arrangements do you need?' he queried, looking at Hirae and Sionan.

'One room, three beds.' Hirae said. 'We should not be separated whilst in this teaming ants' nest of people.'

'Okay, in that case, you can have the south room. Yanie! *Yanie!* Reaser bellowed. The stable hand appeared in the doorway. 'Take these people to the south room.' Reaser handed Chancer a key. 'It will be one bronze per night. Extra for food and washroom.'

'Thanks, Reaser. Out of interest, when is the next Justice Day?' Chancer asked.

'Next one is tomorrow. You're just in time if that's what you have travelled for.'

'You are a true friend, Reaser. Oh, if anyone asks, we're merchants passing through.'

Reaser nodded his understanding and returned to polishing the tankards.

Yanie led the guests out of the back door and across the yard. To the left of the stables was a small staircase leading up to a loft space that had been converted into a long room. Hirae smiled in appreciation, knowing Reaser had placed them here so they could access their horses easily and go in and out of the side gate. There was no need for them to enter the taproom at all if they did not wish to. It was obvious Reaser also wanted to keep Chancer as far removed from temptation as possible.

Thanking the stable hand, the three travellers made their way up the stairs to their room. Three beds, a seat that was propped next to a rickety chest of drawers, and a washstand and screen filled the space. Two small windows looked over the courtyard. Hirae immediately opened the windows to allow the air in, then flopped onto one of the beds. The din of people going about their daily business on the streets pressed in on her, but at least she could feel the breeze on the air. Hirae lay with her eyes closed, breathing slowly, willing herself to acclimatise to this unfamiliar environment.

'What's the plan?' she asked with no desire to go back out on to the streets straight away.

'You both stay here. Recuperate and take some time to rest,' said Chancer. 'I'm going to make some contacts first to see if we can get higher up the list of plaintiffs for Justice

Day. I need to move quickly to have everything in place for tomorrow.'

'What about the bakers? Do you think they made it?' Sionan asked, sinking down onto the seat.

'I'll see if I can find out which plaintiffs are already listed for the day. The bakers should be here already as they left before Kayton's trial. We can only hope they made it safely.'

'Is it safe to bathe?' Sionan asked hopefully.

Hirae barked a short laugh. 'I don't think it is safe *not* to bathe, the way we all must smell.' Sighing, she sat up. 'You go and meet your contact, Chancer. We'll use the washroom, see if we can get our clothes cleaned at the same time.'

Sionan's face lit up with joy, for a moment making her look every bit the young woman she truly was in years.

Chancer handed Hirae the key. 'I'm headed to the public baths to meet my contact. I'll be some while waiting for him, so take your time. I'll knock five times when I return.'

Hirae watched Chancer descend the stairs. He paused as he passed the back door of the inn. Whether it was the smell of ale wafting in the air or because he wanted to speak to his old friend, she was not sure. She watched quietly, ready to intervene if she must, but then Chancer turned decisively away from the taproom and left the yard.

'What is it that causes you to watch him like a hawk?' Sionan asked.

Hirae, startled out of her reverie, looked at the town girl. At first, Sionan had seemed to know so little of the world that Hirae had questioned if she had any steel in her. Having seen Sionan's determination to keep pace during their travelling, she knew she was wrong.

'Chancer has a problem with the drink,' Hirae responded.

'I did wonder, after what Reaser said when we arrived, but I've never seen him drink a drop of alcohol.'

'In fairness, there hasn't really been the opportunity,' Hirae admitted, feeling disloyal to him as soon as the words came out of her mouth. 'Chancer cares, about everyone, and maybe too much. His men used to call him the Ghost Captain. Every person who has died under his command, Chancer carries their ghosts with him like a heavy toll. He cannot let go, and when the pain becomes too much, he drinks to forget… Now he will be carrying Kayton's ghost as well.'

'It wasn't his fault,' Sionan said firmly. 'How can he hold himself responsible for Gelanson's evil? Stegen was the one who put the rope around Kayton's neck.' Her voice broke on the final words.

'I know this, and you know this, Sionan, but you will have a hard time convincing Chancer. He always believes if he had only done a little better or tried a little harder everyone could have been saved, but war is not like that. And believe me, we are in a war with the duke.'

Sionan fell silent. Hirae's words a heavy statement hanging in the room as they settled in, both hoping Chancer's contact would deliver them with the luck they needed to win this part of the battle.

Like clockwork, the man that Chancer was expecting, Hatchen, entered the public baths. Walking comfortably into the steams with the assurance of someone who has the knowledge of how to defend themself and the wisdom to know when it is necessary.

Short and solidly built, the man sat on the bottom step of the steams. The scarring on his shoulders and arms announced to all he was a veteran of the campaign, even if the barrelled muscle of his chest did not already announce his ability as a fighter. After the campaign had ended, this man had taken a role in the Overlord's personal guard, rising quietly to power, not due to his fighting skills, but because of his intellect and astute thinking.

Nobility always dismissed Hatchen from their notice as soon as they saw him. He was not tall, nor handsome, with his nondescript face. People's preconceptions were that he must be less intelligent than them, as though intellect was somehow linked to beauty, but Hatchen was smart enough to use this to his advantage. It was during a long and tedious meeting between the Overlord and some dignitaries from across the Western Seas that he had seen side looks quickly exchanged. Taking it upon himself to follow one of these people, he had learned of a plot to kill one of the dukes of the Manors. Discreetly, he took this information to the Overlord, who had been impressed with his initiative.

Now Hatchen could frequently be found at the Overlord's side, providing observations or deductions in private audiences. Soldiers could stand invisibly, lining the walls in banquets and meetings of state whilst the tongues of those inside became looser as the wine flowed. Hatchen would never have thought of himself as a spy but, as he rose in the Overlord's estimation, he found himself enjoying the subtlety of court politics and intrigue. A different world entirely to the battlefield, but certainly no less dangerous.

Hatchen leant back on the tiled wall. Breathing in the heavy damp air and feeling the sweat trickle down his back, he closed his eyes to mere slits, appearing relaxed, but he had already spotted his old comrade Chancer in the baths.

'Old friend,' Chancer addressed him, keeping his voice low.

Hatchen did not even look Chancer's way, although he had seen him through the steams as soon as he stepped into the room. He had deliberately chosen this place so that, to a casual observer, they would not seem to be sitting together. However, they were close enough to hear each other without anyone else listening in on the conversation.

'Less of the "old", my friend,' he said. 'How goes civilian life, or are you back in the soldering game?' He suspected that Chancer would not be here for anything other than trouble.

'Not quite a game, more of a deadly chase between cat and mouse.'

'Go on,' Hatchen asked, his quick mind already running over the countless possibilities. He knew Chancer had previously been forcibly ejected from Atipac. In fact, it was Hatchen's own unit of men who had completed the task to save Chancer from the less than savoury people he had borrowed money from for drink. Hatchen had decided the safest course of action was to get Chancer out and make it clear to the inebriated man not to return under any circumstances. He had ensured that his men were rough without breaking any bones. They had also placed a small purse of coin on Chancer's person when they deposited him at the city limits and sent him on his way. Thankfully, Chancer had taken the hint and disappeared across the border to become another Manor's problem.

'We need a private audience with the Overlord,' Chancer whispered.

It was only Hatchen's solid training that prevented him from laughing out loud at those words. 'And why would the Overlord be interested in you?'

'We seek a ruling against one of her dukes on Justice Day. I think it would be better if the Overlord knew the details in advance before they are aired throughout the court.'

'I suggest you tell me the details and leave it with me to intercede with the Overlord,' Hatchen said drily, aware that the court was already brimming with plaintiffs, both noble and common folk alike, jostling to get on the hearing list.

Hatchen listened as Chancer quietly told him all that had occurred, pausing when people entered or left the baths. He raised his eyebrows when Chancer came to speak about the sorcery at play. For a moment, he wondered if excessive drink had turned Chancer completely mad. Risking someone observing the interaction, Hatchen turned to face Chancer to scrutinise him in more detail. He could smell no alcohol on him, and when he looked at the man he had called comrade, he knew Chancer spoke only the truth, or at least the truth as he saw it.

'Where are you staying now?' Hatchen asked.

'The Black Bear,' Chancer replied.

'Stay there and stay quiet,' he responded. 'I will speak to the Overlord. Where is this star-stone you speak of?'

Chancer hesitated before responding. 'It is with us.'

Hatchen sucked air in between his teeth in worry. 'If the

item is truly as powerful as you say, it cannot be left with you in an inn. I will send a guard unit to escort you to the Spire. But understand this, Captain, you will not be leaving the Spire with the artefact. Something of that power must remain in the Overlord's custody alone.'

'Agreed, on one condition: you give me your word as a comrade that the stone will not be released to Duke Gelanson.'

Hatchen smiled in response. 'You have a great deal to learn about court politics if you believe the Overlord would release a powerful artefact to a duke of the Manors. Believe me, that stone will not leave the Spire.'

'One more thing,' added Chancer. 'There should be another couple from Clasterne on the plaintiff list; two bakers. They lost their daughter at the hands of Gelanson. Can you see if they made it to the city?'

Hatchen nodded in response. Turning slightly away from Chancer as more people entered the steams, he was already considering the impact of his old comrade's fantastical information. Incantations and artefacts – most people would think it sounded like nonsense – but Hatchen had been privy to some of the trade deals across the Western Seas, and had learned the world was much larger than just the four Manors. This stone would make an interesting new addition to the game.

Hatchen leaned back, taking a deep breath of steam. This would indeed be an intriguing Justice Day.

Chancer left Hatchen to his thoughts and wound his way out

of the steam room, stopping to refresh himself in the cold, freshwater pool fed from the natural springs in the city.

Jumping in and swimming briskly back out, Chancer felt invigorated from the shock of the cool water. Leaving the pool, Chancer sat, willing himself not to pick at the stitches on his side. The itching and tightness of the skin told him the stitches were ready for removal; he'd ask Sionan to take them out later. Thoughts of her conjured up her beautiful face, her green eyes and silvering hair accentuating her natural beauty. He challenged himself to imagine how the relationship would end. Whilst they were out in the forest, he had romanticized about them being together. In the harsh reality of Atipac, he knew he still did not have what was needed to work in partnership with someone to build a home. Walking past the back of the inn earlier, he had felt a shadow pulling him back into darkness. He was still a long way from recovered, he realised, and his heart ached for what he doubted he would ever achieve.

But still he felt more positive than he had in weeks knowing Hatchen would present their case to the Overlord. He had hesitated before promising Hatchen the star-stone, but what other options did he have? Chancer did not have the manpower or ability to keep the stone if Gelanson caught them, and quite honestly, he would be pleased to be well rid of the thing. Sionan's suggestion to use it to heal him the other night had made the hairs stand up on his neck. For someone who had suffered from the use of the stone, there was something strange about the way she was now drawn to using it.

Chancer found his clothes cleaned, and still slightly damp,

drying on the hot rocks by the steams. He dressed, paid his two coppers to the serving woman, and exited the public baths feeling more uplifted. It was freeing to pass the responsibility of the problem of the star-stone onto someone who truly had the power to stand against Gelanson.

Chancer wound his way along the streets back towards the inn, stopping to buy fruit, bread, and meats. He knew Hirae was watching over him like a mother hen; it would probably be no bad thing if he avoided going to the taproom for food. With a lightness in his step he approached the Black Bear, oblivious to the man hugging the shadows behind him.

When he reached the inn, Chancer found Hirae and Sionan waiting in the loft room, appearing to relax on his safe return. Soon afterwards, washed and with clean clothes and full bellies, they were all more hopeful than they had been for weeks. When Chancer shared the good news about Hatchen's willingness to petition the Overlord for help, there was an almost celebratory atmosphere in the room.

Chancer sat back on the bed and kicked off his boots. 'All we have to do is wait,' he said. 'I trust Hatchen. I know he'll intervene with the Overlord for us.'

'Are you sure you were not followed when you returned?' Hirae asked. 'I do not trust the nobility, and I saw somebody hovering at the gate. I am well aware of our vulnerability without Scase's nose scenting for danger.'

'It's certainly possible I was followed,' Chancer said. 'Hatchen is a thorough man and will not leave anything to chance.'

'What if it was Gelanson's people following you?' Sionan asked, her voice rising with fear.

'This is the Overlord's city, not a lawless land,' answered Chancer. 'If something happens in this quarter, then the guard will be here in moments. For now, we rest and wait for Hatchen's escort.'

'We go together to the Overlord, then?' Hirae asked.

'Yes, I don't see any benefit from being apart. If we run into difficulty in the Overlord's palace, one of us will not be enough to perform any rescue attempts. No, we must trust our plan and the Overlord's justice. We go together.' Chancer unconsciously started scratching his side.

'Here, let me,' Sionan said, pulling out one of her sharp throwing knives from the ever-present belt tied round her waist. Chancer lifted his shirt and angled his body toward the light. Sionan gently split and then pulled out the stiches as though it was the most precious piece of cloth she had ever worked on. Chancer barely felt her delicate touch, only the slight tug of skin as each stitch came clear.

Dabbing away a few spots of blood, Sionan leaned back to view her handiwork. A straight scar remained with perfectly spaced dots where each stitch had been removed.

'Not bad for my first piece of sewing on skin,' she remarked, smiling at him.

Chancer walked to the mirror on the wall over the washstand, and reviewed the scar in the reflection. 'Good work,' he responded, impressed. He turned to share a smile with her.

The noise of booted feet echoing around the courtyard and interrupted the jubilant mood in the room.

'Here they come,' Hirae hissed, seeing a troop of six guards marching through the carriageway gate. She reached for her hunting knife, preparing herself to fight.

'Be at peace, Hirae,' Chancer said, aware of his friend's rising fear of being trapped in Atipac. 'They have the Overlord's yellow. They are here as Hatchen said they would be. We need to trust him to help us.'

'Captain Landry?' The call came in unison with a smart rapping on the door. 'The Overlord requires your attendance immediately.'

The trio inside the room looked at each other, sharing with looks the reaffirmation that this was the right course of action. Sionan nodded to Chancer, placing the box with the star-stone inside her travel pack which she held tightly over her shoulder. Hirae stood at the rear to protect Sionan if necessary.

The sergeant of the guards stood to one side to allow them to leave the room in single file. 'Please, sir, follow me and we will escort you to the Overlord.'

'Thank you,' Chancer responded, moving confidently forward, trying to feel as though this was an honour escort rather than an arrest guard.

The walk to the Spire was a difficult one for Hirae. At least on her horse she had breathing space above the press of people. On foot she felt as though she was drowning. The only thing she could be grateful for was the way the crowds respectfully fell back as they saw the Overlord's yellow livery approaching. If they had been delayed on these busy streets by the crush of crowd, Hirae would have been frantic. Trying to regulate her breathing, she felt Sionan's hand take hers and squeeze her palm gently with reassurance. Surprised and unused to human contact, she was unsure how to respond, but realised the friendly gesture of the smaller hand in hers made her feel calmer. She smiled gratefully at the girl, asking herself who was protecting whom as the Spire loomed ever closer.

The streets opened out onto a wide, tree-lined avenue; cobbles gave way to beautiful, natural stone. The magnificence of the Spire was awe-inspiring as the red from the last rays of sun glittered from the tall building. As the structure rose from the ground, it dazzled the eye, becoming thinner and thinner towards the point, so fine it almost seemed to be moving in the breeze. It was a ground-breaking piece of architecture. However, the Overlord's extravagance had been a source of division amongst dukes and common folk alike. Some people revelled in its glory and felt it made their lands more supreme. Others felt the level of taxation to fund its rise from the ground too extreme. None could doubt the impact it had on both those from the Overlord's lands and dignitaries visiting from other principalities. Here, displayed in stone, was the wealth and power the Overlord could call upon. A clear and present reminder for anyone of the prosperity of the Principality of the four Manors.

The group were ushered through a marble arch to pass carefully manicured gardens with soft fountains trickling water. The guards took them along a small walkway towards the Spire rather than via the main entrance. The peaceful solitude in the beautiful grounds was remarkable after the bustle of the main streets. Moving through the gardens, they saw birds of all varieties flitting through the bushes, and Hirae was intrigued to gaze upon bird and plant life she had never seen before in all her travels across the Manors. Way above their heads there was netting of the finest silk keeping the birds within the Spire's gardens.

A stout gate closed behind them in the archway as they made their way into the building. The coolness was marked after the warmth of the evening rays of sun in the garden. Five of the guards remained outside the small doorway.

'Follow me,' the sergeant instructed, leading them further into the circular building. The walls curled away, with no corners around the hallway. The flowing corridor was interrupted only by fine, marble statues and artwork along the curved wall.

They were bought to a white ornate arched door inlaid with gold in the shape of a wolf. The heraldic sign of the Overlord.

'Wait here,' the sergeant instructed.

Hirae and Sionan fidgeted as they stood waiting. The only person who looked relaxed in the formal setting was Chancer. All the walls and adornments were cool colours of white and pastel shades. Everything about the Spire radiated calm and control, but the effect was lost on the two women. After what felt like an interminable wait, the door opened to a young man dressed in the yellow heraldic tunic of the Overlord.

'Please hand your arms to the guard. They will remain outside. I assure you that your weapons will be perfectly safe.'

Chancer followed the request immediately, Hirae and Sionan following his lead. The guard stood heavily laden with their knives and Chancer's sword. Sionan removed the small box from her travel sack, feeling strangely as though the patterns on the box were writhing under her hand. The remainder of the sack she handed to the guard.

'What is in the box?' the herald asked.

'A gift that the Overlord is expecting,' Chancer smoothly responded.

Satisfied, the herald gestured the three to follow him into the room, and closed the door behind them.

They stood in a light, airy, circular room with a soft, pink-white wash on the walls. Most striking was that there was only one piece of furniture, a modest oak throne on a raised dais to the rear of the circular room. They were clearly in the Overlord's private audience chamber. Behind the throne was another door, presumably to the Overlord's private quarters. Hatchen stood, armed with a sword, beside the throne, and Chancer would bet numerous other weapons discreetly placed around his person. Chancer had no doubt there were other armed personnel within close proximity should any foul play be suspected. He did not acknowledge Hatchen. No one spoke, all knowing inherently that they should wait for the Overlord's arrival. This was a formal audience, not a time for idle chatter.

As the door behind the throne opened, everyone drew themselves tighter and taller to receive the scrutiny of the ruler of their lands.

Like a flash of sunlight, the Overlord entered in flowing primrose-yellow robes. Chancer looked upon the countenance of the monarch. The woman was like marble, her face giving away nothing. Despite being of similar age to Chancer, her skin was still smooth, and her eyes a light pink in hue. It was reported that the Overlord's eyes could see directly inside you to find the truth of any falsehood spoken. Her hair was pure white but for a hint of colour reflected from the fine silken threads of her golden robe. She had one adornment: the Chain of the monarchy, golden, with large links, and a blood-red stone shaped like a large teardrop.

The Overlord placed herself upon the throne and looked at the three intently. 'So, Captain Landry, you return to us after all these years with a gift and a tale of woe against one of my most favoured dukes. Speak all, so that I may listen and judge the truth of your accusations.'

Chancer bowed deeply in response and stepped towards the throne. His voice rang out calmly as he spoke. The Overlord listened as Chancer recounted all that had befallen them from the first moment Kayton initially located him in Ascalion, which felt like a lifetime ago. Completing his description of events, Chancer bowed and stepped back.

Silence fell in the room, broken only by the quiet drumming of the Overlord's fingers on the arm of the throne.

The Overlord turned to Sionan. 'Speak of what happened to you. I am interested to hear more about these sorcerous powers Captain Landry alludes to. Speak truly and without exaggeration.' The Overlord leaned forward, and fixed Sionan with a penetrating stare. 'Know that I will see any falsehood in your heart.'

Sionan bowed to the Overlord, and brought her arms forward to show the dark wooden box which contrasted starkly with the light in the room. 'Overlord,' she said reverently.

'This is the star-stone which I saw Duke Gelanson use to turn my hair to grey and strip the youth from my body. His own body became younger as he completed this sorcery. Then I saw, with my own eyes, Gelanson put life into a limb...' Her voice choked on the words. '...My father's arm... it twitched with life.' Sionan's voice rose with emotion as she struggled to contain her feelings. 'It is not only us who speaks of this atrocity to nature. I saw another girl, Leetha, the bakers' daughter, die with a star-shaped wound. Her parents have travelled to attend your Justice Day.'

The Overlord turned her head to look to Hatchen, who nodded in response.

'Majesty, these bakers do appear to be on the plaintiff list for Justice Day tomorrow.'

The Overlord leaned back into her throne, considering all she had been told. 'This is an interesting quandary indeed. One of my most loyal dukes accused of acts against the crown. If the Duke of Clasterne truly has these powers, they should have been declared for the good of the Principality.' The Overlord turned to Hirae, assessing her with an analytical gaze. 'And do you have anything to add?'

'Only to confirm that they speak the truth and to request your justice upon the duke so that the people of Clasterne can live freely without fear for their lives,' Hirae said. '... Majesty,' she quickly added; showing a lack of respect for the ruling classes was not an item to add into the mix at this delicate stage.

'Show me the stone,' the Overlord commanded.

'It may be dangerous, majesty' Chancer said. 'We do not know how this artefact works.'

'I am pleased with your concern for my being, Captain Landry. However, I will have all the facts before I make my decision.' She turned to Sionan, and gestured for her to open the box.

The group tensed as Sionan opened the lid. The star-stone nestled in the silk lining of the box. The Overlord stepped down from her throne. She looked closely at the stone and then into Sionan's eyes.

'Interesting. The stone matches the exact green of your eyes.'

Chancer realised that none of them had mentioned to the Overlord the change that had overcome Sionan after Kayton's death. He tried to catch her eye to warn her not to say anything.

The Overlord lifted the stone from the box, and turned it carefully with her delicate, white hands. 'Such an unassuming jewel to provide such great power. And you say you do not know how to activate this in any way?'

'I do not recall the words the duke was chanting, , but there were many scrolls and books in his research room.'

'Forgive me for speaking, majesty,' Chancer interjected. 'Would we not be better destroying the stone so that its power is never used?'

'Captain Landry, you know little of the struggle the crown faces each day to maintain peaceful lands. Understand that the monarchy will take the best decision for the good of all.'

Chancer bowed in acceptance of the rebuke for his interruption. Who was he to question the ruler of the Principality?

'Hatchen,' announced the Overlord. 'Take the stone and

place it in our safe keep. You three will return tomorrow for Justice Day, where I will hear the bakers' account. You will speak to no one on this matter. To ensure your safety, my guard will remain stationed at your dwelling.'

The Overlord turned and all three bowed deeply as she swept from the room, exiting by the door near the throne. Hatchen stepped forwards to retrieve the box from Sionan, and then followed the Overlord through the exit.

Once the door had closed, the three stood looking at each other uncertainly.

Sionan felt strangely bereft without the stone, as though a future of possibilities had just been closed to her. Hirae and Chancer exchanged a pointed look. Things had not gone as they had hoped. There was no clear signal from the Overlord that the monarch believed their account. Sionan started to speak, but Hirae shook her head at her, gesturing towards the closed door. Sionan tried to ignore the nagging unease gnawing at her insides.

The herald arrived to usher them back to the white entrance door, where the guard returned their weapons. In silence, they strapped them back on before they were escorted back to the inn. Sionan's thoughts whirled with doubts as to whether they had done the right thing in handing over the stone.

Reaching the inn, the guard remained stationed at the bottom of the stairs, and the three trudged up the steps to their loft space. Closing the door firmly, Hirae crossed the room to ensure all the windows were closed.

Finally satisfied that no one could overhear them, Chancer spoke. 'Thoughts?'

Hirae shrugged. 'There is little else we can do. For good or ill, we decided to trust the power of the crown, and that is what we must do. I don't think there's any way Gelanson can retrieve the stone from the monarch.'

'And I don't doubt the Overlord will move to have Gelanson's scrolls and workbooks recovered for the crown, which will surely remove more of the duke's power,' Chancer added.

'Do you think she knows about my eyes changing colour?' Sionan asked nervously. 'When those pale pink eyes rested on me, I felt that she could see into my very core.'

'Doubtful,' Hirae responded. 'No one knows you here. I don't see any point in bringing that up, it's not relevant to Gelanson's guilt.'

'And until we have some idea of why they changed colour, there really isn't anything to tell,' Chancer added. 'We are safer now than we have been,' Chancer continued. 'There are guards outside, we are clean and fed. I say we get some sleep. Tomorrow will come soon enough.'

'Are those guards there to keep us safe or to stop us from talking to anyone?' Hirae asked caustically.

Chancer frowned at Hirae for voicing her concern in front of Sionan, who was now looking anxiously towards the door.

'Either way, it's not safe for us to go out anywhere. If we're stuck here, I for one am going to take the time to rest.' Chancer removed his boots and propped his sword by the bedstead and lay down, closing his eyes.

'Chancer's right on that score, Sionan,' Hirae said. 'There is nothing more to be done today, best to rest and hope for justice tomorrow.'

Sionan managed a brave smile in response and moved to lay down, as always taking her cue from Chancer as soon as she saw he was settled.

Hirae sat on her bed listening to the sound of the revelry growing in the taproom as the night drew in. Hirae wished she could have her companion's solid, unwavering faith in the crown. Even after all that had happened, they were willing to place their trust in someone from the noble classes to resolve everything. Hirae had seen the monarch only once before, on the Overlord's triumphant return from the Ascalion campaign. At the audience today, she had looked like an alabaster carving; her skin flawless and rose-pink eyes bright with intellect. Hirae shifted, her discomfort reflecting the doubts she felt. Likely the concerns were caused by her general distaste for the noble classes.

As the night deepened, she heard the guards quietly changing watch. Determined not to allow the guards stationed outside to lull them into a false sense of security, she remained watchful and alert. Despite Hirae's best intentions, the arduous journey and anxiety from walking through the busy streets soon took its toll and her head fell forward as she lost the battle to remain awake.

Just as she was dropping off to sleep, a niggling doubt crept into the back of her mind. Something in the audience with the Overlord had not been quite right, but she could not quite pull the idea to the fore as she drifted into a fitful sleep.

CHAPTER TWENTY-SEVEN

Sionan woke first, feeling refreshed and hopeful. The reluctance she'd felt at handing over the star-stone had been followed by a strange sensation of loss, as though the stone belonged with her, but now the feeling had evaporated into relief that someone in the highest position of power had listened to their story and believed them. The Overlord had restored peace to the lands after the Ascalion rebellion, and that peace had been maintained for ten years. People had prospered. Sionan had only to keep her faith that justice would be meted out to Gelanson as well.

Quietly moving around the room, she stepped behind the screen to use the washstand and to dress. She felt rested in a way she hadn't since the horrific day when her father had been killed. The sunlight coming through the small loft windows bathed the room in a soft glow, adding to her feeling of positivity. Today was the day when everything would be made right.

Hirae jerked upright, scowling. Unhappy that she had fallen asleep, she was even less happy that she had not awakened when Sionan was moving around the room. Her senses felt dulled without Scase by her side, and she realised how heavily she had come to rely on the dog. A sharp pang of guilt for leaving him lanced through her. She sat up, hopeful that today they would at least have a final resolution. There would be no more running. The Overlord would judge them guilty as rebels or, balanced against Gelanson's evil, she would judge their behaviour acceptable. Either way, Hirae resolved with fatal determination, she would be leaving Atipac today or die trying.

Chancer woke last. He had dreamt of all the banquets and festivities that had occurred in Atipac after the Ascalion rebellion was squashed, the Overlord ever present and smiling warmly at her subjects in their time of victory. Sighing, he got up and pulled his boots on.

'Let's breakfast in the taproom,' he suggested.

Hirae looked steadily at him, making no comment.

'Just breakfast,' Chancer retorted, feeling irritated with her constantly watching him.

'I could eat a horse,' Sionan interjected. Out of the three she was the only one who looked fully refreshed and ready for the day.

'Let's go, then,' Hirae agreed.

Leaving the room, the trio walked with purpose, the knowledge that today would bring an end to their search for justice spurring them on. Gelanson's sorcery would be exposed and the truth would be heard. How the day would close, they could not know, but each of them knew a resolution, or at least an ending was fast approaching to their journey.

The group entered the inn and requested breakfast from Reaser. Platters of sausage, cheese, and bread quickly arrived, and the group ate quietly, talking in hushed tones about the day ahead.

Hirae left Sionan and Chancer to finish their breakfast and walked to the counter. Keeping her thoughts to herself but quietly questioning if they would return to the inn at all, she decided it would be better to settle up now. Hirae paid Reaser for the food, lodging, stabling, and shoeing the horses. Their money was now exhausted, and Reaser was clearly delighted to receive it, announcing that on this one occasion he could tell his husband he was right to have let Chancer and his friends stay. Whistling a merry tune, Reaser cleared their breakfast plates and waved a sunny goodbye to the three as they left the taproom.

'We will ride to the Spire today,' Hirae announced firmly to the troop of guards in the courtyard. If they were not prisoners, she was determined not to subject herself to that walk again. At least on a horse she could see above the heads of the people.

'As you wish,' the sergeant replied.

Collecting their horses from the stables, Chancer commented that they looked in better shape already after their rest and grain-feed. Saddling them up with the assistance of Yanie, the stable lad, he led them out. Hirae and Sionan joined him after packing their few belongings back into their travel packs. Today, Sionan sat her horse like a fine lady as her positive conviction about the outcome of the day shone from her. She smiled warmly at the guards who, without realising, smiled back. The openness of her happiness infected those around her.

They rode to the Spire along the main thoroughfare. The guards guided them along a huge avenue flanked by stone statues of all manner of creatures. The workmanship was so fine it looked as though the sculptures could come to life and climb off their plinths at any moment. The formal approach to the Spire was carefully laid out to inspire awe and reverence for the monarch. Its walls reflected a pearlescent, warm pink in the morning sun.

Despite the early hour, a long queue of people under the shade of canvas shelters stood waiting patiently to be heard, although the queue was still heavily patrolled to maintain the peace. Those who were not seen on this occasion would be given a token to present at the next Justice Day to ensure they were first in line. However, they eyed the new arrivals with annoyance, knowing that anyone escorted by guards would be seen before them.

As the horses moved onwards towards the main archway, Sionan drew a breath in wonder at the exquisite flowers carved into the marble. Everything about Atipac entranced her. She imagined her sisters' faces when they saw all this beauty and hope blossomed in her heart for the future.

The guards halted inside the main archway, and a stable hand appeared to take the three horses. Hirae was relieved at how much easier the ride had been. She'd felt like she had room to breathe. If they were allowed to leave the court, she was glad the horses would be here waiting for them.

A tall, thin herald with a serious face ushered them swiftly via a grand entrance into a long, curved corridor. Again, the building gave the sense that there was no beginning or end, its constantly flowing loops spiralling and rising to the sky. The guards did not follow them inside, but remained stationed outside the entrance. The trio were taken to a small comfortable room with chairs, food and drink, and some books on a small shelf. On a table was a gaming board with pieces set out inviting people to play. It seemed every item had been thought of to keep them occupied as they waited on the pleasure of the Overlord.

'A game?' Sionan queried, impressed by the waiting room.

Hirae had to bite her tongue to keep from answering harshly. *Does she not realise our own lives could be forfeit today?*

'A game,' Chancer agreed, smiling. As they settled to the table to play, Hirae paced the room like a caged animal. 'Enough, Hirae,' Chancer said. 'You stalking the room will not allow us to be seen any sooner. We must be patient.'

Noticing Chancer had not stopped tapping his feet on the floor – a less obvious, but equally clear sign, of nervous energy. Hirae realised she was not the only one concerned about today; he was just covering it better.

In a flash of clarity, she knew he was right. They'd tightened the noose around their own necks when they'd decided to come to the Overlord rather than running. Now they had to wait calmly and see if the noose would be removed. The fact that Sionan was apparently not aware of the threat astonished Hirae, but she knew she should not awaken fear in the girl.

As they whiled the hours away, they could hear doors opening and closing as various plaintiffs were brought before the monarch. On occasion they heard the shouting of obscenities when a judgement had not gone as wished, swiftly followed by the sound of someone being manhandled down the corridor.

Finally, the herald returned. 'Please remove your weapons and leave them in this room. The Overlord will see you now.'

Sionan shot to standing. In her haste she knocked over the gaming board that she and Chancer had been trying to focus on. She bent to start picking the pieces up.

'Please leave that,' said the herald. 'It will be attended to. The monarch must not be kept waiting.'

'Of course, of course,' Sionan flustered in response. She removed her knives and left them on the table next to the other weapons. Smoothing her trousers and tunic, she realised how crumpled they were. Yesterday she had felt on top of the world after bathing and wearing clean clothes. Today she recognised how threadbare and worn they were, and wished she had one of the beautiful sets of clothing her parents made. As a tailor's daughter, she fully understood the power of clothing to give confidence and gravitas to the wearer.

'Trust in the truth,' Hirae said to her, as she strode out of the door to follow the herald. Chancer gave Sionan's shoulder a reassuring squeeze.

Chancer waited for Hirae and Sionan to leave the room before following the herald. As they walked, he judged the distance back to the entrance and on to where their horses were stabled. It was an unconscious action to plan their escape and catalogue the number of guards standing beside each door.

A large set of imposing doors at the end of the corridor stood before them. The doors held none of the ornate carvings they had seen in other areas of the Spire. These were a solid, functional reminder that people entered or left at the Overlord's behest. A full complement of guards lined the open doors, six on each side, fully armed and ready to step in as needed. As the companions entered the imposing room, the doors were pulled shut firmly behind them.

Chancer winced as he heard a heavy lock being put in place. The last time he had been in this Great Hall it had been filled to the brim with celebrating revellers, the room gaily decorated with garlands of flowers. Now in the cavernous room there was only a row of soldiers, armed with sword and shield, standing alert along each wall. The dais at the end of the room held the formal throne used for ceremonious events made of a beautiful, deep-red wood and adorned with yellow cushions. To the left of the throne was another smaller seating area where visiting nobles could view the proceedings. Four of the Overlord's closest advisors filled these chairs. Hatchen stood discreetly behind the throne.

'Captain Landry, Sionan Hellard, and Hirae Stasone. Plaintiffs from Clasterne seeking the Overlord's ruling on this Justice Day.'

As the echoes of the herald's voice bounced around the vaulted ceiling of the room, Sionan realised she had never known Hirae's family name. She spotted the slightest wink from Hirae to her and tamped down a smile. She wondered if Stasone was Hirae's true surname and resolved to discover this later. Glad of the lightness this little conspiratorial wink brought to her heart, she felt the tension in her body ease.

The three bowed deeply, waiting with eyes lowered for the Overlord to speak. They could hear another door opening at the far end of the room and the sound of booted feet entering and crossing the dais to the seating on the left of the Overlord. Chancer resisted the urge to look up, knowing they must remain in this position until the Overlord was ready.

'Approach.' The monarch's powerful voice rang around the room.

As they straightened to move forward, their eyes were yet again drawn to the beauty of the pale woman sat on the throne. Today, the Overlord's robe was the traditional grey of judgment, the colour reflective of the solemnity of the occasion. The robe pooled around the base of the throne; the silken fabric, so fine it shone like moonlight on water, reflecting the light that streamed through the windows. Her Chain of Office sparkled in the light, the red stone reflecting the pink of her eyes. The Sceptre of Judgment was held lightly in her hand and stood the full height of the throne.

The tall golden ornament adorned with red rubies was the most wealth Sionan had ever seen in a single object in one place and her eyes widened at the sight of it. The object must have been heavy, but the Overlord held it lightly as though it was no more than a willow walking stick.

The herald guided them forwards to stand in front of the throne, and then a familiar voice came from the left as a man walked towards them.

'My dear, we have all been so worried about you.'

Sionan felt tendrils of fear clamp her gut as she struggled to come to terms with who faced them. Gelanson smiled charmingly, resplendent in a green tunic which highlighted the amethyst stone in his own Chain of Office.

Hirae and Chancer immediately moved to block the duke's

path. Sionan's mind screamed at her to run as Gelanson bore down on her.

'So, this is the one, Duke Gelanson?' the Overlord asked, ignoring the defensive formation taken by Chancer and Hirae.

The duke paused, eyeing Hirae and Chancer with distaste. 'Yes, majesty. It grieves me deeply that you have been so troubled by my Manor's small, local difficulties. As you can see, the girl is not well. She is only two score years and already looks all of four score. We are afflicted by a terrible wasting disease, but I am placing all my resources into curing this, sire.'

Chancer and Hirae looked at each other, knowing they had no chance of fighting their way out – they were unarmed and outnumbered by the highly trained guards lining the walls.

'I'll not be imprisoned,' Hirae murmured. They both knew the confinement of a cell would kill Hirae far less kindly than a sword thrust.

'Nor I,' Chancer responded quietly, his eyes darting from Gelanson to the guards and desperately searching for a way out.

'I'm sorry to have brought you to this, my friend,' he said. Hirae simply snorted in reply, and Chancer grinned. Even in these dire times, she would not share emotional words with him.

Sionan continued to stand in shock, her eyes locked on Gelanson.

'Be seated, Duke Gelanson,' the Overlord commanded. 'We must go through due process of the Principality's law and assess all the information.'

The duke paused in his stride, his smile held firmly in place while inside he raged at the stupid woman's interruption. His carriage had ridden all day and night after staying in the awful peasant farmstead. They had made it to Atipac as the first rays of light were dawning on the horizon. It was intolerable that he was being subjected to any scrutiny at all in front of these rebels.

At the Overlord's request for him to be seated, he bowed to the throne and returned to his comfortable, if gratingly small, seat below the monarch.

Behind the duke's chair Stegen stood watching the proceedings, her eyes never leaving Chancer and Hirae, as though she could bore a hole through them and kill them with the strength of her hatred.

'Today we have a closed hearing of plaintiffs from the Manor of Clasterne and Duke Gelanson of Clasterne,' the herald announced, his voice ringing clearly around the room. 'All items discussed in our court will remain private to the Throne and the chosen advisors present today. As is written in the Principality law, no party is above scrutiny. Through this fair and just system we maintain peace in the lands. Let us hear from all parties before the ruling of our wise Monarch is bestowed.'

The Overlord indicated to the herald to signal to the guards, who ushered an older couple into the room. Sionan smiled in welcome and relief as she recognised the bakers, who shared a tentative smile as they looked fearfully around the intimidating chamber.

'Sire, plaintiffs from Clasterne also seeking a ruling from

the Overlord on the same matter.'

Gelanson's jaw twitched as the couple approached the throne.

The fear in the hardworking bakers was apparent as they walked with visibly shaking legs. As the Overlord stared down at them, they stood like frightened rabbits caught in the stare of a fox. It was only when they noticed the duke that their fear could be seen draining from them to be replaced by anger.

'Speak and provide all the information you can,' the herald instructed.

And speak they did.

The husband spoke eloquently about his fears for his daughter and how they were barred from seeing their own child. He spoke of their disbelief and dismay, turning to anger at being unable to care for their only daughter during her time of sickness and his subsequent imprisonment. The Overlord encouraged him to continue. As he spoke of the loss of his daughter, his words became choked with grief.

Gelanson walked over to the couple and attempted to place his hands on the wife's shoulder in a show of compassion. The couple stiffened in horror, and their step back away from the duke was obvious to the court. Gelanson tried to cover their actions smoothly with concerned words, his melodic voice radiating around the chamber like a lullaby of empathy.

'I am deeply saddened by the loss of any life in my Manor, sire. You can see how this terrible wasting disease is bringing grief to all. The prison sentence was merely to stop this man's rebellious words leading him to a traitorous action where a more severe penalty would have been imposed. I deemed it prudent to provide a cautionary warning before things became out of hand.'

'A wise approach, Duke Gelanson,' said the Overlord. 'It is always better to douse the sparks before a flame can form.'

The duke bowed. 'Thank you, sire. Please let me request again that we speak about these matters privately. All can easily be explained without putting these poor people through the anguish of recounting the events of their daughter's tragic death.'

'*Murderer!*' the wife screamed, the word echoing throughout the chamber. Exploding in fury, she lunged at Gelanson, whether her intention was to hit or push the man away, no one was certain, but the highly trained guards were already moving to intercede at the first sign of motion. They held her back, and when her husband tried to pull the guards from his wife, he was also easily restrained.

The Overlord banged the sceptre on the dais once. The heavy thud reverberated around the great hall and caused all movement to cease. She spoke calmly into the silence.

'Duke Gelanson, you understand the Justice laws as well as all my nobles. All people of the Principality have the right to request the Overlord's ruling.' She enunciated the words in clipped fashion, clearly becoming impatient with the way the hearing was proceeding. Then she turned to the bakers, who were still restrained. 'Whilst the Throne is saddened to hear of your daughter's death, and we grieve with you, violence in front of your monarch is not tolerated. Due to your grief you will receive leniency for your outburst today. You will serve thirty days' forced labour. Your accusations of the duke have been heard, but you have lost your right to be present for the remainder of the hearing.'

The wife moaned in anguish as her husband looked on in shock. Sionan mirrored their look of disbelief as the couple were forcibly removed. A small triumphant smile played across the duke's face as the bakers' protests faded into the distance.

'Bring forth the star-stone,' the Overlord instructed, watching Gelanson as Hatchen walked to the throne and placed the box on a small table. Gelanson tried unsuccessfully to disguise the avarice in his eyes at the closeness of the precious star-stone.

'It appears we cannot open this box,' the Overlord said.

'Of course, sire, please allow me—' The duke eagerly stepped forwards to open the wooden container.

'No,' interceded the Overlord. 'Hellard, you may open it for us.'

The duke rested back into his chair, surprise evident on his features. Sionan, legs quaking, walked towards the throne and placed a trembling hand on the box. The click of the lock echoed in the chamber along with Gelanson's swiftly indrawn breath. The Overlord watched with interest as Sionan gazed on the stone, her eyes reflecting its deep green of the stone… or was the stone reflecting the green of her eyes?

The creaking of chairs could be heard as the advisors craned forwards to try to catch a glimpse.

'An interesting artefact indeed,' the Overlord said. 'Hellard, for the benefit of my advisors, speak of your experiences of this item at the hands of the duke.'

Chancer and Hirae flanked Sionan in reassurance as she addressed the court. However, only Sionan had witnessed the star-stone at work, and only she could speak of Gelanson's dark experiments. She tried to speak, her voice croaking uncomfortably, a large ball of anxiety blocking her throat. Having seen how the bakers' testimony had been received, she felt her faith in the Overlord's justice tattering to threads around her. The awareness of the depth of her naivety hit her like a crippling blow. It was her word against the duke's, and she was only the daughter of a tailor.

Mechanically, Sionan recited all to the court. The advisors craned forwards to listen avidly, her words nearly drowned out by the startled whispering at the talk of sorcery. In living memory of the four Manors, there had been no reports of powers such as this. She could feel their disbelief wash over her. Their whispering battered at her resolve.

'The girl's mind has turned…'

'What foolish notions are these to lay at the Overlord's door…?'

As Sionan's words drew to a shuddering halt, dizziness swept over her. She had said all she could to gain justice for Kayton, her family, and everyone who had suffered at Gelanson's hand. Chancer placed an arm around her to steady her and she gratefully took the offered support as she looked directly into the Overlord's pink eyes, beseeching her to believe.

The Overlord waited for silence. 'Duke Gelanson, you have informed me yourself of the powers of this stone. The questions I am considering are whether you are at fault for not declaring this astonishing ability to the Throne, and by what right you are treating this *wasting disease* without the input of healers from the Spire. If this disease was to become widely spread, there could be serious ramifications for the Principality.'

The duke stood to face the Overlord and bowed. 'I will, of course, accept any ruling deemed appropriate, sire. Please know that I was only trying to discover more knowledge, which would have been shared with Atipac as soon as I had reliably refined my work.' He paused, mind racing. He simply must have access to the girl at all costs; his desire to study her power was more important than all of his previous ambitions. 'If the crown would allow me permission to proceed with treating Hellard with the stone, I am confident I can cure her madness. I will provide a written report on progress each week for the throne's consideration.'

'Liar!' Sionan shouted. 'There is no disease but what you have given me!' Her frustration welled up, threatening to overwhelm her. Hirae placed a calming hand on her shoulder.

'Silence!' The Overlord's voice thundered from the throne. 'It is the crown's consideration that Hellard should not return to Clasterne but will remain in the Spire where we can study this disease and provide due care. We must determine how much of a threat the disease is to our people.'

Sionan's jaw dropped in horror.

How have I not foreseen this?

'Chancer…' she whispered, his name a talisman to ward off danger.

The Overlord indicated to the guards to remove Sionan from the Throne room, and then the duke's frustration erupted.

'You fool! Do you think *you* have the power here?' Gelanson spat the words with disdain directly at the Overlord. 'I will no longer tolerate the mockery of this hearing, nor the interruption of my study of the girl!'

He lunged forwards for the star-stone and almost had it, but Hatchen grabbed his arm at the same moment the duke's fingers touched the stone. Gelanson spun and pressed the stone against Hatchen's bare hand. Immediately, the hair-raising melody of the duke's chanting spread around the room with sinister promise. Sionan felt her hackles rise as she recognised the cadence of the words. Within the space of a breath, Hatchen dropped to the floor unconscious, felled like a tree. His body withered to that of an old man closer to death than life. Gelanson appeared to grow taller as he sucked in the very life from Hatchen. He turned contemptuously to face the Overlord, who stood stock-still, regal fury emanating from her presence. Chancer and Hirae ran towards the dais, closing on Gelanson as the guards also raced to intercept the duke.

Time seemed to slow. Sionan felt every heartbeat as Gelanson emitted the binding chant. Smoke billowed from his mouth, and his words penetrated the atmosphere. Like a pestilence in a wound, seeping and infecting the whole body, the cloudy miasma vomited out and spread. Chaos reigned as advisors and nobles leapt from their seats to frantically back-pedal from the mist. Overturning their chairs in their haste to escape, some almost made it to the large doors at the end of the hall.

Gelanson revelled in his new power – never had he drained someone so completely or quickly. The life stolen from Hatchen seemed to glow vibrantly from within, making the duke taller and stronger. Youth flowed through his veins again. The ecstasy of power made him incandescent as he raised his arms to guide the fog throughout the room. The guards, some gritting their teeth in agony and others grunting with effort, were trying to move through the mist. Slowly, one by one, they froze in place like the marble statues that lined the avenue to the Spire.

The duke, satisfied with his work, spoke directly to the Overlord.

'I no longer have the time nor inclination to allow this farce to continue. I am the true power in the Principality, and the Instinctual is *mine!*' Gelanson pointed to Sionan, and then looked for Stegen. He noted with pleasure that the fog had responded to his desire that the captain be unaffected.

'Grab the girl. With her mother dead and sisters lost, we cannot allow her to escape again.'

'*Dead?*' Sionan echoed, immobile with shock.

Stegen paused at hearing Gelanson's instructions; her loyalty to the duke was one thing, but treason against the throne quite another. Her moment's hesitation allowed Chancer and Hirae to close the remaining gap, struggling with all their fighting strength against the immobilising mist.

Hirae reached touching distance and made a desperate grab for the duke but, faster than a snake, he struck, grabbed her arm, and pressed the star-stone to it.

Chancer looked on in anger, his feet no longer moving as he bid them. He was so close, but the icy tendrils worked their way up his body and caused his breath to catch in his throat. His fear for Hirae drove him forward one more step before he collapsed, clattering to the floor like a broken toy.

'I'll kill you,' Chancer rasped as the mist constricted his throat and he gasped for breath. 'I swear, I will kill you!'

The Overlord, a statue enshrouded in wispy fog, looked on

in anger as her hearing room fell completely under Gelanson's control.

'You will pay for your treachery,' she hissed at the duke as the sceptre dropped from her now frozen hands. The golden staff clanged to the floor and rolled down the dais steps. One by one, each metallic clang tolled like a bell announcing doom as the Principality's symbol of justice fell to the stone floor.

'Your small mind cannot even conceive the greatness I aspire to,' Gelanson replied with disgust. He viewed the frozen people in the room with satisfaction. Never had he used the dark arts against so many people. The triumph of discovery sent thrills racing along his spine. After today, there would be no need to hide his work in the shadows. The freedom was invigorating, although already he felt his body tiring as the mist started to dissipate. He weighed up the number of people he had controlled against the life-force taken from the collapsed Hatchen. Then his eyes turned to Hirae held immobile in his grasp, a fresh source of energy right at his fingertips.

Hirae's muscles bunched and screamed against the bonds of Gelanson's sorcery as she fought to free herself. Although his grasp was not strong, the miasma of fog held her frozen. When she looked into his eyes, she saw only her death reflected there. She tried to ram her head against the bridge of his nose to break his hold, but found her head barely moved. She could only watch as the duke smiled chillingly at her.

'You are a strong warrior. I'm going to enjoy your taking your life-spirit,' Gelanson said. 'All this time I have used petty servants and townsfolk, when clearly my experiments should have been focused on stronger specimens.' He bared his teeth in a weird parody of a grin before whispering the incantation that would end Hirae's life.

Hirae stared at him. Sadness that she would not see Scase again overwhelmed her as she felt her limbs grow weak.

Sionan watched as Gelanson grabbed Hirae, his earlier words still reverberating in her head.

Her mother was dead, dead, *dead*.

When Sionan saw Gelanson start to drain Hirae's energy, something inside her broke like a bowstring drawn too tight, snapping under pressure. A power unlike anything Sionan had ever felt surged through her body. Her only thought was that, no matter the cost to herself, in this moment, in this room, she would save her friends. She would not fail them as she had Kayton, her father, and now her mother as well. Her whole being raged at the injustice Gelanson had inflicted. Her eyes lit like fire with unnatural brightness and she walked steadily towards the duke.

Gelanson, so focused on the ecstasy of extracting life from Hirae, did not notice the shadow moving across the room and up the dais.

Stegen saw the Instinctual approach and moved reflexively back, away from the sickly green light shining in the girl's eyes and the macabre scene playing out on the podium.

The fog seemed to curl lovingly around Sionan rather than slowing her. Tendrils caressed her body and lifted her silvery hair on a non-existent breeze. From deep inside, Sionan spoke, barely recognising her own voice that rang low with the mastery of power.

'No more. I release all you have stolen!'

There was a brief moment of confusion in Gelanson's eyes

that changed to fear as Sionan's words resounded with deadly promise. Sionan placed an ice-cold hand above Gelanson's over the star-stone. In that catastrophic moment, the duke realised the gravity of his error.

Why did I not consider that this girl could already have grown more powerful than me? A terrified scream was torn from his throat as he felt the life-force being ripped from his body.

Hirae took a gasping breath, fell backwards from Gelanson's weakened grasp, and immediately felt her strength return, in the same moment, Hatchen slowly returned to wakefulness, his years returning as his skin plumped out, wrinkles disappeared, and his hair returned to rusty brown.

'Please stop!' Gelanson begged, voice cracking with age.

But Sionan did not stop.

'Stop!' Gelanson pleaded. 'I can help you understand what is happening to you! I can teach you!'

But still Sionan did not stop, , watching coldly as Gelanson aged at a horrifying rate. Clasping her hand more tightly on to the duke, she leaned in.

'*This* is for my family,' she whispered.

Gelanson stared at her in wild-eyed terror, dropping to his knees as his strength failed. Without his power to maintain the mist, the room cleared. The insidious fog faded and dissipated into nothing.

Sionan watched impassively as the duke – now a withered, white haired ancient, a mere husk of a human – crumpled to the floor.

Chancer, released from his bonds, swiftly ran to Sionan and Hirae, but they no longer needed his protection. The three looked at the decayed form of Gelanson on the floor, his body no longer able to support life as he struggled to draw breath. Gelanson's eyes never left Sionan, his gaze reflecting the disbelief at his altered state.

'What power…' he wheezed in envy.

As the trio looked down at the elderly man who had wrought such terror and destruction, there was no remorse or regret in any of their features. They watched as Gelanson toiled to take another breath.

'For Kayton,' Sionan rasped, clasping her hand tightly on Gelanson's, the edges of the star-stone cutting into her palm. She focused on drawing out his final spark of life.

Slowly, a shudderingly drawn breath was released from Gelanson and he collapsed onto the dais – dead – all the years he had stolen released from his body.

'It's done,' Sionan said.

She looked at the stone in her palm, now tinged with blood where it had cut her skin. Chancer closed his arms around her in an embrace while Sionan wondered just what she had become. All the weeks of hardship, fear, and flight were distilled down into this one moment in the Spire in the centre of Atipac.

'It's over, Sionan. You freed your people from Gelanson's tyranny,' Chancer said earnestly, the pride in his voice touching Sionan's heart. Chancer stepped back and they gazed on Gelanson's withered corpse, wondering what peace his death would bring.

Despite the youth returned to Hatchen, who was levering himself up from the floor, and Hirae, who now looked younger than her years, Sionan still looked the same, with her silvered hair and green eyes.

'We are free of this evil,' Sionan said.

'Time will tell,' Hirae responded quietly. 'Time will tell.'

CHAPTER TWENTY-EIGHT

Morning dawned bright and clear on the following day. The sunshine brought a gift of hope for a new start and peace to heal grieving hearts. Bright light poured through the large windows of the small private audience chamber, giving the room a luminescence as the pearly white walls reflected the daylight.

The Overlord reclined in a chair, looking relaxed and comfortable as she addressed Sionan and Chancer.

'A duke cannot be removed without clearly treasonous actions,' she said, her pink eyes dancing with delight at how events had progressed. Chancer looked at the Overlord, realising how little they had known about the greater game at work in the Manors. 'The duke had been overstepping his boundaries for some time,' the Overlord continued. 'Your plight has thankfully provided the evidence needed to remove him.'

Chancer understood now. Of course, it made perfect sense, the duke must already have been out of favour for them to have been granted an audience at all. Clearly the monarch had already decided Gelanson must go. They had merely provided the necessary means.

'Captain Landry, you will return to Clasterne with my

personal seal and oversee the lands whilst the crown considers who to swear in as the new duke. As Gelanson had no offspring, we will need to review who is the most appropriate out of the wider family of nobility to take on the Manor. When the new duke is in power, you will remain stationed as General of Clasterne Guard, but make no mistake, I will expect you to report to me.'

Sionan laughed with delight at Chancer's befuddled gratitude and confusion; he stood lost for words. How had Kayton brought him from a drunken mess in a rundown bar to becoming a general to the new Duke of Clasterne? That boy's vision for justice had saved not only the town, but transformed Chancer's own life.

He straightened with resolve, surprised at his own relief to have a solid future mapped out before him. 'Thank you, sire,' Chancer replied with a humble bow. 'What of Captain Stegen?'

'We have not yet located Stegen. In the confusion after the...' The Overlord hesitated as she sought the appropriate word. '...Event, she managed to remove herself from the throne room without detection. Nevertheless, I am confident my guards will locate her.' The Overlord poured herself a cup of jasmine tea.

The honour bestowed upon Chancer and Sionan at this private audience with the monarch was not lost on them. She looked resplendent again in a simple sunshine-yellow silk gown, and her red pendant danced in the morning sun. They stood quietly as she delicately sipped at her tea.

'When you return to Clasterne, General Landry, you will see to it that all Gelanson's research work is placed under the protection of the crown and personally ensure its safe transfer to Atipac.'

'Of course, sire,' Chancer replied, getting used to the new sound of "general" being attached to his name. Sionan beamed at him with happiness. Her youth had not returned when she destroyed Gelanson, but the duke's death had alleviated her fear for the future and gave her a lightness of spirit that made her feel young again.

'That brings us to the star-stone,' the Overlord continued, fixing her pink eyes on Sionan. 'We also have the duke's amethyst stone from his chain of office. Interestingly, the stone has changed to a green colour with his death. It now matches the star-stone. My people of science are studying the artefacts as we speak. Hellard, we would invite you to remain in Atipac as our honoured guest, to work with our best minds to understand the power you wield and the secrets the duke unlocked.'

'My sisters!' Sionan interrupted, forgetting court etiquette in her desire to find what remained of her family. 'I must search for my sisters and know what has befallen them.'

'Of course, we will send our best trackers to locate them. Rest assured that your remaining family will be returned to you.'

Sionan's relief was immeasurable. She had no idea where to start looking for her sisters, and no knowledge of how her mother died. The Overlord's assistance would ensure success where she would have floundered.

Sionan looked at Chancer and knew his hope had been that she would return to Clasterne with him, but with her parents dead and siblings scattered to the wind, there was nothing there to return to now. Building a life in Atipac felt like the new start she needed, and maybe in educating herself in the arcane powers with the tuition of the great minds of the city, she could find some method to locate her sisters if the Overlord's trackers were not successful.

She gave Chancer a look of apology, asking for his understanding with her eyes. The small nod he gave her was the acknowledgement she needed, although his shoulders seemed to sag slightly in disappointment.

'I would be delighted to remain in Atipac and support your study of the arts,' Sionan said after a moment, turning back to the Overlord. 'I thank you for your offer to locate my sisters, which I gratefully accept, and beg of you that my siblings are located with every urgency.' Sionan paused. 'I have one favour to ask.'

'Today, you may ask any boon you wish of the crown,' the Overlord replied.

'Please release the bakers from their sentence.'

'Granted,' the Overlord said, quietly surprised that was all that had been asked for, then stood, appraising the two people in front of her. Her sunshine-yellow gown with gold embossed thread glittered. 'And your companion… Hirae? Why has she not attended this audience?' she asked, one eyebrow delicately raised in query.

'Hirae left at first light, majesty.' Chancer scrabbled around for a suitable lie. He couldn't tell the monarch that Hirae desired nothing from the nobility. 'She did not wish to impinge further on your time now that justice has been served.'

Close enough to the truth, Chancer thought.

As the Overlord of the Principality elegantly glided from the room, Chancer wondered if her final words were a kind promise or veiled threat.

'Indeed,' the Overlord replied with a knowing smile. 'We will watch for your friend in the wooded hills.'

EPILOGUE

Out in the forests of Ascalion, a woman roamed with only her large hound for company. Satiated after a successful hunt, the duo sat watching the moon rise to fullness in the night. Hirae scrubbed Scase's head. She felt a pang of regret that she had not said goodbye to Sionan or Chancer, but she had never been one for emotional partings.

After Gelanson's death, her heart had driven her from Atipac in search of Scase before the birds had even broken into their morning song. It had taken some weeks to locate him again. The huge dog bounded and jumped like a puppy when they had been reunited, his joy matched equally by Hirae's. They had travelled steadily west, away from Atipac, enjoying their simple and honest life in the forest.

Hirae watched the moon thoughtfully as she scrubbed the dog's big, square brindle head. He grumbled happily as she scratched his favourite spot behind the left ear.

'Well, my friend, what of the future for us now?'

The dog tilted his head and gave her a serious look. On her travels Hirae had heard the gossip streaking through the taverns and wayside stations about the duke's death and a mysterious girl with silver hair who was now frequently seen at the Overlord's side. People spoke of the girl's emerald-green eyes and the striking counterpart she made to the Overlord's rose-pink gaze. The common folk seemed to delight in tales of the duke's treacherous sorcery and Chancer's rise back to fame. Every person Hirae passed seemed to personally know the new general and have an epic tale about fighting side by side with the daring hero during campaigns.

Standing and stretching, Hirae was pleased that her friends had found happiness and belonging. As she gazed at the ageless beauty of the moon looking down on them, it put her in mind of the Overlord. The uneasy feeling she had felt in Atipac crawled up her spine again as she gazed at the night sky.

'I wish I could just be happy for them, boy,' she sighed as she made tracks back to their camp for the night. Striding silently through the forest, she felt she was being stalked by her unease. Then the feeling coalesced into dread as she turned to look back at the moon.

'*Ageless beauty...*' she whispered, as she realised with sickening certainty what had been troubling her from the first audience with the Overlord. How could she not have seen it immediately, and how, or why, had others not noticed? Like the timeless moon watching the earth impassively from the night sky, the Overlord had not aged since Hirae had seen her in the triumphant procession after the Ascalion rebellion all those years ago.

Scase whined in response to the dread in Hirae's voice.

Hirae, knowing her own path was now set, turned to the east, envisaged the Spire across the leagues of night sky and promised:

'*I'm coming for you.*'

ABOUT THE AUTHOR

Kathryn Ruffell started out writing flash fiction, drawing inspiration from the local legends of Wiltshire. With a prehistoric stone circle practically on her doorstep, Kathryn weaves the mystery of the ancient stones and local lore into her writing, and also takes an active role in developing her medieval fantasy characters, throwing herself into hobbies such as archery, knife throwing and forging axes. The Transference is her debut novel, and the first part of a quintet, bringing readers into her world of heroes, horror, and magic.

Keep up to date on all things *The Transference* by following Kathryn on socials:

Instagram: @kathrynruffellauthor2025
TikTok: @kathrynruffellauthor
Facebook: @kathrynruffellauthor